THE
PAWN

USA TODAY BESTSELLING AUTHOR

T.K. LEIGH

THE PAWN

Published by Carpe Per Diem Publishing, Inc

BOOKS BY T.K. LEIGH

For a full list of all of T.K.'s books, including recommended reading order, please visit T.K.'s website:

www.tkleighauthor.com

For a free eBook, sign up for T.K.'s newsletter.

Content Warning

Some of T.K. Leigh's books may contain content that could be triggering for sensitive readers. For a full list of content warnings for each book and/or series, please visit her website by scanning the code below.

To the readers who know the cost of loving a monster...
But would choose him anyway.

This one's for you.

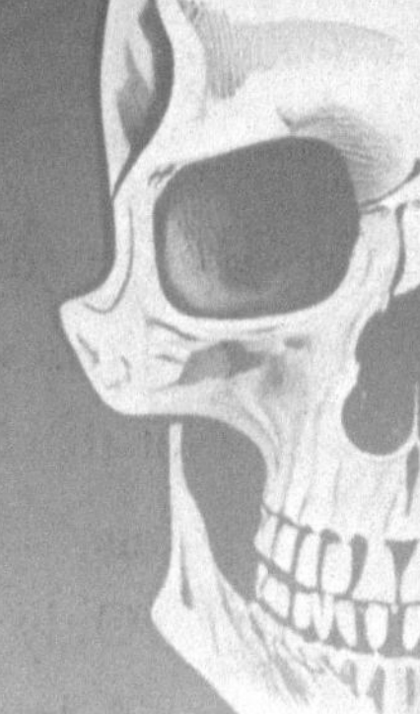

PROLOGUE
(END OF THE HUNTER)

Ariana

The mountain seemed endless.

Twisting switchbacks. Narrow lanes hugged by cliffs on one side and shadowed trees on the other. Every curve looked like the one before it, sharp and unforgiving. I couldn't be sure I was heading in the right direction.

I just knew I had to keep going.

The darkness out here was different. Not just night, but black. Like the earth had exhaled and blew out the stars. A sliver of moon hung behind me, barely enough to light the road. My eyes burned from staring so hard, the yellow and white lines blurring as fatigue clawed at me.

I had no idea how long I'd been driving. A few hours, maybe. My knuckles had gone pale around the steering wheel, my fingers aching from gripping it too tight.

The GPS on Henry's phone had helped. The signal

had been spotty, but it had flickered to life long enough to direct me down the mountain and onto a paved road. Not that I had a plan. I didn't even know where I was going.

Only that it was away from him.

A loud ding cut through the Wrangler, jolting my already fried nerves.

I tore my eyes to the dashboard, looking for what caused that sound. The glowing icon mocked me.

Low fuel.

"Shit," I muttered.

I hadn't thought to check the fuel gauge when I escaped. Rookie mistake. I could only hope I'd find a gas station in the next fifty miles or all of this would have been for nothing.

I peered down the long expanse of road, as if a town might miraculously rise from the trees. But there was nothing. Just mile after mile of dense pine, shadowed hills, and silence so heavy it felt like the world had ended.

This was where Henry grew up? In this isolation? No wonder he was so...broken.

The thought came unbidden, and I shoved it down. I refused to feel sorry for him. Not after what he did. I didn't care what demons he'd inherited from his father. He still made a deal with the fucking Bratva.

There was no coming back from that.

My shoulders ached by the time I finally spotted a flickering sign in the distance — an old gas station tucked beneath towering pine trees. A faded banner flapped beneath the overhang, barely legible through the grime.

But the lights were on.

Relief flooded me so fast I almost forgot to check my surroundings first.

Almost.

I cut the engine and scanned the lot. Not a single car. Just my own headlights reflecting off the glass door and an old pickup truck rusting near the side of the building.

I stepped into the night, the frigid air hitting me like a wall. I tugged Henry's coat tighter and hurried across the lot. The bell above the door chimed when I entered.

It smelled like tobacco and stale coffee. Rows of snack food lined narrow shelves, and behind the counter stood a man who looked like he'd been carved from the very mountain I'd just escaped — gray beard, sun-worn skin, and an oversized flannel shirt with the cuffs rolled up.

"You lost?" he asked with a chuckle.

"What makes you say that?" I asked nervously.

"Ain't too many folks come this way unless they're hunting or hiding. And you don't look like a hunter."

I forced a polite smile. "Just passing through."

He nodded thoughtfully as his eyes crawled over my face. "You look familiar."

I swallowed hard, my heart racing in my chest.

I could tell him the truth. That my name was Ariana Kane. That I was abducted several days ago and held prisoner in some cabin up in the mountains. That the man who took me was hired by the Bratva.

But considering this was the first gas station I'd come across, I worried he might know Henry. I didn't want to do anything that might draw attention to myself. Not until I was far enough away.

So instead, I reached for a pack of crackers on one of the shelves. "I get that a lot."

He didn't argue, but he watched me as I grabbed a bottle of water, a candy bar, then walked to the counter and dug into the roll of cash I'd taken.

"I'd also like forty worth of gas."

The way his eyes lingered on the cash made my skin crawl.

He rang me up without a word, but I made a mental note to move the rest of the money to a safer spot.

"You be careful out there," he said as I turned to leave. "World's not as safe as it used to be."

Didn't I know it?

Outside, the air felt colder. Sharper. The kind that slipped beneath my skin and reminded me I was exposed. Vulnerable.

I filled the tank quickly, glancing over my shoulder every few seconds. I felt like a target, standing out here alone, in the middle of nowhere. Every pine needle that shifted in the wind sounded like footsteps. Every creak from the building could have been someone about to attack from behind.

But no one came.

Once I finished pumping, I closed the gas cap and jumped back into the Wrangler, cranking the ignition.

I turned onto the two-lane road again, trees thick on either side, the pavement stretching on for miles.

Where was I going?

I still didn't know.

I figured I'd know when I got there.

So I kept driving, hoping for a highway. A town. A sign that I was closer to something human again.

Then I saw it.

Headlights.

The first I'd seen since escaping.

I blinked against the brightness, my heart lifting a little. Maybe I was finally getting close to civilization. A diner. A police station. Maybe even a bus stop.

The idea filled me with relief.

But as I glanced in the rearview mirror, my heart dropped when I noticed the SUV I just passed slow its speed, then turn around.

It was probably nothing. Just my paranoia getting the better of me.

They didn't tailgate me, but they stayed behind me.

My grip on the wheel tightened as I continued to float my gaze from the road to the mirror and back again.

Was Henry in that car? I couldn't make out a face in the darkness. Did he know some shortcut off the mountain and had tracked me down here?

Did the gas station attendant recognize the car and call him?

But Henry didn't have an SUV.

At least, I didn't think he did.

My stomach twisted.

I sped up.

So did the car tailing me.

With my heart in my throat, I pressed the gas harder, panic clawing up my spine. Trees whipped past like ghosts. The road narrowed. I gripped the wheel with white-knuckled hands.

Another mile.

Another curve.

Still behind me.

Suddenly, a loud bang reverberated in the silence.

The rear window exploded, glass shattering around me like shards of ice. I screamed, instinct causing me to jerk the wheel as the Wrangler fishtailed on the slick road.

Another shot rang out, and I lost control. The Jeep skidded, veered off the street and down an embankment, snow spraying past the windows, before crashing into a tree with bone-jarring force.

My head whipped forward. The wheel met my forehead with a sickening crack. Pain shot through my skull, bright and searing.

I couldn't breathe. Couldn't move.

My vision blurred, the edges curling inward.

Then I heard it.

Boots.

Crunching snow.

Getting closer.

The door to the Jeep opened.

I tried to speak. To scream. To fight.

But I never got a chance before my world went dark.

CHAPTER ONE

Henry

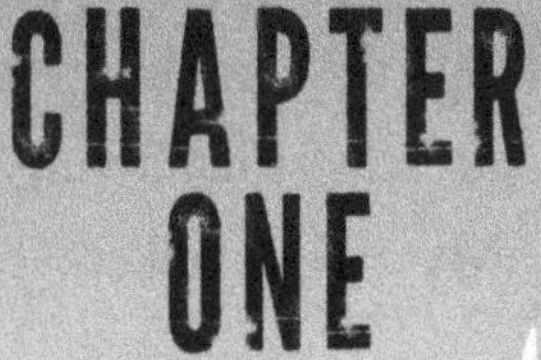

The red dot on my cell phone's tracker app pulsed like a countdown, each blink a reminder that Ariana was too far ahead. That I was too goddamn slow.

My hands choked the steering wheel of my truck, knuckles white as the mountain road blurred beneath my headlights. Sixty miles of distance between us felt like six hundred. Every second that passed was a chance for the Bratva to reach her first. A chance for her to keep believing the worst about me.

I never should have left the duffel bag where she could find it. Never should have allowed myself to forget what happens when I let my guard slip. Now she thought the phone inside belonged to me. Thought I'd been hired to abduct her. She'd drugged me and ran, praying she'd never have to see me again.

But she didn't understand. I wasn't the one who'd been paid to abduct her. I *rescued* her. At the time, I didn't know who I was rescuing her from. Now I did. And I also knew if the Bratva found her, her time left on this planet was dwindling with every beat of her heart.

I kept checking the tracking signal every few seconds, grateful she was still moving. Then her signal slowed. Stopped. My pulse spiked. Had they already caught her?

I zoomed in on the map, trying to figure out where she was. When I saw she'd stopped at a gas station, I blew out a relieved breath. Based on what I could recall, the Jeep didn't have a full tank of gas. That still didn't mean anything. I wouldn't feel better until I saw that little dot move again.

I added pressure to the gas pedal, increasing my speed. Every second that ticked by with no movement on the tracker made my anxiety increase a little more. Finally, the signal started moving again. Relief washed over me, despite the fact she was still over fifty miles ahead of me. At least she was moving.

At least, I *hoped* she was moving.

I had no way of knowing if she was even in the Jeep. She could have been attacked at the gas station and forced back into the vehicle. So many different scenarios floated through my mind, each one worse than the one before. But I pushed them aside, refusing to be consumed with all the what-ifs. Instead, I focused on the road. On what I could control.

On getting to Ariana before someone else did.

I continued following her, gradually closing the distance between us. Thankfully, I could navigate these roads blindfolded. Had driven them on countless occasions. Right now, that worked to my advantage. I was used to driving in the snow and ice. Ariana probably hadn't driven in this sort of weather in years.

After a few minutes, the signal on the Jeep seemed to slow before taking a hard right, veering off the road.

A part of me wondered if she'd found a motel and planned to sleep for the night, not knowing the danger that was after her.

But when I checked the map, there was no motel. Nothing but thick forest.

An unsettled feeling formed in my gut, and I increased my speed even more, my anxiety mounting with every minute that passed. The blinking, unmoving dot continued taunting me. Reminded me this was all my fault. That I could have avoided this if I'd just been honest with her and told her the truth.

When I finally closed in on the signal forty minutes later, the dread was almost unbearable, weighing me down to the point that I wasn't sure if I could muster the strength to get out of my truck. Especially when I saw a pair of tire tracks cutting down the snowy embankment.

Grabbing my gun from the glove box, I stepped into the cold. Cato leapt out behind me, his fur bristling, nose already to the ground. My boots crunched against the snow as I followed the path, praying like hell she'd just hit a patch of black ice and lost control of the Jeep.

But when the vehicle came into view, I knew it was more than that. Tires blown out. A shattered back window. A single set of footprints approaching and retreating. A steady stream of blood lining the path, the dark red stark against the white snow.

I squeezed my eyes shut, forcing down the unbearable ache building in my chest, and continued toward the Wrangler. I already knew what I'd find, but I needed to see it for myself.

The driver's side door was already open with shards of glass from the windshield covering the entire passenger compartment. But that wasn't what had me wanting to scream. It was the blood.

So much blood.

I couldn't think the worst. Not yet. I had to believe Ariana was still breathing.

And I'd do everything in my power to find her.

I may have hated my father with every fiber of my being, but he did teach me one very important life lesson... How to act under pressure. So instead of panicking, I pulled my phone out of my pocket and hit Blake's contact.

"Boss man," he answered on the second ring.

"I need you to pull flight records for every airport within two hundred miles of the cabin," I ordered without so much of a greeting as I shined my flashlight over the site of the crash, searching for anything that might help.

"What's going on?" he asked in concern as he typed on his keyboard in the background.

"Just fucking do it." My voice cracked raw, all the control stripped out of it.

"Anything I should be looking for?" he pressed, ignoring my outburst.

I stared at the carnage in front of me. The blood. The broken glass. The unnerving silence of the woods.

"Ariana..." Her name stuck in my throat, sharp and jagged. "She found the duffel bag. The cash. And the burner phone."

"Shit," he exhaled. "So she—"

"Thinks I abducted her. I mean, I *did*, but not like that." My chest heaved. "And that's not even the worst part." I dug my fingers through my hair as I recalled the news I'd received earlier.

"What is?"

"When we didn't get a hit on who this guy could be, I called in a favor with Salvatore."

"I had a feeling you might."

"He put out some feelers in Miami to see what he could find."

"And what did he uncover?"

"That a Bratva hitman who'd been paid to acquire a high-ticket item went dark."

"And you think that high-ticket item was Ariana?"

"I know it was. Worse, Salvatore called a little while ago to tell me the Bratva enforcer's phone had been turned back on. But I've kept that phone off since I killed him. When I checked, it was gone. Along with Ariana. Now my Jeep looks like a war zone, and she's missing. They fucking found her. If my gut is right and her husband is behind this?" My throat squeezed at the thought.

I knew what he was capable of. Knew the hell he'd put Ariana through for years. I swore I'd keep her safe. Swore no harm would come to her while she was with me. And because I didn't tell her the truth, because I was a fucking coward, I delivered her straight into the devil's arms myself.

"If I'd—"

"Henry," Blake cut me off, his voice sharp. "I think I've got something."

I perked up, hope building inside me.

"A Pilatus landed a few hours ago at a private airstrip about forty miles from you. Came from Miami."

My pulse thudded. "Any information about who the plane is registered to?"

"West Industries. A return flight plan has been filed. Departing in about an hour."

An hour. That was all I had.

"I'm on it. Find out everything you can about West Industries."

"You got it, boss."

I shoved the phone back into my pocket, and sprinted toward the truck, Cato on my heels every step of the way. The tires spit snow as I tore onto the road, the only thought in my head as sharp and relentless as gunfire.

If a single strand of Ariana's hair was out of place, I'd burn their world to ash.

Then I'd take back what was mine.

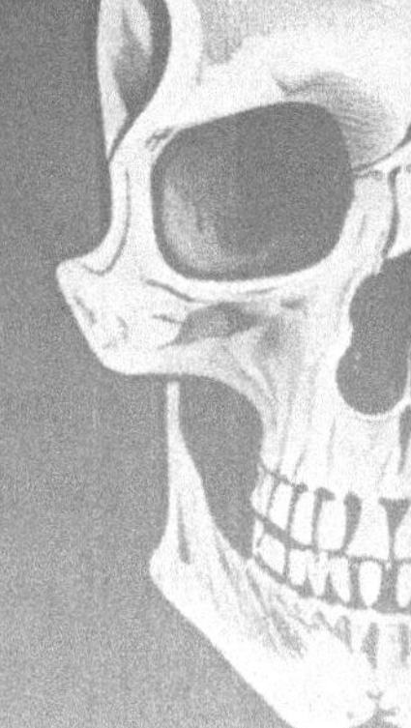

CHAPTER TWO

Henry

I rolled my truck to a stop along the perimeter road and killed the engine, letting the silence swallow me whole. The airstrip loomed ahead, the sole building a dilapidated hangar that was probably built in the 1930s.

I lifted the binoculars to my eyes and surveyed the area. A handful of prop planes sat parked under a weak floodlight. Beyond them, the small Pilatus gleamed, the plane out of place among the tiny two-seaters surrounding it.

Cato nudged my thigh from the passenger seat, a low whine escaping him, as if telling me to hurry. Apparently, he was just as anxious to save Ariana as I was.

"Stay," I ordered, my voice a whisper. His amber eyes locked on mine, steady, and obedient.

I ruffled his head, then stepped into the night, my pistol heavy at my side. On light feet, I jogged toward the fence, muscle memory kicking in as I silently scaled it and dropped onto the other side with barely a sound. A jolt of pain hit my ankle from my still-unhealed injury, but I pushed it down. I had to. For Ariana.

Mere seconds after my boots touched the ground, the hangar's back door flung open.

I dropped flat, the snow damp and sharp against my cheek as I hid in the shadows, my pulse pounding in my ears. But I remained still. Remembered my training. The worst thing anyone could do in this type of situation was panic. And I refused to panic. Especially with Ariana's life on the line.

I kept my eyes glued to the back of the building as a man stepped out. Tall. Broad. Dark hair. Tattoos snaked up his hands and arms, as well as one on his neck. I squinted, focusing on the markings, my stomach twisting when I made out a tattoo of a knife being thrust into his neck. A well-known tattoo for Bratva hitmen.

He leaned against the corrugated wall and lit a cigarette, as if he didn't have a care in the world.

As if he weren't holding a woman prisoner mere feet away.

The door cracked open again, and another figure appeared. He was taller, his head shaved, his arms also covered in ink. He said something in Russian, his voice authoritative. They went back and forth for a few seconds before the bald man vanished inside, leaving the smoker behind.

He took another long drag of his cigarette, closing his eyes as he pushed out a long exhale, smoke floating away in the darkness.

I remained still, mentally reviewing the little information I had.

I knew these men were Bratva. Knew they'd been paid to acquire Ariana as a high-ticket item. Knew there were at least two men. How many more could there be? Based on their choice of aircraft, probably not many.

They flew in on a Pilatus from Miami. It wasn't a plane with a long range. If they wanted to get in and out under the radar, they'd travel as light as possible.

I could have been wrong, but I doubted there would be more than three or four men, especially when I factored in that they were counting on returning with Ariana.

Four against one wasn't great odds.

Three against one was better.

The smoker turned toward the building and widened his stance. When I heard the unmistakable sound of liquid hitting the pavement, I made my move, every muscle tight, every step calculated as I approached, carefully pulling my knife from my pocket. He didn't have a chance to tuck himself back into his pants before I struck.

I hooked my arm around his throat, dragging him away from the building and into the darkness. He thrashed against me, a muffled grunt tearing from him as my blade punctured his side. Blood poured from the wound, coating my knuckles. He clawed at my forearm, his nails breaking skin, but it didn't matter. I tightened my chokehold until his frantic movements stuttered, faltered, then stilled.

I let him drop to the ground with a satisfying thud, his blank eyes wide.

I crept toward the back door, exchanging my knife for my pistol. I had no way of knowing what might be waiting on the other side of the door. Had no idea of the layout. I needed to be ready for whatever I might face.

Taking one deep breath, I reached for the handle and slowly opened the door. The sound of low voices speaking Russian filtered outside, and I paused, listening for several protracted moments to determine how many. I could make out two distinct voices, one that sounded like the shaved-headed man from before, as well as one I didn't recognize. And they didn't sound like they were right by the door, either. They sounded distant.

Distant was good.

Distant gave me room to work with.

I pushed the door wider and slipped behind a stack

of crates, peeking between them. One man paced in front of the open bay door, a cell phone pressed to his ear. The other stood in front of what was probably an office, his back toward me. As if watching something.

Or some*one*.

It took everything I had to remain still as I waited to see if there were any more people. But after a few minutes, no one else appeared.

Even if I was wrong, I couldn't wait. I had to act. Before they loaded Ariana onto that plane and took off into the night.

Needing to be as stealthy as possible, I exchanged my gun for my knife once more, then moved toward the man guarding the office.

He turned just as I reached him, his eyes widening, mouth parting to shout. But he was too late. In one swift move, I sliced his throat. Blood gushed from the wound, staining the hangar floor, his gurgle echoing off steel walls. He dropped, twitching, clawing at the crimson river spilling down his chest.

A string of Russian echoed around me, and I spun as the other man advanced toward me, his gun raised.

He fired but missed, his shot tearing through a crate behind me. I quickly pulled my own gun, hitting him in the hip. He cursed as he fell to the floor, still shooting at me until he was out of rounds.

With a satisfied smirk, I moved toward him. But as I

did, he managed to pull himself upright and charge at me, driving us both to the floor. My gun slipped out of my grip, sliding halfway across the hangar.

We fought dirty. Teeth. Nails. Fists. He slammed his forehead into mine, rattling my skull. I answered with a brutal hook to his jaw, the crack of bone sharp and satisfying. He snarled, wrapping his hands around my throat, cutting off the oxygen.

I was fighting for my life, but at this moment, I couldn't help but think about Ariana. About the bruises she'd had on her throat when I first stole her away to my cabin. How the marks I thought were evidence of rough play in the bedroom were actually proof of her husband's brutality. How he'd done this same thing to her.

My rage returned, and I used every ounce of strength to push him off me and pin him to the cement floor. Then I wrapped my hands around his neck, watching with sick satisfaction as he fought for air before his body went completely still.

I climbed off him, taking a moment to catch my breath, feeling lightheaded. But I pushed myself to my feet and frantically searched for Ariana, finding a limp figure tied up and thrown into the corner of the office.

She was crumpled against the wall, her face smeared with blood, skin too pale, too fragile.

I rushed to her and dropped to my knees, my hands

trembling as I brushed her hair from her face. My chest cracked open at the sight of her swollen cheek and split lip. And it was all my fault. If I'd told her the truth, if I hadn't kept her in the dark, none of this would have happened. She wouldn't have tried to free herself from me. Wouldn't have left. And these assholes would never have found her.

I pressed my fingers to her throat, exhaling a sigh of relief when I felt a pulse. I cradled her in my arms, touching a soft kiss to her forehead and breathing her in, relishing in the feel of her.

But there were more pressing matters.

Like the three dead bodies.

I pulled my phone from my pocket and hit Blake's contact.

"What's the status?" he answered on the first ring.

"I took care of our infestation problem," I replied, looking around at the bodies. "But I may need a cleanup crew."

"Already on it."

"There are two inside and one out back."

"I'll let them know." He dropped his voice. "How is she?"

I looked down at Ariana. "She's unconscious but seems stable."

"Do you know who was behind the hit on her? I looked into the company that owned the plane. It's essentially a holding company. I'm still digging, but knowing how the Bratva operates, I won't find much."

"I figured as much," I exhaled. "I just—"

A shrill ringing cut through, and I tore my attention to the man I'd just killed.

"I'll call you back," I told Blake, then carefully set Ariana onto the floor before moving toward the body. I rummaged through his pockets and pulled out his phone, staring at the screen.

There was no name. Only a letter.

V.

I hit answer and lifted the cell up to my ear. I didn't even have a chance to say anything before a voice came over the line.

"You were supposed to call me an hour ago." His tone was sharp. Arrogant.

Familiar.

Victor *fucking* Kane.

The smug bastard's voice was burned into my memory.

Ever since realizing the same man who tried to abduct Ariana was the same man walking on the beach in the background of Sarah's last posted video, I knew there had to be a connection between the two events. And Victor was that connection.

Hearing his voice on the other end of the phone solidified the feeling in my gut that Victor was involved in both Sarah's murder and Ariana's attempted abduction.

But why?

Why would he hire someone to abduct his own wife?

"What the fuck is going on, Dmitri?" he continued. "Do you have my wife? Was she there? I paid you good money to take care of this so it didn't come back on me, and you're fucking everything up. We had an agreement, and you're not sticking to your end of the bargain here. I essentially served her on a silver platter for your team. And it's been one fuck-up after another. I need some good news, and I need it now."

I didn't respond right away. Just waited.

"Well?" he barked out, obviously impatient. "Are you going to say anything? I'm not paying you to fuck around. I'm paying you to get the job done."

"I'm sorry," I finally said. "Dmitri's unavailable to come to the phone. But don't worry. Your wife is safe with me." I smiled, cold and lethal. "If I were you, I'd be more concerned about your own safety."

"Who is this? Where's Dmitri?" he demanded, but he sounded different. Scared. Agitated. Anxious.

"Like I said... He's unavailable. Permanently."

"W-who are you?"

"I'm the man who's going to destroy you." My tone was casual, as if discussing the weather, not threatening him. "When I'm done, it'll make what I did to your associates look like child's play. For every time you laid your hands on your wife without her permission, every time you made her bleed, every time you made her feel worthless, I'll make you suffer. You'll beg for death. And I won't give it to you. Not until I've had the pleasure of slowly draining every last ounce of life from your pathetic body."

I ended the call and tossed the phone aside.

Then I gathered Ariana in my arms, her head falling against my chest, and carried her out of the hangar.

CHAPTER THREE

Ariana

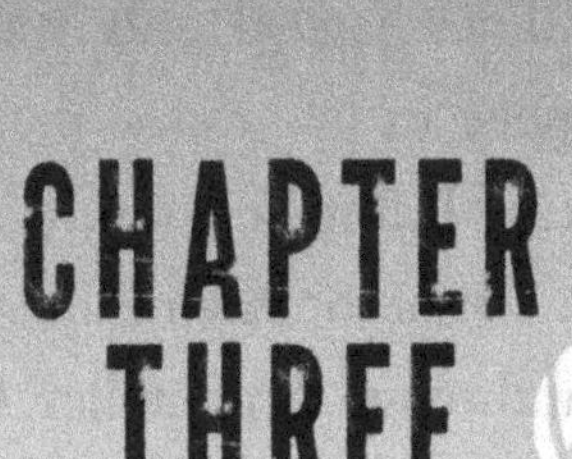

Something rumbled beneath me, deep and constant, like the growl of a caged animal. It pressed into my spine, vibrating through my bones. I shifted, but even the smallest movement sent a flare of pain ricocheting through my body.

Air hissed somewhere nearby, mechanical and steady, underscored by the faint metallic tang of fuel. The scent of it clung to the back of my throat, acrid and bitter, mingling with the coppery taste of blood on my tongue.

I forced my eyelids open, but the light that seared through my lashes was blinding, bright and harsh. It stabbed straight into my skull, making the pounding behind my eyes throb even harder. My vision blurred and doubled, then blurred again. Shapes shifted in and out of focus, swimming like shadows on water.

Two figures stood a few feet away. Both tall. Both shadowed. But they were too unfocused to make out details, their outlines jagged and wavering like heat mirages. They spoke in low tones, muffled at first, like sound underwater. I fought to tune in, every sense straining past the roar of the engine and the hiss of air.

One voice cut through. Unfamiliar. Urgent.

Hope flared so brightly it hurt. Maybe I'd been rescued. Maybe whoever had pulled me out of the Jeep was some stranger with a conscience. Someone who'd seen the wreckage and chose to act. To help.

I clung to that fragile thought, to the promise of salvation.

Right now, it was all I had.

But just as quickly, that small flicker of hope was extinguished when I heard him.

Henry.

The sound of his voice slid through the air like a blade. Deep. Rough. Familiar in a way that made bile rise in my throat.

A memory came rushing back. The stacks of cash filling his duffel bag. The burner phone buried beneath them. The string of texts. The photo of me, bound and gagged, as proof of a job completed. Henry had been paid to abduct me for the Bratva. I drugged him so I could escape. I thought I was free.

But I wasn't.

He'd found me.

I tried to focus, shake off the fog that clung to me, weighing me down. And then I heard it. Something about my mother.

My pulse roared in my ears, drowning out everything else. Panic clawed at me. I had to move. Had to fight. Had to survive. If not for my sake, for my mother's.

I started to sit up, but pain detonated in my ribs, white-hot and blinding. My head split down the middle, nausea churning so hard I thought I'd vomit. My knee burned as if someone had driven a knife straight through it. But I needed to push through the pain. I refused to give up. Not now that it seemed my mother had found her way into Henry's crosshairs.

He could sell me to the Bratva.

I refused to let him target my mother, as well.

I drew in a ragged breath, bracing myself for the pain I knew would come. Then I forced myself upright. The world tilted sideways, my vision exploding with sparks of white and purple. Pain speared through me, intense enough to steal my breath, my knee buckling as I attempted to stand.

The voices cut off, and footsteps pounded toward me, sharp against the low drone of the engines.

"Stay away from her." My plea cracked on my lips, weak and broken.

A pair of arms wrapped around me, dragging me back down to the bed. I thrashed, clawing, punching, but my movements were sluggish, uncoordinated. My hands felt like they belonged to someone else.

"It's okay, baby. You're okay. I'll make sure she's okay, too."

That voice. *His* voice. It made my stomach roil, acid burning my throat.

I fought harder, my nails scraping against fabric, muscles trembling with the effort. My surroundings swam, the edges going gray.

"She's confused and disoriented," another man said, his tone calm. As if this weren't his first abduction.

It probably wasn't.

"I'm going to sedate her so she doesn't injure herself further."

Sedate? No. Not again.

I tried to shake my head. Tried to kick. Tried to scream. But my tongue was thick in my mouth, my body refusing to obey my brain.

A sharp pinch bit into my arm, and what little strength I had to begin with evaporated.

"No..." I begged, the word a whisper.

My limbs turned to sandbags, heavy and useless.

Strong arms closed around me, pulling me against a

chest I knew too well. My head lolled against hard muscle, my body betraying me as it sagged into his hold.

Henry's scent was everywhere, leather and wood and something darker I used to find intoxicating. Now it suffocated me.

"I'm sorry," he murmured, pressing a tender kiss to my temple. "You're safe now." His voice broke with emotion, which only confused me more. "I swear I won't let anyone hurt you again."

The words tangled in my mind.

Safe? With him?

He'd abducted me. Planned to deliver me straight into the hands of the Bratva. And yet, he sounded like he was scared. Like seeing me this way tore him apart.

I wanted to scream at him, shove him away, tell him he was a worse monster than my husband. At least *he'd* never sold me to the Bratva.

But the darkness was already sliding in, thick and merciless.

The last thing I remembered was the steady beat of Henry's heart beneath my ear...and the terrifying uncertainty of what awaited me the next time I woke up.

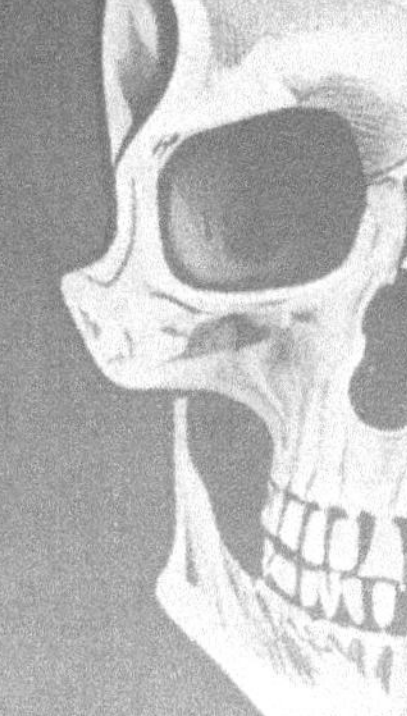

CHAPTER
FOUR

Henry

The glow of the monitors washed the office in blue. I refused to look away despite the exhaustion that had consumed me since we landed in Georgia. Hell, since the adrenaline of finding and rescuing Ariana had worn off.

I rubbed my eyes, but continued to watch the feed of her as she slept in one of my guest bedrooms. She looked so small, her face pale, hair splayed across the pillow, chest rising and falling in a slow, steady rhythm.

Thankfully, her injuries weren't too bad. Mild concussion. Bruised ribs. Sprained knee that would make it difficult to walk for a few days. Nothing that required surgery.

Nothing that wouldn't heal.

For now, all I could do was watch. And wait. And hope when she woke up and I told her the truth, she wouldn't hate me.

That she'd believe me.

She *had* to believe me.

I didn't know what I'd do if she didn't. If she looked at me with the same disgust she did when I first brought her to the cabin.

The door to the office opened, and I glanced away from the monitors. Blake stepped inside, wearing his usual uniform of an all-black suit. Like he'd crawled out of a shadow and forgot to leave it behind.

I once asked him why he always dressed in black, and he joked it was to match the color of his soul.

It was obvious he had demons much like I did. I never pressed him to talk about it. In our line of work, there was an unwritten rule not to ask too many questions. After all, Blake had a certain set of skills that had proven quite useful.

I didn't ask how he knew how to make a body disappear. Or how to clean a crime scene. Or why he kept scouring every corner of the web for a woman named Chandler Meadows. If he wanted me to know, he'd tell me.

"You look like hell," he remarked, his eyes going straight to the monitors as he dropped onto the couch beside Cato and scratched his head.

"It's been a night." I didn't take my gaze off the screen.

"How's she holding up?"

"Good, all things considered."

"And you?" he pressed. "How are *you* doing?"

"Okay." I pushed out a long sigh, running a hand over my face as I fought to stay awake. "All things considered." My words carried a different weight than before.

I was still processing everything that had happened over the last several hours. It wasn't even noon yet. It had only been a little more than twelve hours since Salvatore had called, sending my night into a tailspin. It seemed like so much longer. Days. Weeks.

A lifetime.

"How'd things go up north?" I asked, turning my chair around to face him.

His dark hair was disheveled, and his brown eyes showed signs of exhaustion, probably from pulling an all-nighter to help clean up the mess I'd left in Maine.

"Handled," he replied simply. "All traces you were ever at that bunker are gone. Disposed of the bodies, then drove their car to a remote area and crashed it into a tree to make it look like they lost control before setting out on foot."

"Did you get any hits on who they were?"

"Confirmed Bratva. Lower level, but definitely connected."

I knew they were, but it was good to have confirmation of my suspicions. Unfortunately, with every confirmed piece of information, it just caused more questions.

"Did you find out anything more about the company the plane was registered to?"

"Nothing yet. But I did find something else that might be of interest to you."

I perked up. "What's that?"

He grabbed his phone and pulled up a photo of the art museum seemingly taken the same night of the charity gala I'd attended where I first spoke to Ariana.

Red carpet. Celebrities. Champagne smiles.

"What's so special about celebrities being photographed going into a charity event?"

"Look past that," he instructed. "Far right corner."

I grabbed my glasses and zoomed in, squinting at the two blurry figures. One was Victor Kane. The man beside him was partially obscured, but I recognized him from that night.

"That's the same man I saw approach Victor at the gala." I met Blake's eyes. "Who is he?"

"Maxim Covell."

I furrowed my brow, unfamiliar with the name. "Is that supposed to ring a bell?"

"He's a lawyer for the Bratva. Handles their legitimate business dealings."

He swiped to another photo, then handed the phone back to me. This one showed Victor climbing into an SUV, Covell seeming to scan his surroundings before joining them.

"Do we know who was in the car?"

Blake took his phone from me again, pulling up yet another photo before returning it to me. This one was a darkened image of a man sitting in a black SUV.

"Nikolai Volkov. Obshchak of the Miami Bratva."

"So Victor gets pulled out of a public event to talk to the Obshchak, then mere hours later, a low-level Bratva soldier attempts to abduct his wife?"

"Looks that way," Blake confirmed.

This wasn't exactly earth-shattering. I'd known the Bratva was somehow involved in this after Salvatore confirmed as much.

But one question continued to nag at me.

"Why?"

"I'm still looking into Victor's connection to the Bratva. If there's something to find, I'll find it. He did have his publicist issue a statement late last night."

"What was that?"

"Something to the effect that he's stepping back from public appearances to focus on finding his wife."

"I bet he is." I snorted a humorless laugh.

"He left his estate on Star Island after midnight in a bit of a hurry," Blake continued. "I tried tracking his cell, but it looks like he turned it off. I have people checking his houses, his hotels, every property with his name on it. Every place he's ever visited. He won't hide forever."

I'd expected him to disappear, especially after the threats I'd made last night. Maybe I'd acted a bit rash when I threatened him. But I couldn't help it. Not after confirming he'd put a price on Ariana's head. Not after learning everything he'd put her through. He needed to know his carefully built house of cards was about to fall.

And I was the one who'd make sure it happened.

"He did make one phone call before going off-grid," Blake added after a few seconds.

"To whom?"

"Dr. Wilson Schaffer."

I perked up at the name I knew quite well. The doctor overseeing Ariana's mother's care.

I feared Victor might use Ariana's mother to retaliate against her...or me. So I'd asked Blake to put together a team to pull Daphne out of her care facility and bring her here. Learning Victor had called the doctor after our conversation solidified I'd done the right thing.

"Any idea what they discussed?"

"No, but I can pay him a visit."

I'd known Blake long enough to know a "visit" wouldn't entail a cup of tea and cakes. It would end with the doctor bleeding out and begging for his life.

And if he'd done anything to hurt Ariana's mother, I wanted to be the one to make him bleed.

"Let's hold off for now. See what we can find out about him."

"You think there's something off. Don't you?"

I released a long exhale. "I don't know. But I want to be sure. I'm not taking any chances. Not anymore. Not after everything that's happened with Ariana. Everything I've learned."

I could feel Blake's careful gaze studying me in the silence before he remarked, "You care about her, don't you?"

My first instinct was to deny it. Remind him Ariana was merely a pawn. The queen I'd use to destroy the king.

But that was no longer the case.

"I was wrong about her," I admitted.

"How so?"

I leaned back, staring at the ceiling for a moment before meeting his gaze. So much had happened since I'd spoken to him about my plan. So much had changed.

"Before I took her, I hated what she represented. The dresses. The galas. The easy life. I thought she'd chosen it. That she *loved* it and didn't care who she had to step on to live that lifestyle."

I swallowed hard, cursing myself for not seeing it all

before. Now that I knew the truth, it was so fucking obvious.

"She's not that woman. Every smile. Every laugh. It was just an act. A part she had to play to survive."

"Survive?" Blake pressed.

I slowly nodded. "He's been torturing her. Beating her. Assaulting her. Controlling every part of her fucking existence." My voice cracked, my blood boiling with every word. "She's not his wife. She's his goddamn property. And I was too fucking blinded by my hatred to see it."

Blake's jaw tightened.

He may have been involved in questionable activities from time to time. May have had no problem disposing of a body or cleaning a crime scene. But there was one thing we could both agree on. We despised anyone who harmed a woman or child.

"So what happens now?" he asked.

"Now I tell her the truth." I shifted my gaze to the monitor to see Ariana still sleeping, the faint rise and fall of her chest providing me some semblance of comfort. "And pray she doesn't hate me beyond repair."

"And Victor?"

"What about him?"

"I can leak rumors about his involvement in his wife's disappearance to the press. Feed them some noise. Let public opinion do its thing."

I shook my head. "He deserves more than a scandal or ruined reputation. He needs to understand how it feels to beg for mercy, only to have his pleas fall on deaf ears. Just like Ariana's did for so long. I want him to suffer. And even when I think he's suffered enough, I want him to suffer more. For Ariana. And for Sarah."

He considered my statement for several long moments. When he spoke again, his voice was softer. More concerned.

"This path you're about to go down... There's no going back. There's a difference between taking a life to protect someone, and taking a life out of vengeance. If you do this, it *will* change you. I just want to make sure you understand the stakes. That you'll have to live with it for the rest of your life. Is she worth it?"

"Of course she is. Sarah's my daughter."

He gave me a knowing look. "I wasn't talking about Sarah." He glanced at the monitor where Ariana's peaceful face filled the screen. "Is *she* worth it?"

There wasn't even a question in my mind.

"Without a fucking doubt."

He nodded a single determined nod. "Then that's good enough for me."

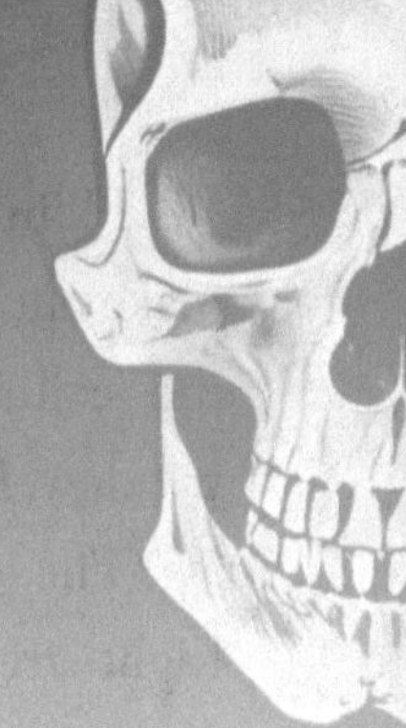

CHAPTER FIVE

Ariana

Waking came in fragments, like a film reel sputtering in and out of focus.

First was the pounding. A heavy throb at the base of my skull that pulsed in rhythm with every sluggish beat of my heart. My stomach cramped, sour and tight, the bitter taste of bile thick on my tongue. My knee burned like it had been branded, the pain sparking sharper each time I moved.

The low hum of something sounded in the background, steady and mechanical. The heater maybe. Then something I hadn't heard in days cut through the silence. The rumble of an airplane flying overhead. Like I was near some sort of civilization. Not hidden away in a mountain cabin like a helpless lamb awaiting slaughter.

I blinked my eyes open, able to focus long enough to make out my surroundings. No log beams running across the ceiling. No snow-capped mountains outside the window. No stone fireplace carved into the wall.

The ceiling above me was smooth, sterile white. Light streamed through the window, the trees outside a mixture of oak and maple. The furniture was modern and impersonal, and the air smelled faintly of detergent, not wood smoke.

I shifted, trying to sit up, but the motion made my head flare with pain so sharp my stomach heaved. I touched a hand to my temple, pressing down as though I could hold my skull together by sheer force, feeling a bandage covering my forehead above my right eye.

I searched my mind for a memory of how I'd gotten it. How I'd gotten *here*. But nothing came.

Had I imagined everything? Had the cabin been some fever-dream I'd conjured to escape my own reality? Was I still dreaming now?

But if this *were* a dream, why did everything hurt so much? Why did my ribs feel like they'd been used for target practice? Why did every slight shift feel like glass lodging deep beneath my skin?

Was this all Victor's doing?

I'd gotten used to his abuse. But it had never been this bad. He'd never left marks on my face. Everywhere else, but never my face.

I forced my eyes wider, blinking until shapes started to form. Something moved in the corner, massive and ominous.

I squinted, willing my vision to sharpen. The shape came into focus, and a tail thumped against the floor.

A dog.

Relief hit me fast. I wasn't with Victor. He would never tolerate a dog in the house.

But I recalled someone who *did* tolerate a dog in the house.

Henry.

Fractured memories played before my eyes as I struggled to piece together the events that led to this moment.

Sheets tangled around us. Henry's weight pressing me into the mattress, his mouth claiming mine. His rough voice calling me a warrior.

Then the duffel bag. Rolls of bills spilling out. The phone. The messages.

The Bratva.

I'd drugged him. Ran. Stopped for gas.

What happened after that?

I closed my eyes, as if that would help me remember better, more snippets coming into focus.

A dark SUV. Headlights in the rearview mirror. Gunfire exploding behind me. The tree. Blood. Pain. Then darkness.

I pressed my lips together until they hurt, smothering

the sob clawing at my throat as the pieces clicked into place.

I should have known better than to think I could outmaneuver Henry Fontaine. He was bigger, faster, stronger.

And from the rolls of cash in his duffel bag, he'd been paid a lot of money for me.

I wasn't a person to him. Just a piece of property.

Like I was to Victor.

And I was stupid enough to fall for his charms.

Like I did with Victor.

I swung my legs over the side of the bed, nearly crying out from the agony coursing through me. I gritted my teeth and breathed through the pain.

Pain was familiar. Pain I could handle. One of the benefits of enduring years of Victor's abuse, I supposed. I had no choice but to function with bruised ribs, broken bones, and scars that would never heal.

With one long inhale, I pushed up to stand. My knee almost gave out, white heat shooting through it, but I caught myself on the nightstand before I fell. Cato jumped to his feet and let out a single sharp bark, the sound echoing like a gunshot.

"Shhh," I hissed, panic snaking through me. My pulse roared in my ears, drowning out everything else.

Except for the sound of footsteps thundering down the hall, fast and unyielding.

I shot my gaze toward the door, my breathing growing ragged as the sound grew closer and closer. Then the door flew open, and Henry's broad physique filled the frame.

His dark hair was rumpled, his eyes shadowed like he hadn't slept in days, his face lined with worry.

Rage surged, burning hotter than the pain. I grabbed the vase from the nightstand, roses and water spilling across the hardwood floor as I fought to maintain my balance. Everything was uneven and blurry. I felt like I was on an unsteady boat that kept rocking back and forth.

"Careful, Ariana." He raised his hands in surrender, his voice low and calm. "You'll hurt yourself."

"I'll take my chances." I tightened my grip on the vase, as if it might help steady me.

"What do you plan on doing with that?"

"I don't know. But I'm not going to do nothing while you sell me to the Bratva. I saw the money. The messages. I know everything. You were paid to abduct me." My voice cracked, but I forced it louder, stronger. Refused to let him see how much his betrayal hurt me.

I'd survived years of being my husband's punching bag. Yet this hurt more than Victor's fists. More than his knife cutting into my skin. More than his cigarettes branding my flesh.

For a brief time, Henry made me feel something I hadn't in years.

Hope.

And it had all been a lie.

"If you'll sit back down, I'll explain—"

"Explain?" I barked out an incredulous laugh. "That's what you'd like, isn't it? For me to sit still, shut up, and let you keep me prisoner."

"You were never—"

"Well, I'll let you in on a little secret, *Mr. Fontaine*," I cut him off, his name venom on my tongue. "I'm done with that. Done with letting some man decide what happens to me. Done letting *you* decide what happens to me."

He flexed his jaw. "Ariana, if you'd—"

"Remember when you called me a warrior? It's probably the only honest thing that's ever come out of your mouth. Because that's exactly what I plan on being. I may not be as big or as strong as you, but I have survived fucking hell."

"I know. I—"

"And I won't stop fighting now. Not for you. Not for Victor. And not for the Bratva. I'd rather—"

"*I'm not working for the fucking Bratva!*" Henry shouted, his voice raw. Explosive.

I startled at the force of it, snapping my mouth shut.

His chest rose and fell like he'd just gone ten rounds, jaw tight, hands clenched into fists.

"I was watching your house when I saw a man break in and take you. I followed. Intervened. *That* man was Bratva. It was *his* duffel you found. *His* phone. *His* money."

The vase trembled in my grip, the weight of it weakening my arms. But I refused to show any hint of weakness.

"Why should I believe you?" I shot back.

He pushed out a long sigh, raking his hand over his face. He looked wary. Exhausted. Like he'd been fighting a war for days.

"You shouldn't. And that's my fault. I own that." He pointed to his chest, raw and determined. "I should have told you the truth the first time you asked. I didn't. And I almost lost you because of it."

His voice caught, and he squeezed his eyes shut. When he returned his gaze to mine, it was fierce. Unwavering.

"I won't make that mistake again. From this moment forward, there are no more secrets. Just..." He stepped closer, his movements measured, as if approaching a wild animal. "Let me explain, Ariana."

He reached for his waistband. I instinctively backed up. A part of me expected him to withdraw zipties, handcuffs, or some other restraints to chain me up like nothing more than property.

Instead, he drew his gun and held it out to me, pointing down.

"If, after hearing me out, you still think I'm lying, still think I'm a monster…" His throat worked as he swallowed. "Then shoot me."

My heart slammed in my chest as I eyed the gun. "You're giving me permission to shoot you?"

"I'm hoping you don't." His lips pressed into a line. "I'm hoping you believe me. I guess I'm trying to prove that you *can* trust me, despite what my past actions may have led you to believe."

I looked from his eyes to the gun and back again, dozens of scenarios playing out before me. If my marriage to Victor taught me anything, it was not to trust anyone. That any promise is yet another chain binding you to someone.

But it also taught me to trust my gut.

And my gut told me to at least listen to what he had to say.

After all, he'd fed me. Clothed me. He may have been cold and aloof, but he was never downright abusive, even though he had every opportunity to hurt me…or worse. Yet he never did. Shouldn't that count for something?

Slowly, I lowered the vase back onto the table. My

knees shook from the strength it took to remain upright, and I eased onto the edge of the bed, my eyes never leaving his.

"I'll listen."

Relief crashed over his expression, the tension leaving his body. "Thank you."

He stepped forward, his gun still outstretched, urging me to take it.

"I don't want your gun, Henry. Just... Don't make me regret this."

He flashed a rare smile. "I'll do my best."

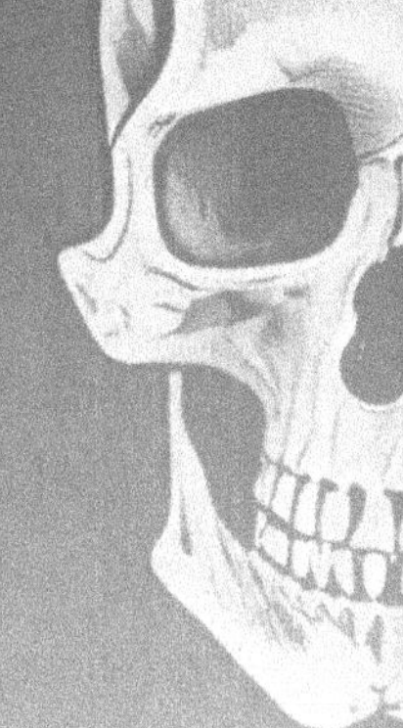

CHAPTER SIX

Ariana

Henry carefully set the gun on the nightstand beside the vase. The muzzle pointed toward the wall, but its presence still felt heavy. Looming.

"In case you change your mind," he said evenly.

I wasn't sure if the gesture was meant as additional proof of his honesty... Or as a manipulative ploy designed to make me lower my guard.

It was something Victor would have done. Which is why I didn't trust it.

Henry picked up a chair from the corner and carried it closer, kicking the roses out of his way and setting it down a few feet from the bed.

"Sorry about your flowers," I muttered, my throat scratchy.

"They're not mine," he replied. "I got them for you."

My heart betrayed me with a sharp, skipping beat. "You did?"

He held my gaze, unwavering. "I did."

It had been so long since anyone had given me flowers. Sure, the household staff routinely refreshed the various floral arrangements scattered throughout Victor's estate, but they were showpieces. Not gifts like these flowers were.

Then again, Victor once bought me flowers on a regular basis.

Until he removed the mask and I saw the monster hiding underneath.

This could simply be another tactic to butter me up.

I refused to fall for it. Not when I knew what was at stake.

"You want to explain?" I began, forcing steel into my voice. "Then explain."

He sank into the chair with a sigh, scrubbing a hand over his face. "I'm not even sure where to start."

"The beginning usually works."

He sat forward, his elbows on his knees, as he stared at the floor for several long moments.

For the first time since I'd met him, he looked uncertain. Not like the relentless man who had tracked me, but someone bowed beneath a weight too heavy to carry.

"The night we first spoke," he said finally, lifting his

eyes to mine. "At the gala. You were right. I'd been watching you. Truth is, I'd been watching you and Victor for months."

A chill prickled down my spine, causing me to shiver. "Why?"

"Because I wanted revenge. I wanted Victor to feel my pain. To lose the person he treasured most."

"Who's that supposed to be?"

"You," he said quietly. "Or I *thought* it was you." His mouth tightened. "I thought you loved being Victor's wife. Thought your soul was as black as his. But I was wrong. So *damn* wrong." His throat worked in a hard swallow, his gaze burning into mine. "I'm so fucking sorry, Ariana."

The words hit harder than I wanted them to. His voice was raw, stripped bare. And I cursed myself for hearing sincerity in it. For wanting to believe him.

But I couldn't afford to cave. Not until I figured out what the hell was going on.

"You said you wanted him to feel your pain. Who did you lose?"

He was silent for a moment. Then he pushed out a long exhale. "Her name was Sarah Laurendeau. She was my daughter."

"Was?" My chest squeezed, despite how much I wanted to hate him.

But hate was a strong word.

I wasn't sure *how* I felt about Henry. Not yet.

"She died this past summer. It was ruled a suicide," he sneered in disbelief.

"You don't think it was."

He slowly shook his head. "I may not have known her that well. Or at all, really. I was only sixteen when I learned my girlfriend was pregnant. She chose to have the baby and gave her up for adoption. It was supposed to be closed."

"But you found her anyway."

He shrugged. "I never spoke to her. I just wanted to make sure she had a good life. And she did. Two loving parents who gave her everything we couldn't. An older brother they'd also adopted. She was happy. Bright. Alive." His expression fell. "Then suddenly, she wasn't."

I recalled the day I'd gone down to the basement in Maine to grab his duffel bag. How I'd thought it was just a man cave but instead came face-to-face with a wall of monitors.

And on one of those screens was the image of a happy brunette who couldn't have been more than a few years younger than me.

Now I knew why she looked familiar.

Because she looked like Henry.

"Why do you think Victor was involved?"

"I don't just think it. I *know* it."

His eyes burned with so much power and determination. And heartache. The heartache was nearly unbearable.

"According to her brother, she'd been seeing someone she met during her travels. A man named Victor. She had a popular travel vlog and traveled all over the world. In the months prior to her death, she stayed at dozens of properties Victor owned."

"I'm not doubting you," I began. "I'm more than aware that Victor hasn't been faithful. But there must have been something more than her seeing a man named Victor."

"A few days after her death, there was a payment from your husband to a charity linked to the District Attorney in LA, where she died. Then, mere days later, the autopsy report was released and the cause of death was determined to be suicide. If you ask me, it all seems a bit too convenient."

"If you're so certain of his involvement, why not go to the police?"

He shot me a sardonic look. "Did *you* ever go to the police?"

The answer lodged like a stone in my throat. Of course, I hadn't. Because men like Victor were untouchable.

Henry leaned closer, his voice low and unshakable as he stated, "I've been around men like Victor my entire life. He's too well-connected, as you know. Nothing would happen to him. He paid off the DA to have the autopsy report falsified. He could just as easily pay off the DA to drop the charges. I knew if I wanted justice, I had to get it myself. So yes, I planned to hurt him. To make him believe he'd lost what mattered most."

My stomach turned, bile searing my throat as my vision blurred, my head throbbing once more. "So what? You were going to...kill me?"

"Absolutely not," he answered without a moment's hesitation. "I planned to *take* you. That's all. I wanted him to wake up every morning, see your empty side of the bed, and feel what I feel every day I wake up.

"I spent months watching you. Galas. Fundraisers. I knew I'd have one chance to do this. And I needed to do it right. But that night at the museum..." He trailed off, staring past me, as if watching the memory unfold before him.

"I didn't plan to approach you that night. Or follow you into that exhibit. But there was just something about you. And when our eyes met..." He licked his lips, as if struggling to find the words. "I felt...alive. And I hated myself for it. You were supposed to be the enemy. I was supposed to hate everything you stood for, but something about you got under my skin."

A spark of something lit up inside me.

Because I'd felt the same thing, too.

For those few moments we were alone in the pastoral

exhibit, I felt alive. Just like he did. I felt like I could be myself again. I could be Ariana Summers.

Not Victor Kane's wife.

Henry was the first person in years who I felt actually saw me.

Or was he just saying this because he knew it was what I wanted to hear?

"The next day, I took my boat out to clear my head. But instead of heading to open water, I found myself steering toward Star Island. That's when I saw a boat pull up to your dock and a man dressed all in black get out. A few minutes later, he emerged with your unconscious body. I followed his boat to a warehouse up the Intracoastal. Took him out. Grabbed you and his duffel, and brought you up to Maine while I figured out who he was and what he wanted."

"Took him out," I repeated slowly. "What do you mean by that?"

"I killed him," Henry responded bluntly. No excuses. No hesitation.

I should have been scared. If anyone else had told me they'd killed a man, I would have been horrified. Fearful for my own welfare.

But Henry wasn't like everyone else.

He never had been.

And that only confused me even more.

"I guess you should be grateful this guy did your

dirty work for you," I snipped out, crossing my arms in front of my chest.

Pain shot through my ribs, but I pushed it down, not wanting to show any weakness. Over the years, I'd become a master at masking pain. I knew if I'd shown any indication of the trauma Victor forced me to endure, it would only be worse the next time.

"That's not it at all." Henry dragged a hand down his face. "I admit that I *did* plan on abducting you, but after seeing someone else take you… I don't know. I was so fucking confused. You put me off balance, Ariana. You made me feel things I didn't think possible. You *make* me feel things I didn't think I ever would. That's why I intervened. I could tell the guy who tried to take you was dangerous. Until I could figure out who the hell it was, I needed to keep you safe."

"You were an ass to me," I reminded him. "Hot one minute, ice cold the next. It was like emotional whiplash living with you. Thankfully, I had years of experience with that sort of thing."

"And I'm sorry for putting you through that. I just…" He looked up at the ceiling, seemingly trying to make sense of his jumbled thoughts. I'd never seen him so on edge. So uncertain. "I didn't want to care about you. In my head, you were just as evil as Victor." His Adam's apple bobbed up and down in a hard swallow. "But then I saw your scars…."

He squeezed his eyes shut, his jaw tight, hands clenched into fists. The anguish in his expression felt so real. So raw. It couldn't have been an act.

Could it?

"All along, my goal was to make Victor pay for what he did to Sarah." He lifted his blazing eyes to mine. "But when I saw what he did to you?" He shook his head. "I'm sorry I didn't realize the truth sooner. The signs were all there. I was just so blinded by my hatred that I ignored them. But I promised myself from that moment on, I'd do everything in my power to protect you. Instead, all I did was put you in harm's way again. If I'd told you the truth, you never would have had a reason to turn on that phone. Never would have read that conversation. Never would have tried to escape. And because of me, you could have died. Those bastards who ran you off the road and—"

"Wait." I straightened, blinking repeatedly. "That wasn't you?"

"Of course not," he replied, indignant.

I searched his face for any indication he was lying. A flinch. An averted gaze. A twitch in his lips. I didn't see one.

"Then who—"

"When you turned on that phone, the Bratva were able to track it. Were able to track *you*. They sent a team."

I kept my face blank, but inside, my thoughts spun. If

he was telling the truth, then he hadn't betrayed me like I'd thought. He was just as caught up in whatever this was as me. But I still didn't know whether I could trust him. I'd trusted Victor at one point, too.

I learned the hard way it was a mistake.

I couldn't afford to make the same mistake again.

"How did I end up here? How did you find me?"

"One of my men tracked a plane from Miami that landed in a small airfield somewhat close to my cabin."

"And the team the Bratva sent?"

"Are no longer breathing."

Even more dead men. Even more blood on his hands. But he didn't seem to care. What did that say about him?

"Why is the Bratva after me?"

"I'm not sure the Bratva *is* after you. Not in that sense. They were paid to do a job. That's all."

My pulse quickened. "By whom?"

His green eyes locked on mine, steady and unflinching. "Your husband."

CHAPTER SEVEN

Henry

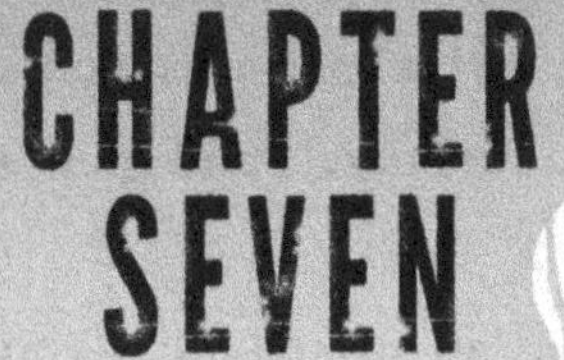

Ariana's face went pale the second the words left my mouth.

Victor Kane put a target on his wife's back.

I hated telling her. Hated being the one to drive that final knife into her chest. It didn't matter that she despised him. That he'd beaten her. Broken her. Stripped her down to nothing but fear and scars.

To learn the man who was supposed to love and protect her had paid to have her abducted still shattered something inside her.

"H-how do you know?" Her voice was strained, like she was holding herself together with fraying threads.

I leaned forward, my elbows on my knees, and exhaled a long breath.

"When I first saw that man try to take you, I figured he was just some schmuck hoping for a big payday. Someone who thought he could grab Victor Kane's wife and cash out." I shook my head. "But after I ran his prints and face through every database and corner of the internet yet still came up empty, I knew it was bigger than that. Deeper. This man was a ghost. You don't hire a ghost for a routine snatch and grab, so to speak. And then…"

"Yes?" she pressed, urging me to continue.

"Then I went back through her videos. The last one was from Santa Monica right before she'd died. I've seen it hundreds of times. Thousands maybe." I paused, pushing down my frustration over everything. "But this time, I noticed something I'd missed before. A man walking in the background." I lifted my eyes to hers. "He only looked at the camera for a split second and he kept to the shadows, but it was him. The same man who tried to abduct you."

"It could have been a coincidence," she suggested.

"I don't believe in coincidences."

Her throat worked around a hard swallow.

"Sarah died shortly after that video," I went on, forcing out the words that were still hard to come to terms with. "A few months later, the same man who appeared in Sarah's last video tried to take you. A ghost with no record. The second I saw him in the background,

I knew Victor had to be behind it. I couldn't prove it yet, but I could feel it in my gut. Which I was able to confirm last night."

"How?"

"After I took care of the men the Bratva sent, one of their phones rang. I answered. Victor was on the other end. Demanded to know what was taking so long. Reminded them he'd paid good money."

"Maybe he hired them to find me." Her voice practically pleaded with me to consider the alternative. But there wasn't one. Not with everything I now knew about Victor Kane.

"We know the man who tried to abduct you was working for the Bratva. What are the chances Victor *also* hired the Bratva to find you? Plus, I uncovered these photos from the gala."

I pulled my phone from my pocket, swiped through the photos Blake sent me, and handed it to her.

"Do you know this man?"

Her brow furrowed. "That's Maxim Covell. One of Victor's lawyers."

"He's the one who pulled him away at the gala, correct? Before you disappeared into the exhibit where we spoke."

"Yes."

"Swipe to the next photo and tell me if you know who *that* is."

She did, her brows furrowing as she studied it. "I've never seen him before. Not that I can recall. Who is it?"

"That's Nikolai Volkov. The Obshchak of the Miami Bratva."

Her head jerked up.

"And the man you know as Maxim Covell," I continued, "was born Maksim Kolokov. He's essentially the Bratva's front man. Handles their legitimate dealings while Volkov is in charge of their *less than* legitimate business. Laundering. Bribes. Trafficking. Drugs. Guns. Stuff like that."

She stared at the phone for several long moments. "So the night before a man broke into your home to take you when your husband was conveniently out of town, Victor was pulled out of a public event to talk to a known criminal. This was planned, Ariana. And Victor's involved."

Her eyes fluttered shut. A single tear cut a clean path down her bruised cheek, glistening under the low light, catching on the shadowed curve of her face. My chest ached watching it. For a heartbeat she looked fragile. Like she was about to shatter into a million pieces. Then steel slammed back into place, her expression hardening, her despair replaced with anger.

"Why? Why go through all this? It doesn't make any sense. If he wanted me dead, he's had plenty of chances over the years. I've lost count of the number of times I was confident he was seconds away from finally killing me. Or is this his way of keeping his hands clean? Allow him to act the part of a grieving husband instead of a murderer?"

"I considered that possibility, too. But I don't think he wants you dead. That man who tried to abduct you? He could have easily killed you. Same with the team they sent to Maine. Hell, one of them had a hitman tattoo inked across his neck. They were all capable of ending you in seconds. But they didn't. You saw the messages on the phone. What did they call you?"

Her jaw tightened. "Merchandise."

Rage burned through me at the reminder, but I forced it down. She needed calm. Logic. Not my fury.

"Exactly," I said tightly. "There's another reason. Something else they want you for."

"What?"

"I don't know. But I'm going to figure it out," I promised her, my voice steadier than I felt with all the uncertainties swirling in my head. "Is there anything you noticed about Victor's behavior in the days leading up to that man taking you? No matter how small or insignificant it may seem, it could help."

Her mouth twisted. "He didn't usually involve me in anything important. I was just supposed to look pretty, keep my mouth shut, and take whatever beating came my way."

My hands curled into fists, my blood running hot. It took everything I had to push down my anger.

"Anything at all, Ariana," I encouraged. "Don't doubt yourself."

She exhaled slowly, shaking her head. Then she stopped, peering into the distance.

"What is it?"

"It's probably nothing."

"Or it could be everything."

"That night at the gala... He never left me alone like that. *Ever.*"

I nodded, contemplating what was so important for Victor to leave Ariana if he usually didn't. I was kicking myself for not following Victor instead of Ariana. If I had, maybe I would have figured out what he was involved in. What Ariana's role was in all of this.

But if I *hadn't* followed her, I never would have spoken to her. Never would have been mesmerized by her. Never would have been on my boat outside her home on Star Island.

And I never would have seen that man try to take her.

As much as I wished I knew what Victor had discussed with Nikolai Volkov outside the art museum, I couldn't regret not tailing him. Not when that one decision may have saved Ariana from whatever Victor had planned.

"How was he afterwards?"

Her laugh was brittle. "Aside from nearly choking me to death for talking to you?"

I gritted my teeth until my jaw ached, my nostrils flaring as guilt collided with rage. What I wouldn't give to wrap my hands around Victor's throat and bring him to the edge of death.

I had to remind myself his time would come. I'd make sure of it.

"I swear to you, Ariana," I began, my voice trembling with the raw fury vibrating through me. "I'll make him pay for every second of fear he instilled in you. Every bruise. Every scar. Every minute he made you wish for death. I'll make him do the same. And I won't fucking rest until he can no longer hurt you or anyone else."

I kept my eyes glued to hers so she could see the truth in my words. I'd never wanted anyone to believe me as much as I wanted Ariana to believe me right now.

To *trust* me.

For one suspended heartbeat, I thought she did. Thought she saw me not as her captor, but as the man who would risk everything for her. Who would *bleed* for her. But just as quickly, her walls went back up, her expression tightening once more.

"I assumed it was because he saw me talking to another man," she admitted, pinching her lips together as she stared past me again, deep in thought. "But now that

I think about it, he was on edge before we left for the gala. He went straight for the scotch when he came home earlier that day. He only did that when something had him rattled."

"So he comes home upset," I began, hoping to make sense out of the various puzzle pieces. "At the gala, he leaves you to discuss something with the Obshchak of the Miami Bratva. The following day, a man tries to abduct you. A man we now know was paid to take you and was working with the Bratva to some extent. It has to be connected. I just don't know what their endgame is."

"What do we do now?"

We. The word hit me straight in my gut. It gave me hope I hadn't completely fucked this up. I didn't expect her to forgive me right away. Or trust me. Not after everything her husband put her through.

Not after everything *I* put her through.

But I was going to do everything in my power to earn her trust. Even if it took me the rest of my life.

"*We* don't do anything," I told her gently. "You have a concussion, along with a sprained knee and some bruised ribs. All you need to do right now is rest."

"You expect me to rest while the Bratva is after me?" She sucked in a sharp breath, flinging her eyes to mine, panic and concern swirling within.

"What is it? Did you remember something?"

"My mom. What about my mom? What if they..." Her voice cracked as tears welled in her eyes.

"Your mother is fine."

She vehemently shook her head. "You don't know that. The day I was taken, she warned me. Said she saw a man with a raven tattoo. I thought it was just her nonsensical rambling, but what if—"

"Ariana." I leaned closer, firm but steady. "I swear to you. She's fine. Would you like to see for yourself?"

Her breath caught, and she snapped her eyes to mine. "How?"

I smiled faintly and stood, sliding my phone back into my pocket. "May I?" I gestured down her frame.

She frowned, not understanding, but nodded anyway.

I bent and carefully lifted her into my arms.

"What are you doing?" She gasped, clutching at my shirt, the heat of her touch searing through the fabric.

My god, it felt good to feel her again. To have her body against mine. To have her hands on me.

"What I promised." I adjusted her gently, mindful of her ribs. "Taking you to see that your mother's fine."

CHAPTER EIGHT

Ariana

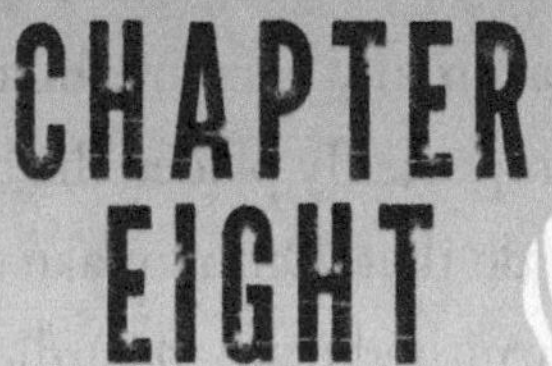

Henry's arms felt impossibly steady around me. I shouldn't have taken comfort in it. Not after what he'd just confessed. How he'd planned to abduct me. How he'd studied me. How I'd been nothing more than a means to an end.

Every instinct I possessed should have been screaming at me to get away. To run as far as I could.

Instead, my body leaned into his warmth like it remembered something my mind refused to accept. His chest rose and fell against me, the scent of cedar and citrus clinging to his shirt as he held me with a tenderness I rarely experienced.

Victor seemed gentle once, too. His hands careful. His voice soft. His concern convincing.

Until it wasn't. Until his care became a cage, his love a weapon. I swore I'd never mistake protection for possession again.

And yet here I was, allowing myself to be carried in the arms of a man who'd confessed to abducting me.

But was he really as bad as Victor?

He'd never taken any accountability for his actions. If anything, he'd repeatedly placed the blame on me.

Henry didn't do that. Didn't make excuses. Just gave me the cold, unvarnished truth, regardless of how I might respond.

Shouldn't that have been enough for me to believe him?

I wasn't sure.

The air shifted as Henry moved through his home. I expected dark wood and oversized furniture, like the cabin he'd kept me in.

But this house was a contradiction. Bright. Open. Comfortable.

I got the feeling this place was his true home. The place he felt most at ease. It made me want to search every inch for greater insight into who he was.

He carried me down a winding staircase and through a great room drenched in what felt like late afternoon light, his footsteps a steady rhythm against the polished wood. The French doors opened, and a petite woman slipped inside, sunlight catching in her auburn hair.

"I was just coming to check on you," she said, her kind brown eyes meeting mine. "How are you feeling, Ms. Summers?"

The name hit me like a soft blow.

Ms. Summers.

My name before Victor. Before I sold my soul to a devil in an expensive suit. It sounded foreign. Like seeing my reflection for the first time in years. I had to resist the urge to correct her out of habit.

I didn't want to be Mrs. Kane anymore.

But I wasn't sure I knew how to be Ariana Summers, either. Wasn't sure who that person was.

Wasn't sure who *I* was.

"A little sore," I managed.

"I'd like to do an exam, if that's okay with you. Check your injuries, especially your head."

I glanced at Henry, uncertain who this woman was.

"This is Krystal," he explained. "She's a nurse I hired." He shifted his attention to her. "Can we hold off on the exam until later? Ms. Summers would like to see her mother."

"Of course, sir." Krystal nodded without hesitation. "Mrs. Summers is out in the garden."

The words barely left her mouth before my pulse spiked, and I snapped my gaze back to Henry.

"She's here?"

"I told you I'd show you she was okay." He gave a small, knowing smile as he stepped outside.

Fresh air wrapped around me, cloaking me in the comforting aroma of freshly cut grass and jasmine. It had been ages since I'd been outside. Since I'd felt the sun's rays. The breeze blowing through my hair.

But that was second to learning my mother was *here*.

When he said he'd take me to see she was okay, I assumed he'd arrange for me to call her at the care facility. I never expected this.

"How?" I asked through the emotion welling in my throat.

"I can be very persuasive." A mischievous smirk curved his lips before his expression turned serious. "Plus, I found some questionable bank transactions between Victor and the head of Serenity Grove...or whatever that place was called."

"He was paying for her care," I explained.

Henry shook his head. "These payments were in addition to what Victor paid the facility."

"Why?"

"I have my suspicions, but I need to do a bit more...digging."

"What do you—"

"Don't worry about it. I promise to tell you everything I uncover. For now, all I want you to focus on is spending time with your mother. After everything you've been through, you deserve that."

The sincerity in his voice unsettled me more than any threat could have. Because it sounded real. *Too* real.

We followed a cobblestone path framed by winter jasmine and the occasional bird chirping. The rhythm of his steps quickened with my heart. I braced myself for disappointment, for illusion. This was the sort of trick Victor would play on me. He reveled in getting my hopes up, then cruelly dashing them, all to remind me who was in control.

But when Henry rounded the corner, I learned this wasn't a trick or a mind game. This was real. My mother was here. And not sitting on a bench, lost in some faraway place only she could see, as was always the case whenever I visited her at the care facility.

She was kneeling in a patch of dirt, sunlight woven through her white hair, planting bursts of marigolds and pansies like it was the most natural thing in the world.

Like the last several years never happened.

Her eyes met mine as she stood. I almost called out for her to be careful, insist Henry put me down and help her.

To my surprise, she didn't waver, her footsteps steadier than I'd seen them in quite a while.

"My girl," she exhaled as Henry gently set me down on a nearby bench.

"Mom," I choked out, tears spilling over before I could stop them. She wrapped her arms around me, and I buried my face in her neck, inhaling the faint scent of lavender and powder that always reminded me of her.

"It's okay, darling," she whispered, rubbing small circles on my back. "I'm here. Everything will be okay."

My chest broke open.

For so long, I'd only seen pieces of the woman she once was, her mind lost somewhere I couldn't follow. And now here she was, lucid and warm, holding me.

How was this possible?

"I'll let you two catch up." Henry's voice cut through, and I pulled my attention back to him. "Krystal will check on you periodically. If you need anything, let her know."

I swallowed hard, peering at him through my tear-stained eyes.

When I'd first woken up in his bed, I'd been convinced he was the enemy. Part of me still wasn't sure whether I could trust what he told me. But this act of kindness undid something in me I didn't know was still holding on.

"Thank you," I whispered.

"Anything to make you happy." His eyes lingered on mine before he looked to my mother. "Mrs. Summers."

She smiled warmly. "Henry."

As he retreated toward the house, the sunlight

glinted off his dark hair, making him look almost ethereal. A hint of light in the darkness that typically consumed him.

"He cares about you," my mother said quietly once he disappeared from view.

I turned my eyes back to her, wiping my cheeks. "You don't—"

"I know." Her voice was calm, clearer than I'd heard it in years. "I can understand your hesitation, especially after Victor."

I didn't say anything. She'd hit the nail on its head. It was precisely what I was thinking.

"But you can always trust your heart, Ariana," she continued. "What does your heart tell you?"

I parted my lips, trying to listen to the same organ that had betrayed me repeatedly. "I don't know."

"Then give it time." She squeezed my hand. "It will know before your head does."

Her words wound their way through me like a vine — fragile, hopeful, terrifying.

Because I already knew what my heart was trying to tell me.

I just didn't know if I was ready to trust it again.

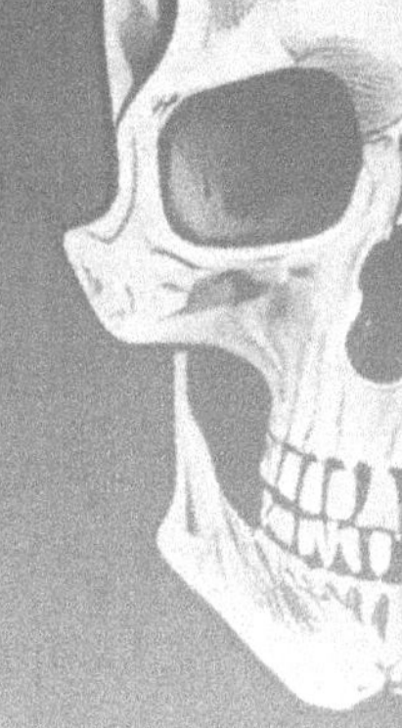

CHAPTER NINE

Henry

My footsteps echoed off the hardwood floor as I stepped back inside the house, but my mind was far away, still caught on the look on Ariana's face when she realized her mother was here.

Pure, unguarded happiness.

I'd never seen her smile like that. I'd seen her laugh out of disbelief, smirk out of defiance, even cry out of frustration. But this? This was different. It was light. Real.

A glimpse of the woman she might have been if Victor Kane hadn't destroyed her life.

And I'd been the one to give it to her. A moment of peace. Of joy.

Hopefully, it would help her see I wasn't the cruel bastard she had every right to think I was.

At least not when it came to her.

"Henry," a voice cut through as I made my way through the living room.

I stopped, my gaze landing on Clark as he stood from the couch, his expression polite, but uneasy.

"I was hoping to have a word."

"Of course." I gestured down the hall. "This way."

I led him into the study, closing the double doors behind us.

I'd never spent much time in this room. It was too polished, too staged. But I didn't want to bring him to my private office. There were things in there he didn't need to see.

As grateful as I was that one of my friends from the navy was now a top neurologist who happily dropped everything to assess Ariana's mother, I didn't want to involve him in this any more than I already had. He had a wife. Kids. With all the uncertainty, I wasn't willing to put them at risk.

I was lucky enough to know someone to call in this type of situation, even if we hadn't spoken in years. That was the thing about going through basic training together. It created a bond we'd carry the rest of our lives. If one of my military brothers was in trouble, I'd drop everything to help. Just like Clark dropped everything to help me.

"How's she doing?" I asked him, gesturing toward the leather couch in the center of the room. "I just saw her outside. She seems...clear." I lowered myself into the armchair opposite him, resting my elbows on my knees.

"I've spent several hours with her this morning, running my own assessment and scans. I've also reviewed the records you provided." He hesitated, and I knew whatever he was about to say wasn't good. "There are...discrepancies."

"Like what?"

He turned his tablet toward me, revealing what appeared to be two different brain scans. He may as well have given me a book written in a foreign language. I had no idea what I was looking at. But Clark did. He'd come a long way from the scrawny kid I met during basic training.

"The image on the left is the scan of Mrs. Summers' brain I performed today," he explained. "The one on the right was in her medical file, supposedly taken by Dr. Schaffer last month."

"Okay...," I drew out, studying the images.

They appeared different, but I didn't know if that was to be expected.

"The scan from today shows no atrophy. No reduced dopamine activity. No plaques or Lewy bodies. No markers of neurodegeneration whatsoever. That level of improvement in four weeks isn't just improbable, Henry. It's impossible."

A slow heat built in my chest. "Could the equipment have been faulty?"

"Not likely. But I repeated the scan on a secondary machine. The results are identical." He narrowed his dark eyes at me. "The scans in her file aren't hers."

I sat back in my chair, letting that sink in. "So you're saying she doesn't have dementia."

"All I'm saying is that based on the scan I performed today, her brain shows no indication of ever having any neurological impairment."

"How do you explain the confusion? Paranoia? Tremors? Ariana observed those with her own eyes. Told me about her slow deterioration over the years."

"I'm not dismissing she may have exhibited those symptoms," he stated evenly. "But I'm not convinced they stem from a neurodegenerative disease. Which is why I ran some panels. Blood. Urine."

"Did you find something?"

He nodded. "I tested for every compound I could think of that might induce cognitive impairment."

"And?"

"I picked up traces of multiple medications. Antipsychotics. Anticholinergics. Barbiturates. Now, these drugs can sometimes be used to treat certain symptoms of

Lewy Body Dementia, but the specific antipsychotic in her system caught my attention."

"How so?"

"If given intermittently, it can induce tremors, rigidity, paranoia. Essentially mimic Parkinsonian or Lewy Body symptoms."

I gritted my teeth. "And the others?"

"The anticholinergic causes confusion and hallucinations. The barbiturates dull cognition. Each one alone might be defensible. Anticholinergics are often used to manage tremors associated with LBD, and benzodiazepines can be given to help with sleep or anxiety, particularly if a patient is suffering from severe moments of paranoia. But when I look at the bigger picture here, specifically the brain scans?" He shook his head. "This looks deliberate. My opinion is that someone wanted her to think she'd lost her mind. Or someone wanted those close to her to think she'd lost her mind."

I stared at the two scans again, my reflection faint in the glass screen — jaw tight, eyes flat, my blood boiling the more I thought about everything. About the reason for all of this.

About *who* would do this.

There was no doubt in my mind Victor was behind it.

According to Ariana, her mother hadn't shown symptoms of impaired brain function until *after* Victor Kane entered their lives. Sure, she suffered from depression after losing her husband, but she'd exhibited no signs of dementia until Victor.

And he'd swooped in like a savior, paying for treatments, handling the logistics, weaving his web of control. He'd found a way to weaponize her fragility, to chain Ariana with it.

My hands curled into fists, the sound of my pulse drowning out everything else.

Victor didn't just ruin Ariana. He destroyed everyone she loved. Hollowed them out. Turned them into tools for his manipulation.

"What do we do now?" My voice was low. Controlled. The kind of calm that came before the most ferocious of storms.

"Assuming you acquired her records through less than legal means, I can make an anonymous tip to the ethics board."

I waved him off. "I'll deal with Schaffer myself. I was talking about Daphne. What's your recommendation for her continuing care?"

"If my theory is correct, we'll need to wean her off these drugs carefully. There could be side effects. I've briefed Krystal on the protocols. She'll monitor Mrs. Summers closely and call me if anything changes. I'll be sure to check in on her regularly, as well, but for now, having a nurse here will ensure she receives any care and treatment she may need."

I nodded, forcing my jaw to unclench. "Thanks, Clark. I really appreciate this."

He offered a faint smile. "It's the least I can do after everything you did for me during basic training. Not sure I would have made it if it weren't for you."

Despite the weight in my chest, I let out a quiet breath of amusement. "You would have. You just needed someone to commiserate with."

"I'm glad it was you, brother," he replied as he stood. "I'll come by in the morning to check on her."

"Let me walk you out." I rose to my feet.

"No need." He waved me off, heading toward the door and pulling it open. "I'll see you tomorrow."

His steps echoed down the hallway as he retreated, and I sank back into my chair.

Every instinct in me screamed for violence.

For retaliation.

I'd had my suspicions Dr. Schaffer was shady, especially after finding large donations from Victor to one of his charities. To most, it would look generous — an extremely philanthropic man supporting the doctor who was helping his wife's mother.

But I knew better.

Victor didn't do anything without expecting something in return.

And now I knew exactly what he'd expected.

"Everything okay?"

I barked out a laugh as Blake walked into the study. "Not even close."

"What did the doc say?" he asked, sitting in the chair opposite me.

I shook my head, unsure where to begin.

But I did know one thing.

"I think it's time Dr. Schaffer answered a few questions."

A slow, dangerous smile curved on Blake's lips. "Consider it done."

CHAPTER TEN

Ariana

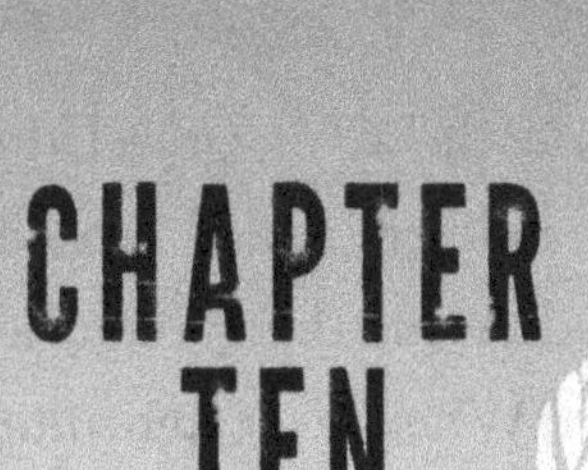

The setting sun washed the garden in hues of pink and blue, the dwindling light catching on my mother's white hair as she leaned over a bed of marigolds. For a few precious hours, it was as if the last decade had never happened.

She hummed softly while she worked, her hands steady as she pressed soil around the roots. She hadn't been steady for years. Every time she glanced up at me, her eyes were clear. Focused in a way I hadn't seen since I was twenty. There were still flashes of confusion, momentary falters as she tried to remember something. But instead of spiraling into panic like before, she listened when I explained. The fog that had swallowed her for so long seemed to lift.

For the first time in years, she felt like my mother again.

I didn't want to question it. Not yet. Instead, I allowed myself to enjoy this without worrying when it would end.

The crunch of boots on gravel drew my attention away from my mother, and I looked up as Henry's shadow stretched across the garden, long and sharp in the fading light. When he came into view, my heart seemed to speed up of its own accord.

His dark hair was damp from a recent shower, curling at the ends, and he wore a pair of jeans and a faded Pink Floyd t-shirt that clung to his chest and biceps. It was such a simple look, but it made him seem real in a way he never had before.

It made me wonder if maybe I was finally seeing the *real* Henry Fontaine.

"Everything okay out here?" His question was low, almost tentative.

"Perfect. Thank you, Henry." My mother smiled at him with an affection and familiarity that surprised me.

She had never looked at Victor this way.

Then again, she'd voiced her concerns about Victor from the beginning.

I replied by insisting she just didn't want me to be happy.

How wrong I'd been.

"But I think I've done enough planting for one day," she continued, rising to her full five-five height and tossing her gardening gloves to the side, brushing off the dirt still clinging to her jeans.

"I'll help you get cleaned up," I offered, standing too quickly.

Pain flared through my knee, and I wavered on my feet. Henry was there in an instant, wrapping an arm around my waist, holding me steady.

The contact sent a pulse of heat straight through me, warm and uninvited.

I hated that my body still reacted to him like this.

"I can manage myself," my mother said, a gentle finality in her tone that left me blinking. For so long, she'd needed help with everything, from brushing her hair to remembering her own name.

Henry inclined his head toward her. "Are you hungry? You're welcome to join me for dinner."

"Was your housekeeper able to get the items on my list?"

"She was," he said. "They're all in your kitchen."

"Then I'd like to cook myself. It's been far too long since I've done anything like that."

"Of course." He gave her a cordial smile. "If you change your mind, the invitation stands."

"I'll come help you," I offered, limping toward her, but she stopped me.

"That's not necessary." There was something knowing in her look, soft but measured. "You two probably have a lot to talk about. And after so many years without privacy, I'd love a little peace."

"Are you sure you feel all right?" I asked, not used to seeing my mother like this.

"I've never felt better." She placed a gentle kiss on my forehead, then turned and walked away.

"She seems like a completely different person," I murmured as I watched her figure disappear into the amber light.

Henry's voice came from behind me, quiet but firm. "That's because she is."

I faced him. "How?"

He parted his lips, as if searching for the words. "I'll explain over dinner."

I raised a brow. "Is this your way of bribing me?"

His mouth lifted in the corners. "Is it working?"

My heart betrayed me with a stutter.

That smile... It reminded me of all the ways he'd once made me feel seen, safe. The way he'd looked at me when he told me none of what Victor did to me was my fault. When he called me a warrior. When he traced my scars like they were something beautiful.

"Please, Ariana. Have dinner with me."

I wanted to say no. Wanted to hate him. Wanted to

keep my distance. But when I saw the pleading look in his eyes, I couldn't seem to form the word.

"Okay," I said quietly. "Dinner."

Relief flickered across his face, as if he'd just won the lottery. He placed a hand on the small of my back, steering me toward the main house.

The kitchen was massive. High ceilings, stainless steel everything, marble counters that gleamed under the recessed lights. He pulled a barstool from the island for me.

"Here. Sit. How's your knee?"

"A little sore," I admitted, wincing as I eased onto the stool. "Krystal gave me a painkiller earlier so that's helped a bit."

"And your ribs?"

"They just feel like I did a really intense workout. The worst pain is probably from the stitches." I touched the bandage over my right brow.

"At least you had a professional stitch you up." He chuckled, opening a bottle of water and setting it in front of me as he passed me a knowing gleam.

"Sorry about that." I stole a glance at the angry red line covering his brow. "First time for me. How's your head? And ankle?"

"I'm fine." He shrugged. "Krystal says I'll have a nice scar to remember you by."

"God. I'm so sorry."

I hadn't even thought about how I might permanently scar or disfigure him when I was patching him up. My sole priority was to stop the bleeding before he lost consciousness.

"It's okay. I've had worse."

I immediately thought of the scars I'd seen across his back — faded pink lines crisscrossing his skin.

"Scars remind us of the battles we fought and won," he said softly, as if able to read my thoughts. "They stop hurting once you stop pretending they never happened."

The words hit somewhere deep inside me. Victor had made me live in denial of every scar, physical and otherwise. Pretend I was whole when I was barely standing. Barely surviving.

But Henry had seen all of them. Instead of looking away, he'd touched each mark like it was proof of my strength.

"So...," he cleared his throat, cutting through the tension. "What are you in the mood for? I have fish, steak, or chicken. Actually, maybe not chicken. I think we've had enough of that particular dish."

Heat flooded my cheeks at the reminder of the night I'd drugged his chicken marsala. Or, more accurately, the mashed potatoes I served *with* the chicken marsala.

"In my defense, I thought you were going to kill me. Or sell me to the Bratva. Or both."

"And now? Do you *still* think I want to kill you?"

"The jury's still out."

"I'll take that as progress." He smiled faintly. "Fish tacos okay with you?"

"Perfect."

He moved around the kitchen with quiet efficiency, seasoning tilapia, chopping tomatoes, mashing an avocado, the scent of lime and cilantro filling the air.

It was fascinating to watch him work, his muscles flexing as he chopped and diced. I could watch him for hours and never get bored.

"What?" he asked without glancing up.

"What do you mean?"

"I can feel your eyes on me."

"I just didn't expect you to cook is all," I lied. I wasn't about to admit I was checking him out. That the sight of him cooking was better than any porn I'd ever seen.

I would take that confession to my grave.

"You've seen me cook before."

"I assumed you'd just reheat something your housekeeper made earlier."

"I like cooking for you," he said simply. "Like taking care of you." His eyes found mine, steady and unguarded. "It's confusing as hell, because I've never been this way. But with you...I don't know. I *want* to do this sort of thing for you."

I wanted to believe him. Wanted to believe this could

be real. That, despite our beginning, maybe something good could come out of this situation.

But life had taught me better. If something seemed too good to be true, it usually was.

When the tilapia was done, he constructed the tacos and set a plate in front of me. The smell alone made my stomach growl. I eagerly lifted one of the tacos and took a large bite, fighting back the moan begging to be set free.

"Good?" he asked.

I nodded, swallowing. "Really good. Thank you."

A faint, satisfied smile ghosted across his lips. He didn't eat right away, just watched me. As if seeing me alive, eating, breathing was a gift he didn't think he deserved.

I shifted my eyes forward, focusing on the food. But the longer we sat in silence, the more unnerved I became.

The more the thousands of questions I'd been asking myself as I sat in the garden with my mother nagged at me.

"Am I still your captive?" I blurted out after several moments. "Is my mother?"

He snapped his eyes toward me, his expression almost offended. "Of course not."

"So we can leave?"

He hesitated, and the pause told me everything I needed to know.

"It's not safe, Ariana. Victor hasn't been seen since

Sunday. If he's running, he's dangerous. And let's not forget he sent the fucking Bratva after you. Until I know there's no longer a threat to you, you're safer here."

"What if I don't *want* to stay?"

"And where would you go? You have no money of your own. No home. Everything you have is tied to Victor."

I parted my lips to argue, but he was right. I'd essentially traded my soul to the devil for a false sense of security. Now, I had nowhere to go. No place to call home.

But did that mean I was willing to stay with Henry?

"Don't ask me to let you go, Ariana. I can't—" He broke off, his voice low and raw. "When I drove up to my Jeep and saw all that blood staining the snow..." He squeezed his eyes shut before returning his pained gaze to mine. "I can't lose you. Please don't make me go through that again. I don't... I don't think I'd survive."

The look on his face made my chest ache.

What must that have been like? To wake up to find me missing? To learn the Bratva was after me?

Then to find the car I'd stolen smashed into a tree with blood everywhere?

I wanted to sympathize with him. Wanted to wrap him in my arms and assure him he'd never lose me.

But I wasn't sure I could trust him.

"How did my mother end up here?" I asked, redirecting the conversation before I allowed his kind words to pull me under.

He tore his eyes from me, clearing his throat. "I wasn't sure how far Victor would go." He took a bite of his taco, washing it down with some water. "I had her brought here just in case. Turns out, I was right. Victor's made substantial donations to a charity Dr. Schaffer is on the board of. My guess is he bribed him to falsify her records. And drug her."

I coughed. "What?"

"She doesn't have dementia, Ariana. The scans didn't match. Her panels showed a cocktail of drugs meant to mimic it. My guess is you only saw your mother when Victor allowed it?"

I slowly nodded.

"Probably made sure she was doped up enough."

"So she's...she's fine?"

"She is."

The words broke something inside me. I covered my mouth, a small sob escaping before I could stop it.

All those years I'd watched her fade. All that guilt. All that grief.

And it was all another lie.

Another game of manipulation.

No wonder doctors couldn't find anything wrong with her until Victor recommended his specialist to us. Dr. Wilson Schaffer.

Without thinking, I reached for Henry. My hand found his, warm and rough. "Thank you."

He squeezed back, his thumb brushing my knuckles. "I'd do anything for you."

There was so much sincerity in his words and, for a moment, I let myself believe him.

Let myself feel the warmth of his touch.

Let myself be happy.

"So what now?" I asked quietly, releasing his hand and refocusing my attention on my taco.

"Now you rest. Spend time with your mother. Make up for the years you lost."

"And you?"

"What about me?"

"What will you do?"

"Whatever it takes to keep you safe," he said. "To make sure no one ever hurts you again."

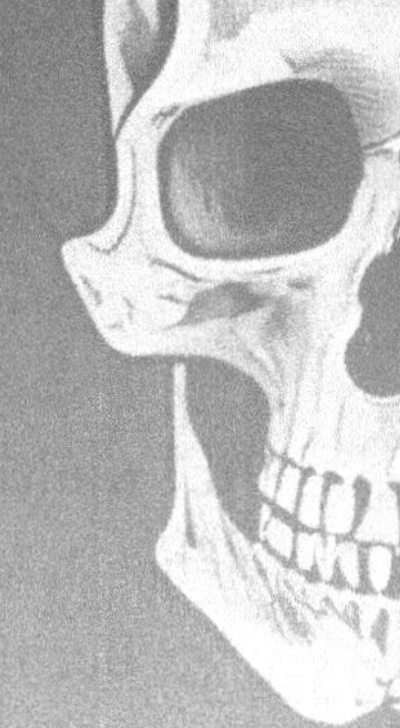

CHAPTER ELEVEN

Henry

The walk to the old barn took just under an hour if I didn't push the pace.

I could have taken the ATV and been there in ten minutes.

But I needed the walk, even if my ankle still throbbed slightly. A walk would do me good.

The night air cut clean through me, heavy with the scent of pine and damp earth. The only sounds were an occasional hoot from an owl and my boots crunching on sticks and dried leaves. Everything else was peaceful. The kind of quiet that settled into my bones and made me feel like the world had stopped turning. It helped me think.

I kept replaying the conversation I'd had with Ariana

during dinner. The way her eyes lit up with hope when she asked if she could leave.

It caught me off guard. I'd assumed once she knew the truth about what Victor had done, she'd understand. That she'd feel safer with me.

But that question had landed like a blade between my ribs.

I wanted to protect her.

But a darker part of me wanted to keep her.

The last of the lights from the house vanished behind a row of trees, leaving me in relative darkness, apart from the moon. But I didn't need it to light the way. I knew every inch of this property. I'd spent hours walking the two-thousand-plus acres of forest, pasture, and hunting ground. Memorized every tree. Every bush. Every path.

Like my father taught me all those years ago during survival training.

After walking a few more miles with nothing but my thoughts to occupy myself, the barn came into view, a gray shape against the darkened sky. I approached the reinforced door and ran my thumb over the biometric scanner. The soft click of the lock disengaging echoed in the quiet. The door groaned when I pulled it open, the smell hitting me the second I stepped inside. Cold air, metal, and disinfectant. Beneath it, something older that soaked too deep into the concrete to ever wash away.

The previous owner had used this building to

process game. I'd meant to convert it to something useful. I never got around to it.

Now I was glad I hadn't.

It was perfect for what I needed tonight. Remote. Sterile. Soundproof.

And already equipped with chains.

I closed the door behind me, then rounded the corner.

Doctor Wilson Schaffer was right where Blake said he'd be. Barefoot on the concrete, wrists suspended from chains bolted to the ceiling. A single floodlight burned down from above, bleaching his skin white and casting long shadows across the floor.

When Blake eagerly agreed to bring Schaffer to me so I could ask some questions, I thought it would take a few days for him to complete his task. Then again, Blake worked with the efficiency of a trained soldier. Once he had his orders, he completed his mission.

My boots echoed on the concrete as I walked toward Schaffer, but he didn't react. His head lolled forward, a dark bruise spreading along his temple from where Blake most likely had introduced him to the butt of his gun.

I studied him for a moment. The sweat-stained shirt. The sagging belly pressing against the fabric. The bald spot he tried to hide with a really bad combover.

Then I drove my fist into his ribs.

He woke with a choked cry, his eyes snapping open, panic flaring as he took in the chains, the light, the space.

"Morning, doc. Or, I guess I should say, 'Evening.'"

"Wh-Where am I?" His voice cracked. "What's going on?"

"I'll be asking the questions." I dragged a folding chair across the floor, the metal legs screeching against the concrete. "You can start by telling me why you *think* you're here." I plopped down in the chair.

"I..." He blinked, confused. "I don't know."

"Think harder. Your life depends on it."

His gaze flicked over my face, searching. Calculating. Like a man trying to determine the rules of a game he didn't realize he'd already lost.

"Is this about Daphne Summers?" he asked somewhat hesitantly.

"There we go." I leaned back, propping one ankle on my knee. "And I was worried I'd have to...jog your memory. Now tell me. What arrangement did you have with Victor Kane?"

"I'm overseeing his mother-in-law's care. I can't tell you anything more without violating privacy laws."

I threw my head back and laughed, the sound echoing through the barren space. "Privacy laws? You disregarded your oath the second you started drugging a woman for money, but now you're worried about patient privacy?"

"I never disregarded my oath."

I leaned forward, resting my elbows on my knees. "I'll give you one more chance to be a decent person. Victor called you Sunday night. What did you talk about?"

"I'm not at liberty to discuss that information."

"Pity."

I stood and crossed to the workbench, my hand brushing the various knives mounted on the wall, all gleaming steel with dark wooden handles. Some long and thin, meant for detailed work. Others thick and brutal to make cutting through bone easier.

"My father taught me how to use each and every one of these," I said softly. "Instead of toy cars or action figures, he gave me a set of hunting knives. Said I needed to know how to take something apart. How to make a clean kill."

Schaffer audibly whimpered.

"I didn't want to at first. I couldn't stomach the thought of taking another life, even an animal's. But he taught me something that stuck. Not every creature deserves compassion." I laughed under my breath. "It's funny. After hearing him say it enough times, it became my mantra, too. Made me realize *he* didn't deserve compassion, either, so I killed him."

My hand hovered over the hacksaw before continuing onto the skinning knife, removing it from its place. I turned, the knife glinting under the light.

"Let's see if you deserve compassion."

He stiffened as I advanced on him, slicing down the front of his shirt, the blade easily tearing apart the fabric. The air hit his damp skin, sweat beading on his brow.

"Have you ever hunted, doc?"

He vehemently shook his head, his sole focus on the knife in my hand.

"It's not as simple as pulling a trigger," I explained. "You see, we lived off the land when I was a boy. Had to kill to survive. I learned how to gut, clean, and quarter the game we killed." I dragged my knife over his skin, but didn't puncture it. Not yet. "Over the years, I got to be quite efficient at it. I could take a freshly killed deer and have it quartered in less than an hour." I gave him a sly grin. "As if the poor soul never even existed."

The stench hit before the sound, a sharp ammonia tang as his bladder gave out, staining his pants. The puddle gathered beneath his feet, trickling toward the drain.

"So let's try again, shall we? What did Victor say when he called you this past Sunday?"

"H-he was worried about Daphne," he stammered. "Mrs. Summers."

"Worried?"

"He's been paying for her treatment. I—"

I cut a line along his abdomen. It was shallow, but sharp enough to draw blood. His groan echoed off the concrete, his breathing growing ragged.

"Don't lie to me," I seethed. "He paid you to falsify her records. Drug her until she couldn't tell up from down. Isn't that right?"

He shook his head frantically. "I only did what—"

"She's under real care now," I interrupted. "The doctor I hired is a top neurologist. He performed another scan. No atrophy. No cognitive decay. In fact, this most recent scan is so different from all the other ones in her medical records, there can be only one explanation." I pressed the blade further into his skin. "Your scans were falsified."

"I may have...adjusted them," he gasped. "But that's all—"

I dug the knife deeper, and he screamed out, his face scrunched up in agony as blood ran down his side.

"Don't worry, doc," I said calmly. "That won't kill you. Not right away. But I don't need to tell you that. You're a doctor. You already know you can survive for a while with a puncture wound in the intestines. I mean, you *will* eventually die if left untreated. And it's a slow, agonizing death. But, hey. At least you're not dead yet. Right?"

"I swear to God," Schaffer began, his voice barely audible as blood fell in streams from his open wound.

"God can't help you now," I taunted. "Only I can. So tell me the truth."

"I *did*. I don't—"

I flipped the knife and pressed the handle into the wound. His scream tore through the silence, raw and anguished.

"Try again."

"I gave her medication," he confessed, "to mimic symptoms."

"Why?" I dug the handle a little deeper.

"He asked me to."

"And you just blindly obeyed?"

His silence was all the answer I needed. It didn't take a genius to put the pieces together. I saw the donations to Schaffer's charity. A bribe masked as benevolence.

"I see." I removed the knife, and Schaffer exhaled a long breath. "As long as someone with enough money asks you to disregard your oath, you're happy to do so. Tell me, doc. What's the going rate for your soul these days?"

"I didn't *hurt* her," he attempted to argue in his defense.

"You drugged her," I snarled, bringing the knife up to his throat. "You stole her memories. A decade of her life was spent in a perpetual state of fog and paranoia. And you think that's not harm?"

"She's alive, isn't she?" he rasped. "He ordered me to kill her, and I didn't. Doesn't that count for something?"

My grip loosened, his statement stealing my breath. I lowered the knife, studying him for any hint of deception. "Who ordered you to kill her?"

He pinched his mouth together, not wanting to utter another word. But I had ways of convincing people to talk.

Stalking over to the workbench, I grabbed the pliers and returned to him, bringing them up to his pinky. He immediately stiffened, trying to yank his hands away, but the chains made it impossible.

"Last chance, doc. Who ordered you to kill her?"

I already knew. I just needed him to say it out loud.

I added pressure to his finger, the sound of breaking bones echoing in the space.

"Victor!" he shouted through his labored breathing. "He told me to kill her, but to make it look natural. Like she'd died from her condition."

"The condition you fabricated."

"I knew it was another test of my loyalty, but this one... It went far beyond the drugs or sterilizations. I never thought he'd ask—"

"Wait. What?" I released his pinky and stepped

back. "What are you talking about? What do you mean by sterilizations?"

He inhaled a sharp breath, as if realizing what he'd just said. "I didn't—"

I brought the pliers up to his next finger, about to squeeze once more, when he blurted out, "He's had me sterilize women."

I took a step back, toiling this new piece of information over in my head.

It was the last thing I expected to come out of his mouth. I figured Victor had been bribing the doctor to falsify Daphne's records as a way to control and manipulate Ariana. Keep her quiet. Keep her compliant.

But to learn this? It seemed out of left field.

"You're a neurologist. Isn't this outside your area of expertise?"

He shrugged. "I'm not technically board certified, but I spent time volunteering overseas during my younger years. I learned the procedure then."

"How many women?"

"I don't know." I approached him once more, and he rushed out, "Four, maybe five."

"For what? Why did he want you to do this?" I demanded, although I had a feeling I already knew.

The last thing Victor needed was a scandal to ruin his squeaky-clean reputation. What better way to make sure there weren't any surprises than to sterilize the women he was sleeping with outside of his marriage?

"It wasn't my place to ask," Schaffer responded.

"Of course. As long as the money's green. Right?" I sneered in disgust as a thought popped into my head.

I yanked my cell out of my pocket and pulled up a photo of Sarah, holding it in front of him.

"Do you recognize this woman? Did you sterilize her?"

He studied her, the seconds seeming to stretch as I waited for him to confirm my suspicions.

"I can't be sure. Maybe. Truthfully, they all looked the same."

I shoved my phone back into my pocket. "And you never questioned Victor as to why he wanted you to sterilize these women instead of them going to their own doctor?"

"I told you. It wasn't my place to ask."

Annoyed by his blind obedience, I whirled on him, thrusting my knife into his stomach.

Deep.

Precise.

Deadly.

His eyes widened, and he made a sound, half gasp, half sob. Then his head fell forward.

I stood there for a long time, watching the red spread

across the concrete, my pulse roaring in my ears, adrenaline eating my veins.

I drew in a calming breath, finding more satisfaction than I should have as I watched the blood trickle down the drain.

"Like I said... Not all creatures deserve compassion."

I tossed the knife onto the workbench. Then I turned and walked away.

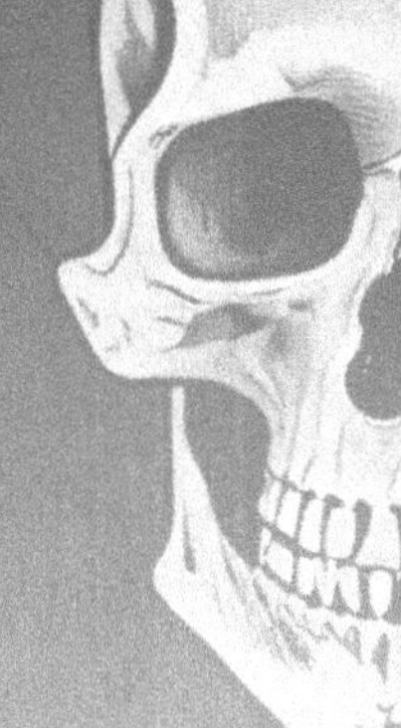

CHAPTER TWELVE

Ariana

Sunlight woke me before I was ready for it. It knifed through the curtains in thin, golden lines, landing across the rumpled sheets. My muscles protested when I moved, especially my knee, but the pain wasn't as sharp as yesterday.

Unfortunately, the ache did nothing to dull the irritation simmering inside.

I'd barely slept, my mind replaying Henry's voice on a loop, telling me I wasn't his captive, but that I still wasn't free. And each time I thought about it, the more frustrated I became with the situation. Sure, he sounded distraught when he spoke of walking up to the Jeep and seeing all my blood. But was that enough of a reason for him to take away my freedom?

I blinked against the light and forced myself to sit up. The room smelled faintly of lemon and tea tree oil — soft, soothing, curated. Everything in this house was like that. Thoughtful. Comfortable. Controlled.

Just like the prison Victor kept me in.

It made my skin itch.

Swinging my legs over the edge of the bed, I limped toward the bathroom and went about my business before washing my hands and splashing cold water on my face. It did nothing to soothe the storm brewing inside me. If anything, the bandage on my forehead was a stark reminder of my captivity.

After twisting my hair into a messy bun, I made my way out of the room, intending to check on Mom in the guest house.

But halfway down the stairs, a familiar sound stopped me in my tracks.

Laughter.

Not just any laughter. My *mom's* laughter.

It had been so long since I'd heard it without the brittle edge of confusion, I almost didn't recognize it.

I followed it down the stairs and into the kitchen, the smell of bacon making my stomach growl. Mom perched on a stool by the island, drinking a tea as Henry moved through the open space.

It brought back memories of the first morning I woke up in the cabin. I'd been so taken aback to see

Henry cooking, let alone for me. I wasn't sure if I should even eat the bacon, since Victor never let me have any.

But Henry did.

He didn't dictate what I did or what I ate.

He didn't control me.

So why was I so eager to put him in the same category as Victor now?

Sensing my presence, Henry looked up from the frying pan, his green eyes locking on mine. "Morning."

"Morning," I replied evenly, turning my attention to my mom, who looked between us with interest.

I still hadn't told her everything about how I met Henry and what led us to this point. I was still coming to terms with it myself. For now, all she knew was he'd witnessed someone try to abduct me and took me to safety.

If his version of events were to be believed, it wasn't that far from the truth.

"How did you sleep, Ma?" I asked.

"Great," she said brightly. "You?"

"Fine."

It was a total lie.

"Bacon and eggs okay for breakfast?" Henry asked, setting a coffee in front of me. It was made exactly how I liked it.

Another small gesture that should have soothed me

but instead made me feel like I was being handled. Controlled.

"Sure."

The first sip burned just enough to wake me. I watched as he tossed a strip of bacon to Cato, who caught it and swallowed it without chewing before resuming his begging position, wagging his tail in the hopes of Henry throwing him even more scraps.

"I was just telling Henry about your ballet days," Mom announced, taking a sip of her tea.

I groaned. "Oh, god. Not this story."

Henry's grin widened. "Is it true you wanted to take karate instead?"

"I wanted to break boards," I deadpanned.

Mom laughed. "Her grandmother got her ballet lessons for her birthday, so we made a deal. Stick it out until the recital, then she could switch. I probably should have specified she had to at least *attempt* to follow the choreography."

I stared at her, stunned by the clarity in her voice. She hadn't told a story this easily in years. Hadn't been able to remember details like this.

"What happened?" Henry asked, leaning against the counter, his smile crooked.

"Well," Mom continued, "she made it to the recital, all right. But when the music started, she did her own thing. Half the class followed her because she'd been so confident in her routine. It was chaos, but in the best way possible."

Henry laughed, a deep, unguarded sound that filled the room, but I refused to let it chip away at the wall around my heart.

"You little rebel," he teased.

"I wanted to take karate."

"And did you?"

"I did," I said. "But I hated that, too."

He chuckled, shaking his head. "So what *did* you enjoy as a kid?"

Before I could respond, a soft voice broke through. "Sorry for the interruption."

I glanced toward the doorway to find Krystal standing there, dressed in her scrubs.

"Dr. Irwin is here to check in on you, Daphne. See how you're doing."

"Can she have something to eat first?"

Krystal opened her mouth to answer, but my mother beat her to it. "I've already eaten," she said with a breezy, matter-of-fact tone I hadn't heard since I was a teenager. "I made myself some oatmeal earlier."

"I'll come with you to see the doctor," I said automatically, already pushing back from my chair.

Mom stopped me with a gentle hand on my forearm. "You stay. Have some breakfast. You don't need to worry about me anymore."

"I don't think I know how," I replied honestly.

She smiled, soft but firm. "You'll figure it out. For now, let me be the mom again, okay?"

The words snagged something deep in my chest. "Okay."

"And as your mom..." She squeezed my arm. "It's my job to remind you that breakfast is the most important meal of the day. So stay. Enjoy your breakfast." She wrapped me in a tight hug and whispered, "He's a good man. Give him a chance."

When she drew back, she had that knowing gleam in her eyes. The same one she used to give me in high school when I claimed the late-night calls from my lab partner were just about our chemistry homework.

With one last smile, she followed Krystal down the hall, leaving me alone with Henry.

At least the dog was a buffer. A warm, breathing distraction following Henry through the kitchen as he set a plate in front of me — eggs, bacon, and a biscuit that smelled like butter and rosemary. He sat beside me, close enough that I could feel the heat radiating off him. There may have been a few feet between us, but his presence seemed to consume everything around me, even the air itself.

I picked up a strip of bacon and took a bite, savoring in the salt and grease. The eggs were runny, just the way I liked them. He'd remembered that, too.

As we ate, the only sounds were the scrape of forks and Cato's occasional whimper for more bacon, which Henry tossed his way every so often.

"Do you have to work today?" I asked, glancing sideways at him, unable to stand the silence any longer. "Or do...whatever it is you do." I furrowed my brow. "What *do* you do?"

"I own a cybersecurity firm."

I tilted my head. "And what does that entail?"

"I help companies protect their networks from outside attacks," he answered, cutting into his eggs. "Set up firewalls. Monitor for breaches. Test vulnerabilities."

"By testing vulnerabilities," I began slowly, "you mean hacking."

"That's one way of testing them."

I studied him, all chiseled muscles and broad physique. He didn't look like the stereotypical computer geek.

"I get the feeling you do more than 'test vulnerabilities.'"

He paused, his knife hovering mid-air. His jaw tightened slightly before he said, "I find holes people don't know exist and fix them. Or erase them." His voice dropped lower. "Permanently."

A shiver traced its way down my spine, and I sensed he wasn't merely talking about deleting files.

"And yes," he went on, "I do need to work today.

There have been some recent developments I need to look into."

"Is it about Victor?" I swallowed hard. "Do you know where he is?"

"Not yet." He lifted his gaze to mine. "But I had a chat with Dr. Schaffer last night."

"What did he say?" I asked somewhat cautiously.

Henry hesitated. His silence felt deliberate. Measured. Like he was deciding whether I could handle the truth.

"I have a right to know," I pressed.

"I know you do." He sighed. "I'm just trying to find a good way of telling you. But I don't think there is one."

My stomach knotted. "What is it?"

"Victor called him Sunday night," Henry said finally.

"And?"

"According to Schaffer, Victor asked him to kill your mother. Make it look like natural causes."

I sucked in a sharp breath, the sound catching in my throat.

"It looks like Victor's in panic mode," Henry went on, calm and clinical, though I could hear the tension underneath the surface. "In my experience, whenever someone's panicking like this, they don't last long. It's only a matter of time before he makes a mistake. And when he does, I'll be there."

I stayed silent, my mind spinning. As much as I questioned whether to trust Henry, I couldn't ignore the truth. If he hadn't pulled my mother out of that care facility, she may have already been dead.

Or was this all yet another lie to endear me to him?

"Schaffer also told me about his arrangement with Victor," Henry added.

"To make my mom think she was losing her mind," I whispered. "More or less."

"Yes. But that was just one part of it."

My pulse quickened. "What else did he do to her?"

"Not to her. To other women. Victor paid him to sterilize them."

I nodded, taking a bite of my biscuit.

"You don't seem surprised by this," Henry remarked.

"Victor is nothing if not cautious. I wouldn't put it past him to send each of his mistresses to his doctor of choice so no one would find out about his indiscretions."

Then I darted my wide eyes toward his, remembering what he'd shared about his daughter. How he believed Victor had been having an affair with her and killed her.

"Did you ask him about Sarah? Was she one of them?"

"He wasn't sure. Said they all looked alike. I'm hoping he kept records somewhere I can access. It's a long shot, but maybe Victor's hiding out with one of these women."

"Can't you just ask Dr. Schaffer for their names? He's obviously cooperating if he told you everything else."

He looked at me, and I immediately knew that was no longer possible.

"Oh." My voice dropped to a whisper.

"He hurt someone you care about," Henry murmured. "So I hurt him. Made sure he can never hurt anyone else. Trust me. For what he did to your mother for over ten years, he got off easy. He deserved so much worse."

His words hung heavy between us. He didn't sound proud. Just resolute. Like it was a fact of life. I wasn't sure whether to be horrified or grateful.

He tore his gaze from mine and pushed back from the table. Gathering our plates, he moved to the sink with the same quiet efficiency that somehow made him seem even more dangerous.

"If you need anything, my housekeeper, Shelby, is around. As is Krystal." He turned and started down the hallway, Cato following obediently behind him.

"So that's it?" I called after him, carefully sliding off the stool.

He faced me once more, furrowing his brow. "What do you mean?"

"I can do whatever I want? Have free rein of your house?"

A small smile curved on his lips. "Of course."

"I can leave then? Because that's something I'd like to do."

His shoulders tensed, his jaw ticking. "I told you last night. It's not safe."

"According to you," I retorted, folding my arms.

"I'm trying to keep you alive, Ariana. That's all."

"And I'm trying not to feel like property again!" The words cracked out of me before I could stop them. "I lived ten years with someone who controlled every breath I took. And now you're doing the exact same thing."

His fists clenched at his sides. "I am *nothing* like that monster."

"Then stop acting like him!"

"I'm *protecting* you," he declared, leaning into me. "That's not the same as controlling you."

"Isn't it?" My voice rose, trembling with anger I couldn't swallow down. "You say I'm not your captive, but you won't let me step off your property. You say I have choices, but every time I make one that doesn't align with yours, it's suddenly too dangerous."

"I'm not going to apologize for wanting to keep you alive."

"You don't have to apologize," I shot back. "But don't pretend this is freedom. It's not."

He raked both hands through his hair, exhaling in

frustration. "I'm sorry you feel like I'm keeping you prisoner. Truly. If you want to hate me for it, fine. Hate me. But I'd rather you hate me and live than love me and die because I let you walk into a death trap."

My breath hitched, my traitorous heart skipping a beat at the mere sound of the word "love" rolling off his lips. But I didn't have a chance to formulate a response before he turned sharply and stormed down the hallway, Cato trotting uncertainly after him.

The echo of his footsteps faded, leaving me standing alone in his quiet house.

Furious.

Shaken.

And more confused than ever.

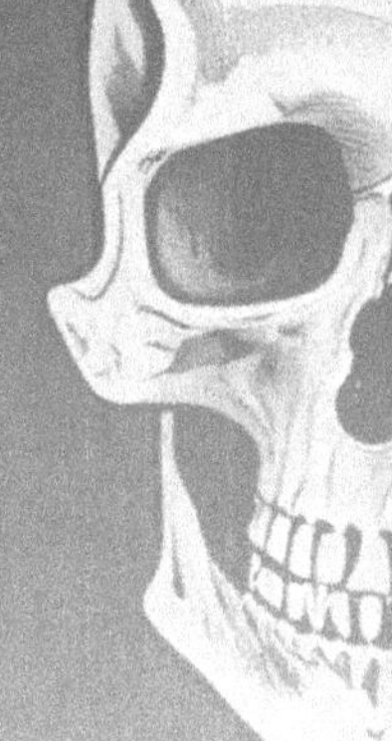

CHAPTER THIRTEEN

Henry

I sat behind my desk, the glow from the monitors washing the room in cold blue light. The hum of the servers filled the silence, steady and low, like a heartbeat I couldn't shut off. Schaffer's files filled the screen in an endless scroll. Appointment calendars. Billing statements. Encrypted medical reports.

But instead of focusing on it and trying to find a clue, my thoughts kept returning to Ariana.

Her voice echoed in my head, telling me I was treating her just like Victor had.

It stung.

But she was wrong.

I was *nothing* like Victor.

Was I keeping her here?

Of course, but it was for her own good.

What was it going to take for her to see that?

The door beeped, and I looked up as Blake walked in, ensuring the door locked behind him before strolling across the room.

"How'd last night go?" he asked, dropping onto the couch.

"Schaffer admitted to drugging Daphne."

He leaned back, resting his ankle on his knee. "Did you ask about the call from Victor?"

I nodded. "He told Schaffer to kill Daphne."

"Bastard." Blake scrubbed a hand down his face. "Why would he want her dead? He'd already made it so she was halfway out of her mind."

"Maybe to manipulate Ariana? Or flush her out of hiding? He knows how much she loves her mother. If Daphne died, Ariana would want to say goodbye." I paused. "It sounds like something he'd do."

Blake nodded grimly, then glanced toward the monitors. "What's all that?"

"Schaffer's patient files. At least the ones I could access."

He narrowed his gaze on me. "Do you think there are others like Daphne?"

"There could be. But that's not what I'm looking for."

"What are you then?"

"Schaffer mentioned that Victor had also been having him sterilize women. My guess is they're the women he'd been sleeping with to ensure there wouldn't be any Victor Juniors."

"I'd say he did us all a favor." He flashed a smile before his expression sobered. "Did you ask about Sarah?"

I blew out a breath. "He couldn't confirm anything. It's most likely a complete waste of time, but maybe Victor's hiding out with one of these women."

"Like you taught me years ago... Leave no stone unturned."

"True." I rubbed the back of my neck. "Except every stone seems to lead to more questions than answers."

"We probably have a few days before anyone notices Schaffer's missing and the police start sniffing around. I can sweep his house and office. See what I can find."

I stared into the distance, unable to shake the feeling we were missing a giant piece of this convoluted puzzle. I doubted this had anything to do with why Victor paid the Bratva to abduct his own wife, but I needed to rule it out.

"Do it," I ordered, shifting my eyes back to the monitors.

My attention caught on the live feed of the second floor as Ariana poked through her bedroom, opening and shutting drawers harder than necessary, pacing the length of the room. Every line of her body radiated frustration and barely contained fury.

Her hand slapped the edge of the dresser before she braced herself against it, shoulders rising and falling with a rough breath. When she turned toward the window, her posture was defensive. Coiled.

Like she resented every inch of distance between her and the freedom that existed on the horizon.

"Do I sense trouble in paradise?" Blake teased.

I exhaled, slowly shifting my eyes toward him. "She asked to leave."

"Let me guess. You told her no."

"What else was I supposed to say?" I threw up my hands in exasperation. "It's not safe. But when I tried to explain that to her, she told me she feels like my prisoner. Which is ridiculous. She's not my captive. I've told her so repeatedly. She needs to stay here for her own safety. Until the threat's gone."

Blake didn't say anything right away. He didn't need to. His silence said everything.

"You think I'm overreacting, don't you?"

He gave a small shrug. "I think you should try seeing things from her perspective. You *did* confess you'd planned to abduct her. And now you're keeping her here, refusing to let her leave."

"To keep her safe."

Blake exhaled, long and slow. "I get it. Between her

asshole husband and the Bratva, there are a lot of factors at play. But you can't ignore how she feels and dictate what you believe is best. You know who else ignored her feelings and dictated her actions?"

I squeezed my eyes shut. "I'm not like Victor."

"I know that," he said evenly. "And deep down, I'm pretty sure Ariana knows that too. But that doesn't give you the right to disregard her reality. You want to prove you're not like that asshole?"

Blake gestured at the monitors.

On the screen, Ariana spun away from the window, grabbed the closest throw pillow, and hurled it against the wall, muttering something under her breath.

"Then give her the one thing Victor never did." He paused. "Give her a choice."

A cold, hollow ache opened in my chest. "Are you suggesting I let her go?"

"Not necessarily." He leaned forward. "But right now you're sacrificing everything, including her trust, for the illusion of control. And she knows it. Hell, she's *reacting* to it. You two are at opposite ends of the same rope, pulling until one of you snaps. And if you keep tightening your grip, *she's* the one who's going to break."

I looked back at the screen, watching as she continued to pace, despite her limp. I wanted to go up there, tell her she needed to rest, but I had a feeling that wouldn't go over very well right now. Not after our last conversation.

"You can keep her safe *and* still give her room to breathe." Blake's voice cut through the static in my head.

"How?" I glanced his way as he stood, buttoning his suit jacket.

"You need to meet her halfway. If you want her to stop seeing you as the enemy, you need to stop acting like you are. That starts with giving her some semblance of freedom."

CHAPTER FOURTEEN

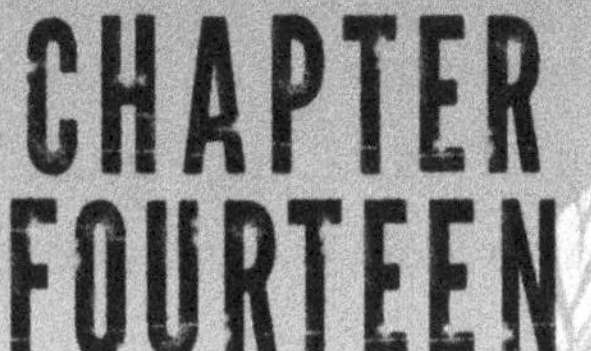

Henry

I'd barely left my office after my conversation with Blake.

Not because I had anything urgent to finish, apart from continuing to dig through Schaffer's patient files. But that wasn't the reason I'd locked myself in here.

Instead, it was to give Ariana space.

If I hovered too much or made it seem like I was constantly watching her, she'd see it as proof I was her warden and she my prisoner. So I stayed in my office, surrounded by the low hum of computers and the faint, bitter scent of stale coffee.

I'd spent most of the day combing through Schaffer's records, searching for anything that might help me figure out what the hell was going on. By late afternoon, the words on the screen had all begun to blur together — names, dates, fragments of medical jargon that led nowhere. I pinched the bridge of my nose and leaned back in my chair, the leather groaning beneath me. I'd been chasing shadows for hours, and all I'd managed to accomplish was to come up with more questions.

What was I missing?

Why couldn't I shake the certainty that whatever Victor had Schaffer doing was worse than anything I'd uncovered so far?

I exhaled slowly, pushing back from the desk. Staring at these files wasn't going to suddenly make the answers materialize. And the longer I sat in here, stewing, the more my thoughts kept drifting to Ariana.

And to my conversation with Blake.

How I needed to meet her halfway.

Was there a halfway? What would it take for her to understand I only wanted to keep her safe? There was no middle ground when it came to her safety. But how did I make her stop being so damn stubborn so she'd realize that?

I needed to clear my head. Move. Sweat. Do something other than spiral in my own damn thoughts.

Standing, I stretched my neck and back, rolling the tension out of my shoulders before stepping into the hallway, taking a moment to adjust to the natural late afternoon light filling the space. The door shut behind me with a soft click, but it still seemed to echo loudly in the quiet house.

As I moved down the hallway, I picked up the faintest trace of lavender and powder drifting through the air, growing stronger with every step I took. And when I emerged into the living room, I knew why.

Because Ariana was there.

She was dragging a suitcase I recognized as one that typically lived in the back of my closet, her expression set with quiet determination.

"I told you it's not safe for you to leave," I said. My voice came out rougher than I intended, seeming to thunder against the high ceilings.

She startled, her eyes wide as she snapped her head in my direction. She blinked repeatedly, her lips parting, obviously taken aback by my presence.

"Here's a little tip. If you're trying to make a quick getaway, it's easier and faster if you leave everything behind."

She straightened, lifting her chin in defiance. "For your information, I'm not leaving."

"Oh, no?" I crossed my arms in front of my chest. "Then explain the suitcase."

"If I'm to be kept here against my will, I'd prefer to choose *where* I stay. And I'd rather stay with my mother. You did say I could go anywhere on your property, correct?"

The challenge in her tone was unmistakable. It reminded me of those first few days at the cabin when every word between us was a test. When I didn't know whether I wanted to comfort her, avoid her, or kiss her senseless.

Hell, most days, I wanted to do all three.

I still did.

From the very beginning, I was drawn to her spirit. Her fire. Her determination.

It was so different from the poised and perfect trophy wife I thought her to be.

"I did…," I drew out.

"Then that's where I'm going. That's what I choose."

"I don't—"

"You wouldn't want to deprive me of this choice." Her gaze met mine, steady and defiant. "Would you?"

Her question held everything… Her anger. Her fear. Her hope. But mixed within was a silent plea, begging me to prove I wasn't like Victor.

A war raged inside me, every instinct screaming to keep her close and protect her. But layered beneath it all was something quieter. Harder. More honest.

I wanted her to trust me. She never would if I kept her caged.

Blake was right. Control was an illusion anyway. If she wanted to run, she'd find a way. If she wanted to stay, that had to be her decision. Her choice.

So, for the first time in a long time, I forced myself to let go. To give up the control I'd held on to for years.

She wanted space and a sense of autonomy.

I could give her that.

"Okay," I said finally.

Her brows rose, her mouth slightly agape. "Okay?"

"Yes," I responded evenly. "I understand why you might want some space. If you prefer to stay with your mother, I won't stand in your way."

"You won't?"

I shrugged dismissively, as if the idea of giving up this much control didn't pain me.

"You're safe as long as you remain on my property. The guesthouse is on my property. No harm will come to you there. Do you want me to help carry your bag?" I gestured toward it, but kept my distance.

She stared at me for several protracted moments, obviously dumbfounded by my sudden about-face. I had a feeling this entire situation was a test. She most likely expected me to push back. But I wasn't going to. I was going to give her some rope.

Some freedom.

"I can manage," she replied.

I stepped aside, letting her pass.

As much as I hated watching her limp through the great room and toward the French doors, I gave her the space she needed, her steps echoing against the polished floors in the cavernous room.

When she opened the door, she paused, glancing back at me. Our eyes met — hers conflicted, mine hopefully confident and reassuring.

Then she faced forward and stepped into the sunlight. I watched until she disappeared from view, the sound of her suitcase on the gravel path fading with her.

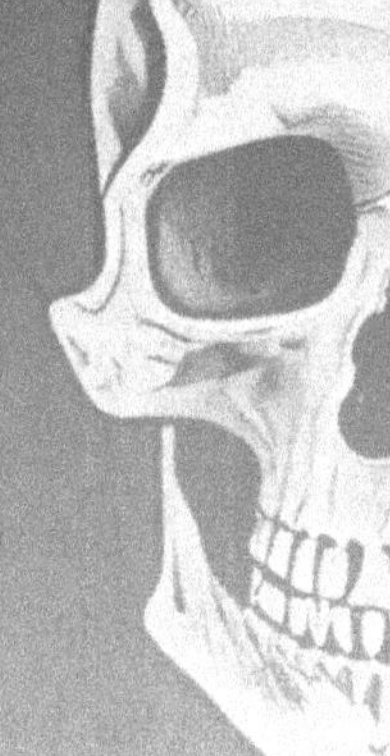

CHAPTER FIFTEEN

Ariana

I t was hard to call this a guesthouse.

The ceilings stretched high enough to swallow sound. Afternoon light spilled through the tall windows, catching on the polished floors and the faint specks of dust dancing in the air. Everything smelled faintly of fresh linen — expensive, clean, impersonal. It was probably twice the size of the house I grew up in, but what mattered most wasn't the luxury.

It was the *space*.

Space to think.

Space to breathe.

Space from Henry.

Especially after he let me go so easily. I'd expected a

fight. Another argument. For him to prove what I'd spent all day convincing myself of.

That he was exactly like Victor.

But that didn't happen.

He let me go, even though I could tell by the tension in his body it was the hardest thing he'd done in a long time.

Yet he did.

Because it was what I wanted.

What I *chose*.

I tossed the suitcase onto the ottoman in one of the spare bedrooms and started unpacking. I folded each item with unnecessary precision — yoga pants, soft t-shirts, everything brand-new. The kind of clothes Victor never allowed me to wear.

Of course Henry would choose them.

Or have someone choose them for me.

As if he knew what I'd been forbidden and wanted to undo it.

Or maybe he just wanted to remind me who held the power now.

I still hadn't decided which.

"You know you don't have to stay here," my mom said gently as she lowered herself onto the bed. "I can manage on my own."

"I know I don't have to." I refolded a t-shirt that didn't need it, careful not to meet her eyes. "I *want* to."

For a while, only the quiet rustle of fabric filled the room, accompanied by the low hum of the HVAC. I could feel her studying me with the same scrutiny she did when I was a little girl.

"You're not just staying here to avoid a certain green-eyed, dark-haired man, are you?"

I kept my gaze trained on the t-shirt, ignoring the teasing lilt in her voice. "Henry has nothing to do with this."

"Ari, sweetie....," she began in a soothing tone, "I think he does. Talk to me, baby. Tell me what's going on."

A breath escaped me before I could stop it, long, shaky, and full of everything I'd been holding in for the past several days.

Hell, probably for the past several years.

I never thought I'd get moments like this again. Never thought my mom would be lucid enough to ask questions, let alone see me.

But because of Henry, she was here.

Because of Henry, she was getting better.

And because of Henry, I didn't know what to feel anymore.

One second, I wanted to hate him with every fiber of my being. The next, I wanted to throw my arms around him and jump head first into all the strange feelings he brought out of me.

"I'm so confused," I admitted, the words tumbling out. I sank down beside her, the mattress dipping under our combined weight.

"What are you confused about? It's obvious he cares about you. Deeply."

I twisted a loose thread from my t-shirt around my finger until it bit into the skin. "Do you remember what I told you about how we met?" My gaze lifted to hers.

"You said he was in the right place at the right time. Someone tried to hurt you, and he intervened."

"That's true," I stated. "But the reason he was in the right place at the right time is because he was *watching* me, Mama. He wanted to hurt me. To get to Victor."

Her eyes sharpened, her posture going still. "*Did* he hurt you?"

"Yes. No. I don't know." I pinched the bridge of my nose. "Here's this man who admitted he planned to abduct me to hurt Victor. So what if he intervened when someone Victor hired tried to do the same thing?"

Her expression changed, eyes widening as my words registered in her brain. "Victor did that?"

"Victor's done a lot of horrible things," I muttered under my breath, unsure if I was ready to discuss the last ten years in detail.

But I didn't have to.

My mother took my hand and squeezed, her fingers thin but steady.

As if she already knew everything I'd endured.

Everything I'd survived.

"And I'm sorry you had to go through that," she whispered, her eyes glistening. "Why did Henry want to hurt him? Apart from Victor being a worthless piece of shit."

"He thinks Victor had something to do with his daughter's death."

"Henry has a daughter?"

"He did." I smiled sadly. "Her body was found in a suite at Victor's hotel in Santa Monica a few months ago. It was ruled a suicide. But according to her brother, she'd been seeing someone older. Someone named Victor. Henry also found a payment from Victor to a DA around that time. He thinks Victor killed her and paid to cover it up."

"I see." Her thumb brushed over my knuckles, slow and thoughtful. "And because of your...unconventional beginnings, you're not sure you can trust him."

"Can you blame me? I trusted Victor in the beginning, too." My throat tightened. "He ended up being the monster you warned me about. I should have listened to you."

"Hey." She squeezed again, firmer this time. "That's no way to live, baby. Regret's too heavy a thing to carry. We can't change the past. We can only use it to navigate what comes next." Her eyes softened. "I told you yesterday. Listen to your heart."

"I'm not sure I can trust my heart."

"Do me a favor and close your eyes."

"Why?"

"Because you're stuck in your head." Her smile grew wistful. "You're like your father that way. He'd get lost up there too, turning problems over until he couldn't see the answer that had been right in front of him all along. But some choices need the heart, not the head. So... Close. Your. Eyes."

I sighed, not seeing how this could help.

My mother had always been a little *woo-woo*, as she called it. Psychics. Meditation circles. Tarot decks on the kitchen table. She used to drag me to yoga class on Saturdays, where we'd sit cross-legged and breathe while I tried not to roll my eyes.

After she started slipping away, I longed to have those Saturday morning yoga classes again.

So instead of insisting this wouldn't make a world of difference, I did as she asked and closed my eyes.

"What are you feeling?" she asked.

"I'm feeling like I'd rather have my eyes open."

She playfully swatted my arm. "Focus. Think about the time you've spent with Henry. What color do you see?"

"Color?" I arched a brow. "All I see is black. Because my eyes are closed."

"Take a deep breath. Inhale for three, exhale for

four." Her voice turned calm and rhythmic. "Push out all the negativity that's been festering, blocking your inner eye."

For once, I didn't tell her there was no such thing, inhaling for three before pushing out a long exhale.

It reminded me of that first night in the cabin. The panic that had consumed me, threatening to suffocate me.

But then Henry's voice had broken through the chaos, low and steady, his touch grounding me when I thought I'd never breathe again.

"Green," I whispered. "I see green."

She breathed out a soft *ah*. "Green."

My eyes snapped open. "Is that bad?"

Her face lit up. "Just the opposite. Green is filled with positive energy, Ari. It represents harmony, balance, rebirth, security." Her smile deepened. "It's the color of growth. If you see green when you think of Henry, that's your heart telling you to trust him. That he'll give you the peace you crave."

I jumped to my feet, pacing the length of the room. "He's still keeping me prisoner here."

She gestured around us, her eyes twinkling. "I don't see bars on the windows. And that door looks plenty open."

"He won't let me leave the property."

"For good reason." Her gaze briefly floated to the

bandage at my temple. "Victor sent dangerous men after you. Let's not forget everything else Victor's done to you. And to me." Her throat worked on a swallow. "He's only trying to keep you safe."

I parted my lips to argue my point further.

What *was* my point?

That freedom mattered more than safety?

That I didn't want to need Henry, even if I already did?

I didn't know.

All I *did* know was that I was petrified of falling into the same trap I did with Victor.

Petrified of losing what little sense of self I'd regained.

Petrified of letting another man control me.

But was Henry controlling me?

"You may not like it..." Mom stood and grabbed my hand. "But I'm grateful. Victor Kane has already taken so much from us. If this is the price to make sure he can't take any more, I'll gladly pay it." She squeezed my hand again.

I looked past her for a long moment, torn between my head and my heart.

The former whispered caution.

The latter whispered green.

"What do you suggest I do? Tell him I'm content being his prisoner?" I plopped onto the mattress.

"I didn't say that." She sat beside me once more. "You need to make him work for it a little."

I frowned. "Work for it?"

She nodded, grinning mischievously. "Every good romantic hero has to grovel. And that man looks like he's capable of an epic one when it comes to you."

For a heartbeat, I just stared at her. Then a laugh broke free, shaky but real. I threw my arms around her, squeezing her tightly.

"I've missed you."

She hugged me back, her breath warm against my skin. "I've missed me, too."

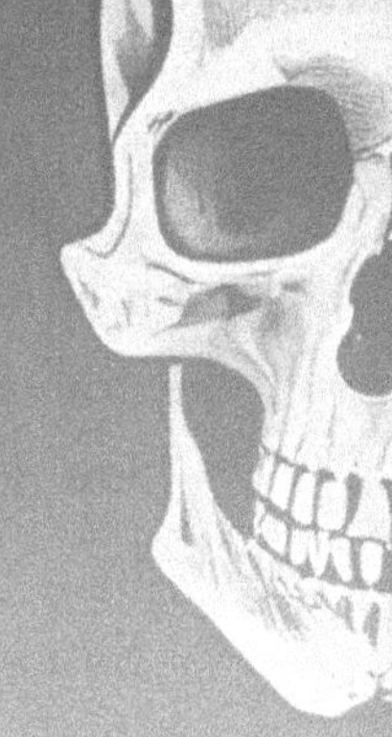

CHAPTER SIXTEEN

Ariana

For years, I couldn't stand the smell of garlic and tomatoes. After my mother started slipping away, it only reminded me of everything I'd lost. Of laughter in a kitchen that no longer existed.

Not anymore.

Now it reminded me of our second chance.

To most, tonight would have seemed ordinary. Just a mother and daughter cooking dinner together.

To me, it felt monumental.

Like reclaiming something sacred I'd thought was gone forever.

We'd made lasagna from scratch, her guiding me through the steps the way she used to when I was a teenager.

There were still moments she got tired or lost her train of thought, but the doctor said that would fade as the drugs continued to work their way out of her system.

For now, he wanted her to rest when her body told her to.

So after we'd finished eating, I helped her up the stairs and into her bedroom.

When I came back down, the kitchen felt both too quiet and too loud, my thoughts immediately drifting to Henry.

Had he eaten dinner? Or was he still locked in his office, surrounded by a wall of screens and unanswered questions?

The image of him all alone in that big house tugged at my heartstrings.

I tried to ignore it. Told myself to finish cleaning and go to bed. That Henry was a grown man and could take care of himself.

But I couldn't stop thinking about him.

Despite my better judgment, I spooned a few pieces of leftover lasagna into a glass container, sealed the lid tight, and grabbed a sweatshirt.

The air outside was cooler than I expected. Crisp. Clean. It carried the scent of pine and something faintly metallic, like rain on gravel.

The path to the main house wound through the

garden, lined with solar lights that spilled a soft glow across the stone.

It wasn't until I reached the back door that I considered it might be locked. But as I touched my hand to the knob, it gave way and I stepped inside.

The house was dark except for the dim under-cabinet lighting that bathed the kitchen in warm, golden tones. The only sounds came from the faint hum of the refrigerator and the steady tick of the clock on the wall.

I tiptoed to the fridge and was about to open the door when a movement flickered in the corner of my vision.

I turned and froze.

Henry stood in the doorway, his broad shoulders backlit by the hallway light. His sleeves were pushed up, revealing his strong forearm muscles.

For a heartbeat, neither of us said anything. Then I lifted the container with a small, awkward gesture.

"I didn't know if you'd eaten. I, uh, brought you some leftovers. We made lasagna."

He stepped closer, the movement unhurried but deliberate. When he reached for the container, his fingers brushed mine. It was just a graze, but it ignited a spark inside me.

"Thanks."

No smile. No follow-up. Just a single word, hanging in the space between us.

Since he didn't seem interested in talking, I turned to head back to the guesthouse.

"How have you settled in?" his voice cut through.

I came to an abrupt stop and glanced over my shoulder. "Fine. I didn't have much to unpack."

"And your mother?" he asked, setting the container down on the counter. "How's she doing?"

"Better." I fully faced him. "She still gets confused sometimes, but the doctor says it'll pass."

"Good."

The word felt strained, and I hated how we'd become strangers in all the spaces that once felt charged and alive.

"I'm not sure if I ever properly thanked you," I said, trying to fill the silence, if for no other reason than to remain in his presence a little longer.

It was a strange thought, considering I wanted to put as much distance between us as possible earlier.

But was that *really* what I wanted?

Or did I just want to see how far I could push him? Prove to myself he *was* an asshole keeping me prisoner.

Instead, he let me go.

He *listened*.

I'd forgotten what that felt like.

"For what you did," I continued. "Getting her out of that place. And..." I hesitated, searching for the right words. "Taking care of Schaffer."

His jaw tensed. "It was nothing."

I shook my head, taking a step toward him. "It was everything to me. Having her back, the woman she used to be. It's the greatest gift anyone's ever given me. So... thank you."

He looked at me for a long moment, something shifting in his expression. "Despite what you may think," he said quietly, "or what my previous actions made you believe, I do care about you, Ariana."

He took a step closer. Then another.

Each one chipped away at my resolve.

The familiar pull I'd tried so hard to suppress roared to life, everything I shouldn't still crave returning to the surface. The memory of his touch. His breath. His voice.

"More than I've cared about anyone in a very long time." His throat worked in a hard swallow. "Maybe ever."

Time seemed to stand still as he leaned in, hesitation etched in every movement. As if giving me a chance to stop him.

Or, more accurately, a choice.

I should have stepped back. Reminded myself who he was. What he'd done.

But all I could think about was the way his voice could strip my defenses bare, the way his touch once made me feel safe and seen in a way no one else ever had.

So I remained perfectly still as he inched closer and closer, his lips gently brushing against mine.

The kiss was barely there, just a whisper of contact. But it was enough to unravel me.

My breath caught, my pulse stuttered. Every nerve in my body seemed to awaken at once, remembering what it felt like to want him. To need him.

To *choose* him.

But before I had a chance to deepen it, he pulled back.

"You should get some sleep."

His voice was full of restraint, as if he had to force the words out.

I blinked, trying to steady my breathing. "You should, too. You look...tired."

His mouth quirked. "Is that your polite way of saying I look like shit?"

Despite myself, I let out a small laugh. "You could never look like shit, Henry. You're far too handsome for that."

"Glad you think so."

I felt my cheeks heat. "I just meant you look like you're carrying the weight of the world again. Some sleep might do you good. And *not* in your office. In your actual bed."

He waggled his brows. "Care to join me?"

My lips parted. I wasn't sure whether I was shocked or tempted. Maybe both.

"I'm kidding." He winked, and warmth bloomed in my chest.

God, I'd missed this. The teasing. The hint of light beneath all his darkness. The reminder he was still human.

"I promise not to stay up all night working," he said when I remained mute.

"Good."

Another silence fell as we stared at each other. But this one felt different. Gentler somehow. Easier to breathe in.

"Well..." I stepped back, increasing the distance. "Good night, Henry."

His gaze held mine. "Good night, Ariana."

I lingered for a beat, unsure what more I wanted him to say.

Unsure if I *wanted* him to say anything more.

So I turned and continued through the house, stepping into the night.

The air outside felt colder now, but my skin still burned from where his lips had touched mine, a quiet fire I didn't think I'd ever be able to put out.

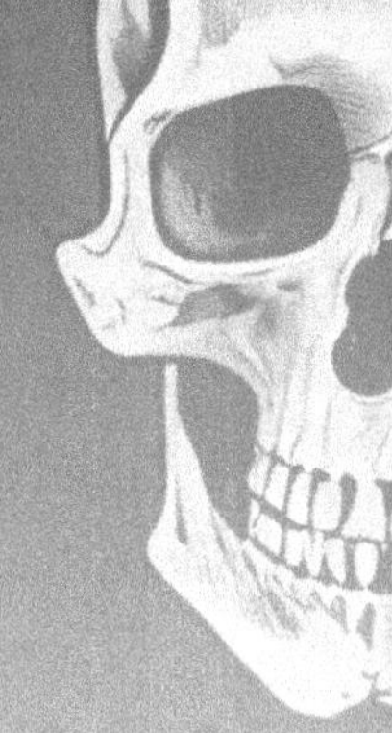

CHAPTER SEVENTEEN

Henry

The horizon was still smeared in shades of silver and pale pink when I stepped outside the following morning. The air held a crisp February bite. Sharp enough to sting your cheeks, but soft enough to remind you that you're alive.

Sometimes I forgot how much I needed mornings like this. How much I craved them.

When my father had moved us to the middle of nowhere, isolation felt like punishment.

I needed noise. Lights. Movement. Wanted to drown out the echoes of everything he forced me to endure.

After I left the military, that was precisely what I did.

Atlanta gave me all the chaos I could handle...and

then some. Traffic, sidewalks teeming with people, a constant barrage of sights and sounds.

Somewhere between long hours and sleepless nights, I started dreaming about quiet. About air that didn't taste like exhaust. About somewhere I could just breathe.

That was why I bought this place. At first, it was a weekend retreat. A place I could go to recharge my batteries.

Now, it was home. I worked out of the city one or two days a week. The rest of the time, I stayed here, where the only thing demanding my attention was the dog at my side.

At least before Ariana.

Now, I didn't want to leave because of her.

Not out of worry. I had eyes everywhere. The entire property was wired into my system. If anyone stepped foot on the land, I'd know.

I stayed because every second I spent in her presence, I found another reason not to go.

Cato dropped a mud-stained tennis ball at my feet, whining softly. I tossed it into the pasture and watched him tear after it, kicking up dust in his wake. As he zoomed through the grass, my gaze drifted toward the guesthouse.

And my thoughts drifted to Ariana.

To last night.

To the moment in the kitchen she'd stood before me, the soft light glinting off her hair, her eyes hesitant but warm. The way her voice trembled when she thanked me. The way her lips parted when I leaned in.

A brush.

A whisper.

A spark.

It had taken everything in me not to push it further. Not to drag her against me and lose myself in her the way I'd been craving for days now.

But she needed space.

And I'd promised myself I'd give it to her.

Even if it killed me.

Cato pawed at my leg, panting heavily through the ball in his mouth.

I reached down and took it from him. "Good boy."

The sound of a door slamming closed caught my attention. I looked toward the guesthouse in time to see Ariana step onto the back deck, bundled in a sweatshirt and leggings, her hair loosely tied back. The morning light shining on her made her appear almost ethereal. Like something out of a dream.

Cato immediately abandoned all loyalty and bolted toward her.

"Careful, bud," I called out, jogging after him. "She's still healing."

"I'm fine," she said, laughing as Cato bounded up the steps and pressed his head against her hip. She scratched between his ears, her voice low and tender. "Hey, pal. You're happy to see me. Aren't you?"

"Do you blame him?" I remarked, leaning against the railing. A subtle blush bloomed on her cheeks. "I'm about to take him for a long walk to tire him out."

"Sounds invigorating."

"Want to come?" I asked before I could stop myself. "If you're feeling up for it."

She hesitated, biting her lower lip. That same lip I'd kissed less than twelve hours ago.

Then she nodded. "I'd like that."

She held the railing as she carefully stepped down the stairs. She still had a slight limp, but every day it got better. I still took it slow, allowing Cato to dart ahead.

When he stopped and looked back at me expectantly, I threw the ball. It arced high against the pastel sky, cutting through a veil of morning mist.

"He's so playful," Ariana remarked.

"He still has a bit of puppy in him, I suppose."

"How old is he?"

"About three. The vet guessed he was ten or eleven months when I found him."

She tilted her head. "You didn't go to a breeder or something?"

"Absolutely not," I scoffed. "To each their own, but I prefer to help the animals who need it."

"So you rescued him," she exhaled, as if another piece of the puzzle had just snapped into place.

"Yeah." I glanced at her, admiring her silhouette in the early morning light. "Let me guess. Victor only allowed dogs with pedigrees worth more than most cars."

"I wish." She rolled her eyes. "He hated animals. That should have been my first clue he wasn't a good person."

"What kind of sociopath doesn't like animals?" I mused as Cato flopped down in the grass, rolling happily around in the dust. "Especially dogs."

"The worst kind," she said with a laugh. "Where did you find him?"

"Here," I said, motioning toward the north edge of the property. "Near the old graveyard."

She stopped mid-step. "There's an old graveyard?"

"By the original house. A log cabin from the mid-1700s."

"There's a log cabin?"

I chuckled, my smile growing. "Sure is. Even survived the Civil War. The current main house wasn't built until the early 1900s."

"Wow."

"I'll take you up there sometime," I offered. "When your knee's a little stronger. It's a bit of a hike."

She smiled softly. "Sounds wonderful."

I tried not to read too much into her answer, but it warmed something in my chest all the same. Gave me hope she wasn't counting down the seconds until she could be free of me.

"So you found Cato by the graveyard?" she pressed after a few moments.

"Poor guy was skin and bones. I didn't plan on keeping him. Just wanted to help him get healthy." I tossed the ball again. "Two years later and he's still here. Now I can't imagine *not* having him in my life. He's definitely happy to be back here, that's for sure."

Ariana's smile turned wistful. "He didn't like the snow up in Maine?"

"He actually loves the snow. Miami, though?" I grimaced. "Not so much. He likes space. Freedom."

"I can't blame him there," she said quietly, and I could hear the hidden meaning in her words.

"Guess so." I shoved my hands into my pockets, unsure what to say.

As much as I wanted to remind her she was here for her own safety, I knew it was a sore spot. I didn't want to argue. Not now. Now when we were finally getting along.

"I've never been a fan of Miami myself," she admitted after a beat. "Everything there feels fake. The people. The places. Nothing's real. It's definitely not the life I imagined when I was a kid."

"What kind of life *did* you imagine? What did you want to be when you grew up?"

There was so much I wanted to learn about her now that I knew the woman I thought her to be was nothing but a façade. An act she put on to protect herself from her husband.

"You mean *other* than a ballerina or black belt in karate?"

A chuckle escaped. "Naturally."

She looked across the field, a wistful smile tugging on her lips. "I had lots of dreams when I was younger, but the one I always returned to was landscape architecture."

"Really?"

She nodded. "I always liked the idea of taking something ugly or forgotten and making it beautiful again."

I studied her profile. The quiet conviction. The spark of who she might have been before all of this. Before Victor.

"It's not too late, you know," I offered softly. "You're still young."

"Can't say the same for you, old man." She smirked, cutting through the tension.

"Don't they say forty is the new thirty?"

"I think people who are forty say that." She playfully nudged me.

"You're only as old as you feel," I countered.

She slowed to a stop and faced me, peering at me through her lashes. "And how do you feel?"

The air between us shifted, becoming thicker, charged. I could have told her the truth. That I felt alive for the first time in years. That I wanted to touch her. Taste her. Breathe her in until she filled every empty space I'd once been content to ignore.

Instead, I said, "Peaceful."

She stepped closer. "Peaceful?"

"Yeah."

Her lips curved faintly. "I like peaceful."

"Me, too."

The words came out low and rough.

I leaned toward her, drawn by a magnetism I couldn't control, the world narrowing to just her and me. Not the lies I told. Not the constant threat to her safety. Right now, nothing else mattered except this moment. This heat. This want...

Until Cato barreled into my side, almost throwing me off balance.

He dropped the ball at my feet, looking at me expectantly, his tail wagging like he'd done me a favor.

"Cockblocker," I muttered.

"Doesn't look like he cares."

"What can I say? He likes my balls."

Her laughter echoed around us, bright and

unguarded. The sound of it reached deep inside me, thawing pieces I thought had died years ago. I'd do anything to hear her laugh again. To give her a life where she had a reason to laugh like this every damn day.

"What about you?"

"What about me?" I threw the ball again, and Cato sprinted after it.

"What was *your* dream as a kid? Did you always want to be a hacker?"

"I'm in cybersecurity," I corrected.

"Same thing."

I chuckled and stared ahead. "I'm not sure I ever had dreams as a child. My dad ripped us away from our normal life when I was young. After that, my one dream was surviving. Getting my mom and brother out of that hellhole." I released a humorless laugh. "You already know how that turned out."

Ariana stopped and reached for my hand. Her fingers were cool, but her touch was warm and grounding.

"It's not your fault." She held my gaze for several long moments, allowing her statement to sink in. "Say it," she murmured, like she did when I first told her about my fucked-up family.

"It's not my fault."

"Good."

She dropped her hold on me and continued through the dusty pasture. "What about after?"

"It's hard to have dreams when you're constantly moved from foster home to foster home. Back then, my dream was to one day have a suitcase to put my belongings in, instead of a garbage bag."

I had no idea why I was sharing all of this with her. I never spoke about my past, especially my time in foster care. But with Ariana, I found myself *wanting* her to know this side of me.

I wanted her to know the *real* me.

And maybe that was exactly what she needed in order to finally trust me.

"Computers offered me an escape. I liked how predictable they were. There was no gray area. Just zeroes and ones, when it all comes down to it. After I left the military, the NSA tried to recruit me. I decided I'd rather make my own rules, so I started a private firm instead."

She tilted her head. "What is it about 'cybersecurity' you like?"

"I guess I like the idea of outsmarting people who try to hide their misdeeds."

Her lips curved. "Like Batman."

"I suppose. Just without the leather suit."

"That's a pity. I think I'd like you in leather."

A chuckle rumbled from my throat. Twenty-four

hours ago, I never expected to see this side of Ariana. To be able to joke and talk so easily like this.

I'd never admit it to him, but Blake was right.

I met Ariana halfway, and now the taut rope between us had loosened.

"I'll keep that in mind," I said as my phone buzzed. I pulled it from my pocket, Blake's name flashing on the screen.

I gave Ariana an apologetic smile. "I need a second."

"Sure."

Turning away slightly, I answered. "Yeah?"

"There was nothing at Schaffer's," Blake said, his voice tight. "His place was clean. *Too* clean if you ask me."

I pushed out a long sigh, pinching the bridge of my nose.

I knew the chances of Schaffer keeping incriminating files easily accessible were slim. But I was still hoping for something to go our way.

"I'm looking into other property holdings to see if he kept them somewhere else," he continued.

"Where are you? Are you still in Miami?"

"Nah. Flew back to Atlanta this morning. I'm already at the house. Didn't expect to find you gone, though."

"I'm walking Cato. I'll be there in a few."

I ended the call and pocketed my phone.

"Everything okay?" Ariana asked.

"Blake couldn't find anything at Schaffer's home or office relating to the women he sterilized."

"Does Blake work for you?"

"More or less. I forgot you haven't met him yet. He's sort of...secretive," I explained, unsure how else to describe him.

"And these files... They're important?"

I blew out a long breath. "Until we know why Victor paid those men to abduct you, *everything* is important."

"You need to go. Don't you?"

"I'm sorry."

She waved me off. "It's okay. My knee's getting a little sore anyway."

"Why didn't you say anything?"

She shrugged. "I liked learning about this side of you."

"I'm glad," I replied, my mouth curving up in the corners.

We made the short walk in silence, but it wasn't awkward. It was comfortable. Whatever tension was between us yesterday had evaporated. As if it were all a dream.

When we reached the guest house, we said our good-byes, and I watched as she climbed the steps.

But before she could slip inside, I called out, "Ariana."

She paused, glancing over her shoulder at me.

I hesitated, debating my next course of action, not wanting her to feel pressured. But I wanted more of this.

More of her.

In whatever way she'd let me have her.

"Want to walk with me again tomorrow?"

"I'd like that." Her smile was small but real.

"Me, too."

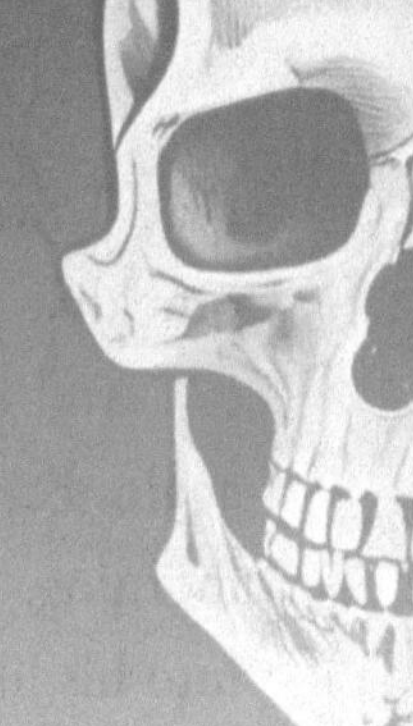

CHAPTER EIGHTEEN

Ariana

I curled my hands around the mug of coffee and scanned the sprawling property for any sign of Henry.

Still nothing.

When he'd asked if I wanted to walk with him again this morning, I hadn't thought to ask what time. He was always up early. Always moving. Always disciplined. But the light had been creeping higher for a while now, and still no Henry.

Maybe he was sleeping.

Maybe he forgot.

Neither possibility felt like him.

I considered walking up to the main house to check, but I didn't want him to think I was eager to see him. Or that I was willing to forgive him for everything so quickly.

And yet, I'd been looking forward to seeing him again. Especially since I hadn't seen him since yesterday morning. I'd even gone up to the main house and snuck into his library to borrow a book. He must have known I was there. I saw the red light from the cameras.

But he didn't leave his office.

I shouldn't have been surprised.

He'd barely left his office in Maine. Spent every waking moment locked in that dark room, surrounded only by computers and monitors.

But his absence was more profound than I expected it to be.

The sharp sound of barking cut through, and my heart leapt as a blur of brown and white fur came barreling down the dirt path.

And when Henry came into view seconds later, my stomach did little backflips.

His hands were tucked into the pockets of a gray hoodie with NAVY emblazoned on it, the fabric stretched across his broad chest. His jeans hung low on his hips, and his hair was a disheveled mess that should've looked careless, but it only made him look more breathtakingly human.

Cato circled him, barking impatiently, as if urging him to move faster.

I walked down the porch steps and met him halfway, holding out one of the travel coffee mugs I'd prepared earlier.

"Black. Just the way you like it."

"Thanks." He took the mug, his voice low and a little rough.

It reminded me of waking up beside him in Maine, his body curved against mine, his voice tired and raspy first thing in the morning.

Before that day, I'd always woken up alone. It was safer that way. Or so I thought.

Until I woke up in Henry's arms. Even now, even with the lies between us, I still found myself craving the comfort I felt when wrapped in his embrace.

"Ready?" he asked.

"Of course."

We fell into step together, our shoes crunching over the gravel path as he led me toward the open pastures. Henry pulled a faded tennis ball from his hoodie and threw it across the field. Cato took off after it, kicking up dust in his wake.

"How did yesterday go?" I asked, trying to sound casual. "Any news about Victor?" My throat tightened around his name. "Where he might be?"

He exhaled, long and tired. I could feel the frustration radiating off him. "Nothing yet. Blake has eyes on his hotels and clubs, but as you know, there are a lot of them."

"I wish I could be more help," I offered. "I learned early on it was safer to only speak when spoken to. To not ask questions. Otherwise—"

He turned to me so abruptly I nearly ran into him. His hand came up to cradle my cheek, his palm warm, his thumb brushing my skin.

"It's okay," he assured me softly. "I'll find him."

"But—"

"I. Will. Find. Him," he repeated, emphasizing each word, his determined green eyes unwavering as they bored into mine. Then, as if realizing the intensity of his touch, he let go.

Cato approached, dropping the ball at Henry's feet. He threw it again, his motion easy and fluid.

"Tell me more about landscape architecture," he said, the abrupt change in subject taking me by surprise.

I blinked. "What?"

"What about it interested you?"

I narrowed my eyes. "Do you really care, or are you just trying to change the subject?"

"I'm absolutely trying to change the subject," he admitted with a faint smile. "I've spent the past twenty-four hours chasing down every lead I came across, no matter how obscure. My brain needs a break from all this for a minute." He paused, his expression sobering. "But I also care. I want to learn these things about you. Want to learn what makes you tick. What you're passionate about. What makes you happy."

It was such a simple admission. Most people wouldn't think twice about it. But it struck something deep inside me.

Victor never seemed interested in learning about me. Not really. He'd decided who I should be, dressed me in his version of perfection, and called it love.

Henry's genuine interest felt like sunlight hitting skin that had gone too long without warmth.

"What is it?" he asked, noticing my reaction.

"It feels strange to talk about this stuff again."

"Why?"

"Victor never understood why I liked gardening and landscaping. In his mind, that was work for 'the help'. He said my time was better spent attending luncheons and organizing charitable events with the other wives. Things much more fitting for the wife of Victor Kane." I rolled my eyes.

"Well, I'm not him. Forget about being the person he forced you to be. Just be Ariana Summers."

"I'm not sure I know who that is anymore," I whispered to myself.

At least, I *thought* it was to myself.

But Henry heard me.

He turned me toward him and brushed a loose strand of hair from my face, his touch lingering long enough to make my breath catch.

"Then let me help you figure that out."

I didn't move as his gaze dropped to my mouth. The air between us grew heavy with the pull I'd been trying so hard to ignore. Every inch of me tingled with anticipation, longing to feel his lips on mine, especially after that tease of a kiss the other night.

He curved toward me, and I held my breath, the seconds seeming to stretch.

"And you can start," he murmured, "by telling me more about the things you once loved." He stepped back, his absence causing a chill to overwhelm me.

"Tease," I muttered.

"What do you mean?" His tone was innocent. His smirk was not.

"Don't play dumb, Henry," I chastised, walking beside him once more. "It doesn't suit you. You know what you're doing."

"And what am I doing?"

"Like I said. You're being a tease."

"How so?"

"By not kissing me when I know you want to."

"I want to do a lot more than kiss you, Ariana."

"Why haven't you? You get so close, then pull away. Or is this all a part of your game?"

He stopped walking, and I did the same.

"There's no game. It doesn't matter what *I* want." He stepped closer, our bodies a whisper away. "All that matters is what *you* want. I know I've hurt you. Know you're not sure if you can trust me. I *want* you to. But I also understand trust is difficult for you. I hope I'll eventually earn back your trust. Until then, we can just spend time learning about each other in order to help you figure out what you want. That's the only way this will work."

I tilted my head back, my chest tightening. "You want this to work?"

"More than anything."

Something inside me cracked open at the sincerity in his voice. The emotion. The care. No one had ever spoken to me like this. With desire wrapped in restraint. With patience that didn't feel performative.

"But I need your trust first," he continued. "Need you to believe me when I say I'm not keeping you here to imprison you. I understand why you're skeptical about taking my word for it. If I were in your shoes, I would be, too. But my offer of protection isn't a trap. If I could ensure your safety, I'd happily let you go. Let you live the life you deserve. But Victor's still out there. He paid dangerous men a lot of money to find you. And if something happened to you because I let you walk away, I'd never forgive myself.

"I hope you'll eventually come to understand my actions aren't to control you. I just... I care about you, Ariana. More than I thought possible. But I want you to *choose* me. Not because you feel any sort of obligation to me. But because you trust me. So until that happens, I'll wait."

I stared at him, my throat tight. His words hit somewhere deep, somewhere that hadn't felt warmth in a long time. I wanted to trust him. Wanted to let myself believe he wasn't like Victor. But wanting and being able to were two very different things.

"It's hard for me," I admitted. "Victor... He said all the right things, too."

"I'm not him. Even if I can be...a little overbearing."

"A little?" I retorted playfully, arching an eyebrow.

"Okay. More than a little," he said with a self-deprecating laugh. "You bring out a side of me I didn't know existed. And it's not because I want to own or possess you, show you off as a trophy. It's because I can't stomach the idea of not having you in my life."

He reached out and cupped my cheek again, his touch gentle. Reverent.

"It doesn't matter how long it takes for you to realize what I'm saying is true," he murmured. "A week. A month. A lifetime. I won't give up. Won't stop trying to earn your trust. Earn *you*."

I fought back the tears forming in my eyes. For so long, I'd done everything in my power to hide all my emotions. Victor would only use them against me.

But with Henry, I felt like I could let him see all my fractured pieces.

Just like he'd allowed me to see all *his* broken pieces.

"I don't know if I'd go *that* far," I retorted in a shaky breath. "You *are* over forty. I'm not sure how many good years you have left."

His laughter cut through the tension like sunlight breaking through the clouds, bathing everything in light once more.

"Am I always going to have to put up with the age jokes?"

"And if you are?"

"I can handle it."

He flashed me a wink, then turned back toward the path, as if he hadn't just cracked himself open and handed me everything inside to do with as I pleased.

"So landscape architecture." He cleared his throat. "Tell me about it."

"What do you want to know?" I asked, catching up to him.

"Everything, Ariana." His gaze locked on mine, his

eyes filled with an emotion I was too scared to label. "I want to know everything about you."

And for the first time in years, I wanted someone to know everything about me.

So I did the one thing I didn't think I'd ever be able to do again.

I let him in.

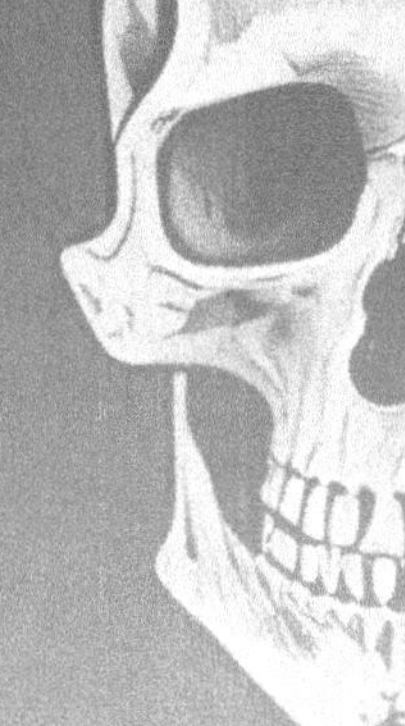

CHAPTER NINETEEN

Ariana

I couldn't remember ever being this at peace.

For years, I dreaded waking up in the morning.

There was a part of me that hoped I wouldn't. That prayed for death. It would be a welcome alternative to the hell I'd been living with Victor.

That was no longer the case.

Now I couldn't wait to wake up each day, knowing I'd soon see Henry.

A week had passed since we began our morning walks, and they'd quickly become the highlight of my day.

I'd gotten into a routine of waking up as the sun started to rise. After making two cups of coffee, I'd head out onto the porch. Within minutes, Cato would come bounding around the bend first, tail wagging furiously, with Henry close behind.

I told myself it was the fresh air I looked forward to. The way the mist lifted from the fields. The quiet peace of being surrounded by nature.

Deep down, I knew better.

It was him.

Our walks had stretched longer each day. What started as a half-hour around the fields had turned into two-hour explorations that left my legs pleasantly sore and my heart doing strange things I couldn't seem to control.

Today, we'd hiked to the old cemetery, where the weathered stones leaned like sleepy sentinels in the grass, and stopped by the original log cabin, the one Henry said had been built when this land was first settled.

He spoke about history the way I spoke about gardens. As though he understood the importance of things that took root. It made me want to stay out here with him for even longer just to listen to him talk.

Thankfully, the pain in my knee was now down to a dull throb. Even the gash on my forehead was doing better. Krystal had removed the stitches yesterday. There was a scar, but it didn't bother me. Every time I looked at it, Henry's words echoed in my mind.

Scars remind us of the battles we fought and won.

I liked that.

He'd fought plenty of battles of his own. Some he was still fighting. But lately, he'd been lighter. So had I.

With every morning we spent together, he somehow brought back pieces of me I'd forgotten existed.

He'd asked about my father, and I'd told him how I loved spending time in the floral shop with him. How he'd taught me every plant had its own language. Different light. Different soil. Different needs.

Henry had listened like he actually cared, not because he was trying to fix or analyze me, but because he genuinely wanted to know these things.

In return, he'd shared things I hadn't expected. About his mother reading to him. The struggles he had with his father. What prompted him to join the military.

He was the first person I'd met in years I didn't have to pretend around. The first person I could be myself around.

And thanks to him, I was slowly figuring out who that was again.

Now, as we approached the guesthouse, that bittersweet ache returned to the surface. The one that became more profound every morning when we said goodbye.

My mother had started dropping hints about me moving back up to the main house. I kept insisting it made more sense to stay here since Henry worked long hours, and I spent most of my days with her.

While it *was* true, it wasn't the whole truth.

In reality, I wasn't sure if I was ready to live under the same roof with Henry again. Not because I didn't want to. But because of what it might mean if I did.

"Thanks for the walk," I said, turning to face him when we reached the porch. "And the conversation."

"Hope I didn't bore you too much." He shoved his hands in his pockets, rocking on his feet. "I've always been a bit of a history buff. It's why I couldn't say no to this place when I found it."

"Not at all." I smiled. "I like learning more about you. What you're passionate about. You're a very... intriguing person, Henry Fontaine."

"I'm glad you think so."

He held my gaze for several long moments. Long enough for heat to pool low in my belly. Long enough for the air to hum with something electric and undeniable, especially when I stole a glance at his lips.

I wanted to close the distance. Press my mouth to his and stop pretending I wasn't thinking about it every time I was with him.

But fear held me still. Fear that I might have been wrong about him.

Or worse... That I might have been right.

"I'll let you get on with your day." I cleared my throat and increased the distance between us. "Same time tomorrow?"

"Of course."

I turned toward the door, my fingers curling around the cool metal of the knob when his voice stopped me.

"Ariana?"

I looked back. "Yes?"

He hesitated, as if warring with himself. Then he asked, "What if we did something else instead?"

"What do you mean?" I fully faced him.

He shrugged, the normally confident man I'd gotten to know nowhere to be found. It reminded me of the vulnerability he showed me when he was injured. When I held his fate in my hands.

"Maybe we could go somewhere."

"Go...somewhere?" I repeated, furrowing my brow.

"I thought you might like a change of scenery."

"Like, back to Maine?"

He laughed quietly. "No. Not to Maine. Somewhere else. I want to show you more of my life. This..." He gestured to the fields stretching out for miles around us. "This is just one part of it."

I tilted my head. "I thought it wasn't safe."

"You'll be with me. We won't be going anywhere someone might recognize you. You'll be protected, Ariana. I never want you to feel anything but safe when you're with me."

A week ago, I would have jumped at the opportunity to leave. Run, even.

Now, the thought terrified me.

Not because of the danger outside these walls. But because of what might happen between us if we were truly alone. No distractions. No buffers. Just Henry and me.

"I don't know if I should leave my mom," I started. "She—"

"Yes, you should," came my mother's voice from behind me.

I spun around, startled to see her standing in the doorway. "Were you listening to our conversation?"

"Of course." She smiled sweetly. "And stop being so stubborn, Ari."

"I'm not being stubborn. You've been through a lot these past few years. I just want to make sure you're okay."

"And you've been through a lot, too," she replied, her eyes softening. "I'll be fine here. Honestly, I could use a little peace and quiet. Some alone time." Her lips curved in a knowing grin. "Consider yourself banned from this house for the weekend."

She winked at Henry, and he returned it with a conspiratorial smile that told me this wasn't entirely spontaneous. Then she slipped back inside, giving us some semblance of privacy.

But I had no doubt she was still listening.

"What do you say?" he asked.

"I don't know," I replied.

"Ariana…" He stepped toward me and grabbed my hand, gently brushing his thumb along my knuckles. "I told you I'd do whatever it takes to earn your trust. Consider this me showing you that you're *not* a prisoner here."

"So you're doing this for me?"

He reached up, brushing a strand of hair behind my ear. His fingers grazed my cheek, sending shivers down my spine.

"Everything I've done since that gala has been for you." His unwavering gaze held mine, not allowing me to escape the truth in his words. "Let me show you more of my world. Who I am."

I looked over the field, sunlight shimmering across the tall grass, reminding me of freedom. Beauty. Possibility.

And him.

The man I was slowly learning to trust.

"Okay," I said with a smile.

The transformation on his face nearly undid me. His entire expression lit up, becoming boyish even. Like a weight had lifted from his shoulders.

"Do you think you can be ready to leave around noon?" he asked.

"Sure."

"Great." He leaned down, pressing a tender kiss to my cheek.

The warmth of his lips lingered long after he retreated, leaving me standing there, my pulse racing and skin tingling.

And wishing he hadn't stopped at just a kiss.

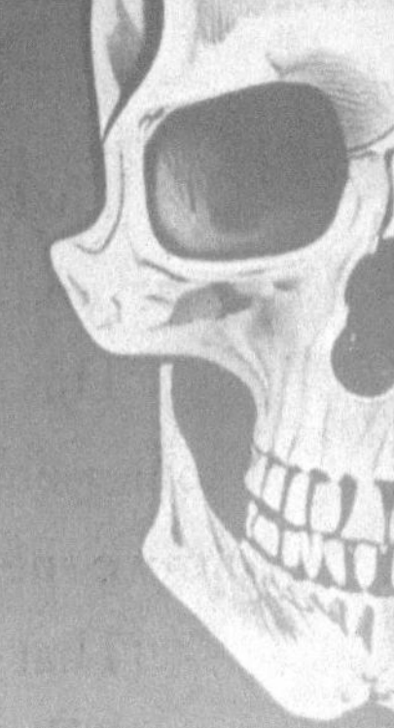

CHAPTER TWENTY

Henry

The highway stretched before me like a gray ribbon, cars flickering past in a blur of color and motion. Every flash of chrome made my pulse hitch, my grip tighten on the wheel. It was probably irrational to worry that someone could be following us, but old instincts died hard. If anyone *were* following us, I'd know. I'd see them coming. I'd stop them.

Ariana seemed completely oblivious to the anxiety filling me as she sat in the passenger seat. Her lips curved into a faint smile as she admired the passing landscape, sunlight flickering over her face in golden bands.

For a fleeting moment, I let myself imagine this was normal.

That we were a regular couple going away for the weekend.

This was why I wanted to get away. To help her feel some semblance of normalcy. To do something more to prove she wasn't my captive. That I wasn't like Victor.

That I could meet her halfway.

"What are you thinking about?" I asked, stealing a glance at her.

"Just taking it all in," she replied, still watching the world fly by. "I've never been to Atlanta before."

"Really?" I furrowed my brows. "I thought you'd have been everywhere."

She shrugged. "I went wherever Victor demanded I be." Her expression fell, becoming distant.

"I'm sorry. I didn't mean to bring him up. I hoped this could be a Victor-free weekend."

"I didn't take you for an idealist," she teased, glancing my way.

"What do you mean?"

"Thinking we can have a Victor-free weekend. At least right now." Her gaze softened, becoming almost wistful. "Maybe one day, the years I spent with him will feel like nothing more than a distant dream. But right now, I'm constantly having to remind myself he doesn't control me anymore."

Without thinking, I reached across the console and

threaded my fingers through hers. Her skin was warm. Soft. Grounding.

"He'll never hurt you again, Ariana. I won't let him. Not while I'm still breathing. I swear to you."

She didn't answer, but her fingers curled gently around mine before she slipped them free, turning her gaze back to the passing trees.

"Has this always been home?" she asked, her change of subject obvious. "After you...left Maine?"

"My mom's sister lived outside the city," I responded. "I was sent to live with her and her husband. A few months later, she learned she was pregnant and told my social worker she couldn't handle me anymore."

"But she was your aunt."

"In her defense, I was a really angry kid. Angry at my dad. At the world. But at myself more than anything. I don't blame her for sending me away. I was a lot to handle."

"I'd say you're *still* a lot to handle," she shot back playfully.

"Truer words have never been spoken." I flashed her a grin.

"Is that when you were sent to your first foster family?"

"It was."

"How was that?" she asked, almost hesitant.

"Some decent families. But the system's stretched thin. Troubled kids like me don't exactly make life easy, so I got moved around a lot. I learned not to get too attached to any one place. Or person."

"That sounds so lonely."

"It was. But then..."

"Yes?" She perked up, obviously interested in this part of my life. A part I hadn't talked about much.

Which was why I wanted to take her to Atlanta. To meet one of the people who knew me then.

"I met Samuel. He goes by Gideon now, but that's a story for another time. He was another foster kid. We lived in the same home for a bit." I laughed to myself at the memory. "God, we butted heads at first."

"You?" she said in mock disbelief.

"I know. Shocking." I huffed a laugh. "But he's like a brother now. You'll meet him tonight. He lives in Atlanta with his wife."

Her head turned sharply toward me. "Really?"

"If you're okay with it," I added quickly. "If you'd rather do something else, we can. I want to show you who I really am. And Gideon... He's family."

"Sounds like the perfect opportunity for some payback."

I raised an eyebrow. "Payback?"

"For the morning I walked in on you and my mom

talking about me as a little girl. I plan to get all the dirt on you from your friend."

"On second thought, maybe we *won't* go see him."

"Too late. You promised. I can't wait to learn all your secrets, Henry Fontaine."

"I'm looking forward to it, Ariana Summers."

She relaxed into her seat. "I like that."

"What?"

She shifted her eyes toward me. "Hearing you call me that."

"It's who you are to me."

"Thank you."

She peered at me for a protracted beat, something unspoken simmering between us. Then she turned back to the window, a smile still playing on her mouth.

The rest of the drive passed in comfortable silence, and soon the Atlanta skyline swallowed us in a wall of glass and noise.

After navigating through the typical Friday afternoon traffic in downtown, I turned into the garage beneath my building and punched in my code. The gate lifted and I steered toward my reserved spot.

With our bags in hand, I led Ariana toward the private elevator tucked behind a steel security door and keyed in the code before pressing my thumb to the scanner.

"A bit of overkill for an apartment building, don't you think?" she teased at the doors slid open.

"This isn't an apartment building," I replied.

"Oh?"

"It's *my* building. As in I own it. My firm's headquarters are here."

"So...we're at your office?"

"Yes."

"Do you sleep in your office here, too?"

"Not exactly. I have an apartment on the top floor. Makes for a much quicker commute."

"Workaholic." She rolled her eyes. "You do know there's more to life than work, right?"

I narrowed my gaze at her as the doors closed. "I'm starting to realize that."

The elevator began its rapid descent, the hum of the motor filling the silence. I was grateful for the speed because being in this small space with her — so close I could feel her warmth, see each subtle breath — was testing the limits of my restraint.

She looked at me like she saw something I didn't even know I was showing. Like she'd already peeled away the armor and found what was underneath.

She always had that effect on me.

When the doors opened again, I guided her into a small foyer, keyed another code into the security panel, and pressed my thumb against the next scanner.

"So much security," she murmured.

"I needed to know you'd be safe here."

She darted her eyes to mine. "Did you have all of this put in...for me?"

I gave a noncommittal shrug. "I'm trying a new thing."

"What's that?"

"Compromise."

"Compromise," she repeated like she'd never heard the word before.

"You've obviously been restless. And while I want you to feel like you're free to go wherever you want, that's not possible quite yet, so I had additional security measures installed in my apartment here so I could be assured of your safety. I know it's not ideal, but—"

Before I could finish my statement, she threw her arms around me, wrapping me in a tight squeeze.

For a second, I didn't move, completely taken aback. Then I slid my hand along the curve of her spine and pulled her closer. Her scent consumed me, and I lowered my head, breathing her in. Lavender, powder, something uniquely her.

She curved back slightly, pressing her hand to my cheek, her thumb grazing the stubble along my jaw.

"How do you always manage to surprise me?" she whispered. "And confuse me?"

"I don't mean to. I'm just trying to show you who I am. The real me."

"I think I've always seen the real you, Henry. Even when you didn't want me to."

"Maybe so." I swallowed hard. "But now I want you to. All of it. The good *and* the bad."

"I want you to know me, too. The good and the bad."

Her tongue swept across her lower lip, drawing my attention to her mouth. It would've been so easy to close the distance. To take what I'd been wanting for weeks.

But I couldn't. Not yet. I needed her to choose me. To trust me.

So I did the hardest thing I'd done in quite a while. I let her go.

"Come on. I'll give you the grand tour."

Pushing out what sounded like a frustrated sigh, she followed me into the open space, then froze, her eyes wide as she took in the wall of glass overlooking the city. Sunlight poured through, illuminating everything in sight.

"It's no Star Island," I said sheepishly, "but I hope you'll be comfortable here."

"Star Island was nothing more than a prison."

"Then I hope you'll feel free here. Like you can breathe."

"That's how I feel whenever I'm around you." She held my gaze, allowing her words to sink in. Then her expression brightened. "Even if you drive me fucking crazy at least once a day."

"It's my superpower."

With a wink, I placed a hand on her lower back and steered her deeper into the penthouse, unable to shake the feeling in my gut that this weekend was about to change everything.

I only hoped it was for the better.

CHAPTER TWENTY-ONE

Ariana

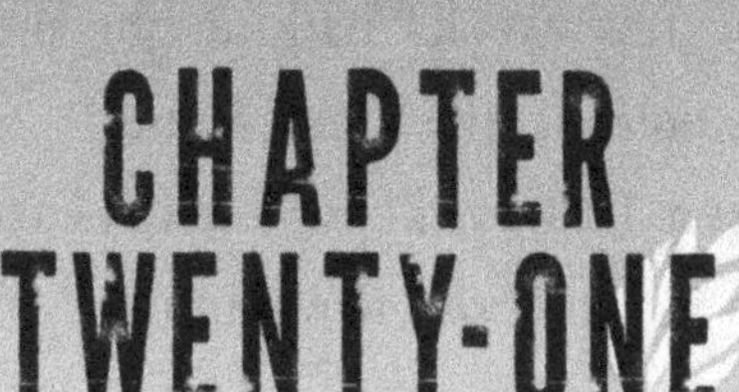

I stood in front of the vanity, my palms flat against the cool marble, trying to calm the flutter in my stomach. Dinner with Henry's friend shouldn't make me nervous, but this wasn't just any friend. It was someone Henry had known for decades. Someone he considered family.

I tried to picture Henry as a teen. All sharp edges and unmitigated rage, the version he hinted at when he spoke of his past. But there must have been something softer beneath the façade, too. The kind of boy who wanted to protect people, even when he didn't know how.

He liked to tell me he wasn't a good man. But he was wrong. Yes, he'd done things. *Illegal* things. Maybe even unforgivable things in some peoples' eyes.

Yet, I'd seen the goodness in him, too. The restraint. The quiet decency Victor never possessed.

He was a bad person. I refused to put Henry in the same classification as Victor, despite my earlier insistence otherwise.

The past few weeks had taught me that Henry Fontaine was *nothing* like Victor Kane.

Deep down, I always knew that to be true.

I was just too stubborn to admit it.

Or maybe I was just too *scared* to admit it.

I leaned closer to the mirror, tracing the edge of my crimson lipstick. It was the same shade I wore the night I first met Henry. I remembered how he couldn't seem to look away from my mouth, like every word I spoke might undo him. I'd be lying if I said I didn't wear it tonight hoping for the same reaction.

My heart gave a nervous skip at the thought.

The rest of my makeup was soft. Barely-there eyeliner. A hint of blush. Subtle shadowing around my eyes.

The woman staring back at me didn't look like Victor's carefully curated doll. She looked like someone real. Someone reclaiming herself one small rebellion at a time.

I smoothed the hem of my thigh-length sweater dress, the knit fabric warm against my skin, and tugged on my knee-high boots. Two things Victor hated. Two things that made me feel...free.

When I stepped into the hallway, the air carried a faint scent of cedar that would always remind me of Henry. The penthouse was modern and polished, all stainless steel and glass. Beautiful in a way that felt distant. Lonely. Like a place designed for someone who didn't expect to be cared for and didn't trust himself to want it.

But I saw beneath the mask. Saw him for who he truly was.

As I emerged into the living room, my heart stuttered at the sight of Henry standing in front of the window, dressed in dark jeans and a charcoal button-down with the sleeves rolled just enough to reveal the muscles in his forearms.

He was silhouetted against the darkened sky, the city lights below burning like the fires of some underworld kingdom. For a heartbeat, he looked like something mythic. Like Hades himself. Commanding. Solitary. The King of Shadows watching over the souls below. Haunted by things no one knew.

But when he turned and saw me, everything changed.

Heat sparked in his eyes as they traced the line of my body. Like he was trying to take me in all at once and failing because there was too much he wanted to look at.

It struck me that I'd never worn anything but yoga pants and pajamas around him. Sure, he'd seen me draped in the designer gowns Victor clothed me in, but that wasn't who I really was.

"Is this okay?" I asked nervously, gesturing at my dress.

He crossed the room in three purposeful strides, stopping close enough that I could feel the heat coming off him. He tilted my chin, his eyes dark and reverent.

"You look fucking amazing, Ariana."

Warmth bloomed in my chest, spreading outward.

"But you could wear a paper sack," he added, his thumb brushing the corner of my jaw, "and I'd still find you beautiful."

A nervous laugh slipped out of me. "That might be a little itchy. I'll stick with the sweater dress."

"Lucky me." His mouth curved into something bordering on wicked. Then he stepped back, and a chill washed over me from the lack of touch. "You ready?"

I nodded, not trusting my voice, and he helped me into my coat, a simple gesture that felt intimate in a way I hadn't expected. Then he led me out of the penthouse and into the elevator.

When we reached his dark SUV, he opened the door for me, helping me in. It didn't escape my notice that his gaze lingered on my legs longer than one would consider platonic.

And I certainly enjoyed having his eyes on me.

As he pulled out of the garage, the hum of the city surrounded us — horns, tires on asphalt, the pulse of the Atlanta nightlife. As much as I claimed to hate the isolation of the Maine cabin, then the farmhouse, I couldn't help but feel like everything here was too loud. Too intrusive. Too many possibilities for danger.

"You're safe with me," Henry said, threading his fingers with mine and squeezing, as if able to sense my thoughts.

I gave him a grateful smile, this one gesture relaxing me. "Thank you."

But unlike before, he didn't release his hold on me. He kept my hand in his throughout the twenty-minute drive, not letting go until we pulled up to a gated driveway and he lowered the window to enter a code into the box.

After the gate sprung open, granting us access, Henry steered the SUV down a long drive, parking in front of a stunning colonial before jumping out to open my door with a quiet urgency that made me smile. It was such a little thing, but I loved the effort he went through just to open my door.

Victor never did.

He always had his driver open my door, even when we were dating. Hell, there were times Victor couldn't even be bothered to walk me to my door.

But Henry rushed so he could do this one small thing for me, proving he wasn't only thinking about himself. He was thinking about me.

Always.

I took his hand with a smile, relishing in his warmth as he helped me out. Once I had my footing, he steered me toward the house with a gentle hand on my lower back.

As we approached the front door, he entered a code into the keypad.

"You're just going to let yourself in?" I asked.

"He does the same at my place."

"Guess I'll make sure not to walk around naked then," I teased, hoping to tame the nervous butterflies dancing in my stomach.

Henry froze, his eyes snapping to mine, predatory and hungry.

"That settles it." He reached into his pocket and pulled out his phone.

"What are you doing?"

"Deleting his access." His lips twitched. "Feel free to walk around naked all you want, Ariana."

I laughed. "I was kidding."

"I wasn't."

The intensity in his gaze stole my breath, so much heat and want in those green orbs. It sent a rush of excitement through me, destroying every single defense I'd built over the years.

"Is that what you want?" I whispered, stepping closer, drawn by something magnetic and reckless. "To get me naked?"

His Adam's apple bobbed up and down on a hard swallow. "You already know the answer to that."

"I wouldn't want to presume, Mr. Fontaine." I tilted my head back, my voice husky. Wanton.

"Ariana..."

He took half a step toward me, then the door swung open.

A very pregnant blonde filled the doorway, wide-eyed as she looked between us. "Oh! I'm sorry. I heard voices, and I... Well, I didn't mean to interrupt...your moment."

"We can pick it back up later." He gave me a wink that sent another wave of exhilaration through me before turning his attention toward the blonde. "Good to see you, Imogene."

He kissed her cheek, and I tried not to notice how effortlessly he shifted from predator to friend.

Or how much I liked the idea of being his prey.

"How are you feeling?" he asked.

"Like I want to evict this kid," she groaned, rubbing her belly. "But apparently, she needs to cook for six more weeks."

"Enjoy the quiet while you can."

"I plan on it." She smiled, then turned to me. "You must be Ariana. I'm Imogene."

Before I could react, she wrapped me in a hug. The contact startled me. I'd spent so long in a world where affection was calculated, where smiles were rehearsed and hugs were performative. This felt different. *Real.*

When she sensed my hesitation, she drew back with an apologetic grin. "Too forward? Sorry. I'm a hugger."

"No," I said quickly. "It's okay. I don't mind."

"Good." She gave my arm a squeeze. "Come on in. Gideon's in the kitchen."

Henry guided me inside, the house warm with soft light and the smell of garlic and rosemary. As we reached the kitchen, a tall, built man turned from the stove, his grin wide and unguarded.

"Good to see you, brother."

"You too," Henry said, clasping him in a hug that spoke of years of trust.

I couldn't remember the last time I'd seen a friendship like this — simple, loyal, untainted. I'd had some good friends in high school. But then Victor entered my life and managed to isolate me from everything and everyone I once held dear. I didn't understand what he was doing at the time.

My mother did.

She tried to warn me.

And Victor silenced her.

"Ariana," Henry said, drawing me forward. "This is Gideon Saint."

I frowned. "Why does that name sound familiar?"

"Probably because it is," Henry said dryly. "He used to pretend to be a venture capitalist, so you probably heard his name in your old circles."

"Pretend?" I asked, confused.

"It's a long story," Gideon said with a slight laugh.

"Are you still in that field? Or *pretending* to be in that field?" I had a feeling whatever Henry meant by that had something to do with the reason he went by Gideon now instead of Samuel, as he'd mentioned was his name when they first met.

"Not anymore." His gaze softened as he pulled Imogene against him and placed a hand on her stomach. "Figured it was time to focus on the only good investment I ever made."

He pressed a kiss to her lips. The tender and unguarded gesture hit me right in the chest.

I didn't realize until this moment how much I missed seeing love like that. Unhidden. Unashamed. Real.

And when I looked at Henry, at the faint smile tugging at his mouth and the warmth in his eyes, I felt a flicker of something fragile and dangerous bloom inside me.

For the first time in years, I didn't force myself to smother it.

Instead, I allowed myself the one thing Victor tried to take from me.

I let myself hope.

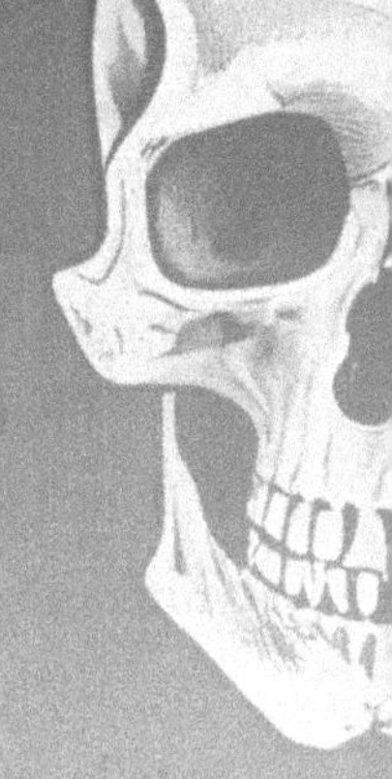

CHAPTER TWENTY-TWO

Ariana

"This looks incredible," I said, inhaling the mouthwatering aroma of garlic and butter as Gideon set down a plate containing a beautiful cut of filet mignon in front of me.

"Hope you enjoy it. I've been brushing up on my cooking skills these past few months." He sat at the head of the table and reached for his wife's hand, smoothing his thumb over her knuckles with an easy familiarity. "That way, Imogene can stay off her feet."

"I *am* turning food into a human," she said dryly, rubbing her round belly. "And you've definitely gotten better in the kitchen."

"You have, actually. It's been...what? At least three

months since you last gave me food poisoning," Henry teased, taking a slow sip of his wine.

"That was *one* time," Gideon argued, pointing his fork at Henry. "And I still contend it wasn't my fault. I think the spinach had salmonella or something."

"Right." Henry rolled his eyes. "Whatever you need to tell yourself."

"Boys…" Imogene sighed, but her tone carried more affection than annoyance.

I hid my smile behind my wineglass.

I loved this. Loved seeing Henry like this — looser, lighter, his edges softened by comfort. An ordinary man surrounded by people who loved him.

And maybe a man capable of loving in return.

"How about a toast?" Imogene lifted her glass of sparkling water.

We all followed suit.

"To new friends," she said warmly. "To finding family in unexpected places, and to the kind of company that makes even the darkest days feel a little lighter. Cheers."

"To new friends," I murmured in response, and we all clinked our glasses together.

Everything about tonight felt strange. Not because I didn't enjoy being here. But because it felt so normal. My life had been anything but normal for so long, I didn't know how to act. I kept thinking it was all a dream I'd soon wake up from. But I didn't. This was real.

And maybe this could be my life. This could be my new normal. I could be the type of woman to be able to enjoy a laid back, unpretentious dinner with friends.

Real friends.

Not people who pretended to care one minute, then stabbed me in the back the next.

"Thanks again for cooking," I said to Gideon as I carved into the steak with my knife. "And for including me."

"Are you kidding?" Imogene interjected. "When Henry said he was bringing you to Atlanta, I threatened to revoke his future godfather status if he didn't bring you to dinner."

"When are you due?" I asked, sliding a piece of steak into my mouth. The first bite nearly made me moan. Tender. Buttery. Rich with flavor.

It had been so long since I'd had steak.

Victor never allowed me to eat it.

But he could eat all the steak he wanted.

Hypocrite.

"March fifteenth, but I'm really hoping she comes before then. I already feel like a beached whale."

I smiled, spearing a brussels sprout. It was caramelized with a hint of maple.

"Henry mentioned you've known each other since you were teens," I remarked to Gideon with a sly smile.

"Don't fall for it," Henry warned, his voice playful. "She's hoping to get dirt on me."

"It's only fair," Gideon shot back. "You gave Imogene the dirt on *me* when we started dating." He turned to me, grinning. "Let me tell you something about Henry Fontaine."

Gideon and Henry may not have been brothers, but they shared many similar features. Dark hair. Tall stature. Strong physique. They both had the look of someone who'd been through hell and survived. I got the feeling they only survived because they had each other.

"He pretends to be tough on the outside, but he's a complete softie on the inside. You just need to know how to crack him."

"And how did you crack him?"

"Easy." He shrugged, taking a bite of steak. "I kicked his ass."

"Do you have to tell this story?" Henry groaned, but the warm smile on his face told a different tale.

"We were both in the same foster home," Gideon explained, sipping on his wine. "He hated me on sight. To be fair, I wasn't exactly easy to like, either. I challenged anyone who looked at me wrong... Including him."

"He still does," Henry muttered.

"One day, our social worker got so fed up with us constantly trying to kill each other that he dragged us into the car. Said if we wanted to fight, we needed to learn how to do it properly." A nostalgic gleam lit up his eyes as he looked into the distance.

"What happened?" I pressed, fascinated by the story. By this part of Henry he'd yet to share with me. It made me want to learn everything about him. The good *and* the bad.

But I had a feeling even his bad parts were shadowed in good.

"He drove us to a local community center run by Mr. Cooper, a retired Marine who taught martial arts to troubled kids like us. Angry. Lost. Impossible to control. Coop taught us how to channel our anger into something productive."

"If it hadn't been for him, we'd probably both be in prison," Henry commented.

"Or worse," Gideon added.

They shared a look that said more than words could. It showed the quiet bond between two men who'd walked through the same fire and survived.

"When do we get to the part where you kicked his ass?"

Gideon's lips curved into a mischievous grin. "Ah. My favorite part." He leaned closer. "Want to know what Henry's biggest weakness is?"

"What's that?"

"He's one cocky bastard. Thinks he's invincible, even though he's just as human as the rest of us." He gave Henry a long, knowing look that felt like it carried more meaning than just a teenage memory. "I used that weakness against him."

"You got lucky," Henry replied flatly.

"Coop told us no more fighting outside the gym," Gideon continued, ignoring Henry's remark. "But one day, he could tell we were both irritated with each other. So he called us to the mat. Back then, Henry was all brawn. No brain." He laughed under his breath. "I guess he's still that way."

"I'm sorry. Were *you* offered a job by the NSA because of your computer skills?" Henry snipped back.

"You mean hacking skills?" Gideon jabbed.

"Same difference." Henry winked at me before allowing Gideon to continue his story.

"Anyway, he wasn't as...methodical as he is now. He was very much of the mindset to shoot first and ask questions later. I've always been more of a thinker. Always strategizing before making my first move. That's what I did here, too. Henry may have been bigger and faster, but I'd been studying him. I knew exactly what to do to take him out. He was expecting me to block his jab. Instead, I stepped into him. Knocked him off his feet and pinned him in three seconds."

"Three-and-a-half," Henry corrected. "And I *let* you pin me. Madison Winthrop was watching, and I knew you had a thing for her. I was just trying to help you out with the ladies."

"Sure you were."

"We can settle it right here and now," Henry challenged.

"I wouldn't want to embarrass you in front of Ariana."

"Or maybe you're afraid I'll embarrass *you* in front of Imogene," Henry retorted.

"Trust me." Gideon shifted his attention to his wife, taking her hand in his. "She's seen me at my absolute worst."

Something in his tone changed, a subtle shift from teasing to tender.

"And yet she still chose me."

"It wasn't even a choice," Imogene whispered.

Her words echoed in the air, hitting me in a way I hadn't expected.

I'd spent so long believing love was weakness, a weapon someone could turn against you. Victor had taught me that. He'd made me think trust was just another way to hand someone the knife they'd use to cut you open.

But as I watched Gideon brush his thumb along Imogene's hand, I realized how wrong I'd been. There was nothing weak about what I saw between them. No games. No masks.

It was *real*.

I felt Henry's gaze on me, a slow, steady pull that made it hard to breathe. He wasn't smiling anymore. The teasing warmth from a few moments ago had been replaced with something deeper. As if he'd been thinking the same thing I had.

I looked away, afraid he might see too much.

If Imogene was right, if love wasn't a choice, then I was already in trouble.

Because somewhere between Henry's tender admissions and rare, unguarded smiles, between the way he touched me like I was something fragile and the way he looked at me like I was anything but, I'd already stopped choosing.

And maybe I never had a say in it at all.

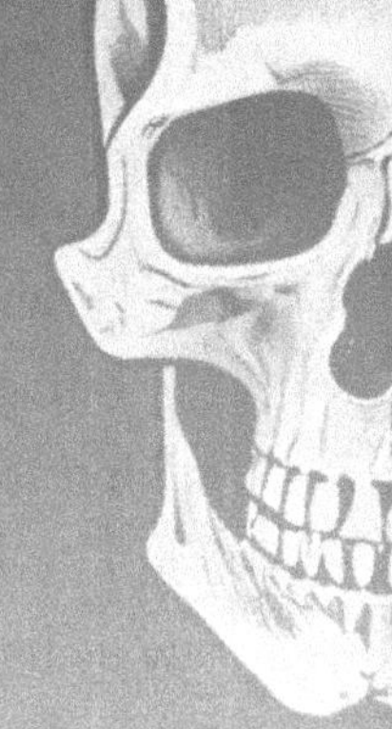

CHAPTER TWENTY-THREE

Henry

I stacked plates beside the sink while Gideon rinsed them, the low hum of conversation drifting from the living room where Imogene and Ariana sat curled up on the couch. Every few seconds, I found my gaze drifting toward them.

Ariana was laughing at something Imogene said, her head tipped back, eyes bright, shoulders loose in a way I'd never seen. Not once in all the months I'd watched her from afar. Not once in the weeks since she'd been under my roof.

Something warm worked its way through me every time her smile broke free.

Something I didn't have a name for.

Something I wasn't sure I *wanted* to have a name for.

"I never thought I'd see the day," Gideon remarked.

I dragged my eyes away from Ariana. "What are you talking about?"

The kitchen light cast shadows across his stubbled jaw as he bumped his shoulder with mine, like we were teenagers again instead of two men with more scars than we could count.

"You. In love."

"I'm not—"

"Don't even try with that bullshit," he snorted. "I've known you for nearly thirty years. You're fooling exactly zero people in this room."

"You don't know what you're talking about."

"And you're in denial." He grinned. "But I'm happy for you. Even if it's a hell of a twist, considering a few weeks ago you despised her. I'm sure there's a story."

There was. One I hadn't told him. Not fully. I hadn't wanted to drag him into it. Not when he had a baby on the way and more to lose than either of us ever had growing up. I'd only given him surface-level updates, reassuring him I was fine and had everything under control, especially once news of Ariana's disappearance broke. He knew my plan. But he didn't realize nothing had gone according to plan since I'd attended the gala at the museum.

Even so, when I'd called to let him know I'd be in Atlanta with Ariana, he didn't question it. That was the sort of friend he was.

"There definitely is," I admitted, glancing toward the living room again. Ariana's profile glowed in the warm light, soft and relaxed.

"So what is it?"

I picked up my wineglass and took a long sip. Then I told him everything.

The gala.

The pull I couldn't explain.

The boat drifting toward her dock.

The man carrying her limp body from her property.

The instinct that made me follow.

The killing.

The cash and burner phone.

The cabin.

The failed leads.

The Bratva.

By the time I finished, the dishwasher was rumbling quietly, the kitchen wiped clean.

"That's all...a lot," Gideon said finally. "But honestly?" He smirked. "I'm more interested in the story between you and Ariana. How you went from hating her to staring at her like you'd burn down the world if she stopped breathing."

A smile tugged at my mouth before I could stop it. "She could have left me. But she stayed."

"What do you mean?"

"You know the ravine on my property up in Maine?"

He nodded.

"One night, I got a motion alert. Went to check it out. I was...distracted."

He glanced toward Ariana and laughed. "I wonder what had you distracted."

"I slipped. Fell down the ravine. Hit my head." I touched the healing cut on my brow.

"So that explains it," he said with a smirk.

"Somehow I managed to crawl out. Cato must have gone to alert Ariana and led her to me. Instead of using the opportunity to run, she helped me back to the cabin. Stitched up my head. And then..."

Gideon leaned closer. "Yes?"

I shifted my eyes toward Ariana, then back to him, lowering my voice.

"Then I learned the truth."

"What truth?"

"I thought she was like him," I admitted. "Thought she was content being the trophy wife of a monster. That she didn't care who he hurt as long as she benefitted." I swallowed hard. "But she was a victim like Sarah was. Even worse."

Gideon sobered immediately.

"She showed me," I said quietly. "Showed me what he'd done to her. The bruises. The scars." My grip tightened around the wineglass. "He tortured her, Gideon. Assaulted her. Controlled every aspect of her life. Paid off a doctor to falsify her mother's medical records and drug her to make Ariana think she was losing her mind. She stayed because he held her mother's care over her."

"Jesus," Gideon whispered, staring past me as he processed everything I just shared about what the man with a sparkling reputation had done to his wife behind closed doors.

But Gideon knew firsthand how men with the most sterling reputations are usually the ones capable of the worst atrocities.

"So what's next?" he asked, shifting his hardened gaze back to mine.

"I find Victor." My jaw flexed. "He disappeared after our...conversation."

"When did you talk to him?"

"He called one of the Bratva soldiers he'd sent to Maine. I answered and may have threatened him."

Gideon huffed a laugh. "See? Shoot first, ask questions later."

"I guess." I ran a hand through my hair. "He disappeared after that. No activity. No sightings."

"So you have no idea where he is?"

"No. But I'll find him."

He hesitated. "You could...," he started before trailing off.

I set my glass down a bit too sharply. "What?"

He stepped closer, lowering his voice. "You could use Ariana."

"No." It tore out of me, loud enough that both women looked over. I forced a calm smile for their sake, then turned back to Gideon, dropping my voice to a lethal whisper. "Absolutely not."

But even the glare I gave him didn't make him back down. Nothing did.

"It could work."

"I'm not involving the police," I snapped. "They won't do shit. He's too well-connected."

"I didn't say anything about the police. But think about it. He's obviously looking for her. He sent the fucking Bratva up to Maine. If she resurfaced under circumstances *you* control, he'd come out of hiding. I guarantee it."

He wasn't wrong. I'd already considered the same thing. More than once.

That didn't mean I'd do it.

"No," I repeated. "She's been through enough. I'm not using her to get to Victor."

Gideon's mouth lifted. "Wasn't that your plan in the beginning?"

My stomach twisted, all the guilt and shame I'd been

burying since I learned what Ariana had endured roiling like acid. "You, of all people, should know plans change."

His gaze flicked toward Imogene. He'd once intended to use her for revenge, too. Until he learned the truth. Until he fell in love.

"If you were in my shoes, would you use Imogene as bait?"

Gideon's expression softened instantly, and he pushed out a long sigh. "No. I'd shield her from everything."

"And that's what I'm trying to do. Shielding Ariana. Keeping her safe."

He studied me for a moment before a slow smile curved on his face. "I'm happy for you, brother. You deserve this."

I let out a dry, humorless laugh, leaning against the counter. "I don't know about that."

He squeezed my shoulder. "You do. Stop letting the guilt eat you alive. Stop letting your past dictate your present. Or your future." He dropped his hand. "God knows I did. And if someone hadn't smacked some sense into me, I might have lost everything."

He didn't have to spell it out. I remembered every conversation, every argument, every time I'd tried to keep him from drowning in revenge.

But this wasn't the same.

This wasn't about settling a score. Not anymore.

This was about Ariana. Protecting her. Giving her something she'd never had.

A life free from fear.

A chance at something better.

And she'd never have that while Victor's heart still beat.

CHAPTER TWENTY-FOUR

Ariana

Imogene hugged me at the door, her arms warm as they wrapped around me. Unlike earlier this evening when I'd stiffened at her unexpected affection, now I melted into her embrace, letting myself accept the kindness. The warmth. The unspoken understanding.

"Henry's a really good man," she whispered in a barely audible voice as she leaned in. "One I'd trust with my life. And my baby's life." She pulled back, allowing me to see the truth in her words.

I may have just met her, but there was no denying she sensed I needed to hear them. Needed some sort of reassurance I was on the right path. That I didn't need to doubt my growing affection for this man who'd entered my life in such an unexpected way.

"Thank you," I whispered back.

"Of course."

She gave me one last squeeze before releasing me. Gideon swooped in next, pressing a kiss to my cheek before wrapping me in a brief, but surprisingly gentle bear hug.

"Visit again anytime," he said with a grin. "If for no other reason than to drag this guy out from the Underworld."

"The Underworld?" I arched a brow, looking between Henry and Gideon.

"It's what he calls my various offices," Henry explained.

"Dark. Windowless. It suits." Gideon shrugged.

"So you *are* like Hades then."

"Maybe a little." He winked, then gave Gideon a quick hug goodbye before steering me down the path toward the SUV with a steady palm on the small of my back.

The night air was crisp, smelling faintly of wood smoke from nearby chimneys. Henry opened the passenger door and helped me inside, his hand firm around mine. The moment he closed my door, the world outside dimmed, cocooning me inside the quiet vehicle.

As he drove down the residential street lined with lamplit porches and sleeping houses, I found myself watching him. His profile looked softer tonight. Or maybe it wasn't Henry who was different at all.

Maybe it was me.

My feelings.

"I hope you had fun tonight." His voice was low, almost hesitant. "And that Gideon and Imogene didn't scare you off too much."

"It was exactly what I needed."

His grip tightened slightly on the steering wheel. "Good."

We fell into a comfortable silence, one that let my thoughts drift and settle. I replayed the evening in my mind like a favorite movie — the laughter, the teasing, the smells of home-cooked food. No forced smiles. No rules. Just warmth and familiarity.

That feeling stayed with me the entire drive back to Henry's penthouse.

"Want to watch a movie?" he asked after helping me out of my coat and draping it over one of the barstools by the kitchen island.

"I'm pretty tired," I said around a yawn. "Maybe tomorrow."

"Sure." He nodded once. "I'll walk you up."

He gestured toward the winding staircase, letting me go first. As we climbed to the upper floor, I felt his presence behind me — solid, warm, protective.

"Thanks again for tonight," I said, turning toward

him when we reached my room. "I really enjoyed myself. Especially Gideon's story about you crashing your brand-new car because you were checking out a girl."

He groaned. "I'm going to kill him for that. Slowly."

I laughed. "If you do, Imogene will kill you. Honestly, I think she scares me more than Gideon."

"Me, too." He leaned in and brushed a soft kiss on my temple. "Good night, Ariana."

I closed my eyes, basking in the feel of his lips on me, even if it wasn't as deep or sensual as I hoped.

"Good night, Henry."

I met his gaze one last time, a thousand thoughts on the tip of my tongue. But I didn't allow myself to utter them. Instead, I slipped into my room and closed the door, already feeling the chill of his absence as I listened to his retreating footsteps.

On a long sigh, I kicked off my boots and peeled off my sweater dress before pulling on a t-shirt and sleep shorts. But as I went through my nightly routine of washing my face and brushing my teeth, my thoughts kept returning to Henry.

My head warned me not to trust so easily. Not after everything Victor put me through.

But my heart whispered of everything Henry had done for me. Every sacrifice. Every risk. Every moment of gentleness he didn't think I saw.

He'd proven again and again he wasn't like Victor.

That questionable choices didn't make him a bad man.

That he would stand between me and danger every time, even if it cost him everything.

That he was the only person I *trusted* to stand between me and danger.

I froze, my heart dropping to the pit of my stomach.

He was the only person I trusted.

The realization hit me like a brick wall, nearly stealing my breath.

I *trusted* Henry. I probably had for a while now.

I just hadn't trusted myself.

I moved before I could think, flinging open the door. The hallway was quiet and dim, except for the sliver of warm light glowing beneath Henry's bedroom door. My heart pounded, but not with fear. With anticipation.

With want.

With certainty.

I padded down the hall and stopped outside his door, lifting my hand to knock. The sound seemed deafening in the silence, echoing around me.

For a few agonizing seconds, nothing happened. Maybe he wasn't here. Maybe he'd gone down to the office.

I was about to turn away, take this as a sign, when I heard footsteps, and the door swung open.

Henry stood there, jeans low on his hips, shirt unbuttoned, the lamplight catching on the muscles of his chest. The tattoos. The scars.

"Is everything okay?" he asked, his voice rough with concern.

I opened my mouth, but every thought in my head scattered like leaves in the wind.

Words felt inadequate. Too small to contain everything I felt. Everything I wanted to convey.

So I didn't use them.

Instead, I reached for the hem of my t-shirt and pulled it over my head before sliding my shorts down my legs, kicking them to the side, allowing him to see all my scars.

Trusting him to see all my scars.

Henry's gaze darkened instantly, his breath going ragged.

Then I sank to my knees, bowing my head.

It was a position Victor had forced on me. One he took pleasure in. One that made my body lock up, dread coiling through every muscle.

But with Henry, I didn't tremble with fear.

Every inch of me hummed with raw, undeniable need.

"What are you doing, Ariana?" Henry asked, his question dripping with a hunger he could barely control.

"Trusting you."

His bare feet came into view and he touched my

chin, lifting my gaze to meet his. His eyes were fierce. Reverent.

"You don't have to do this to prove you trust me."

"I know," I whispered. "I *want* to. Want to replace the bad memories with good ones. With memories of you. I need this. Need to reclaim what he stole."

His jaw clenched, his nostrils flaring. Then he dropped to his knees, too, cupping my nape as he pressed his forehead against mine. Our breaths mingled, heat sparking between us.

"You're a fucking warrior, Ariana."

I expected him to kiss me. Take control. Set the tone.

But he didn't.

He waited.

For me.

For my choice.

But it wasn't a choice at all.

Not with Henry.

So I surged forward and crushed my lips to his.

CHAPTER TWENTY-FIVE

Ariana

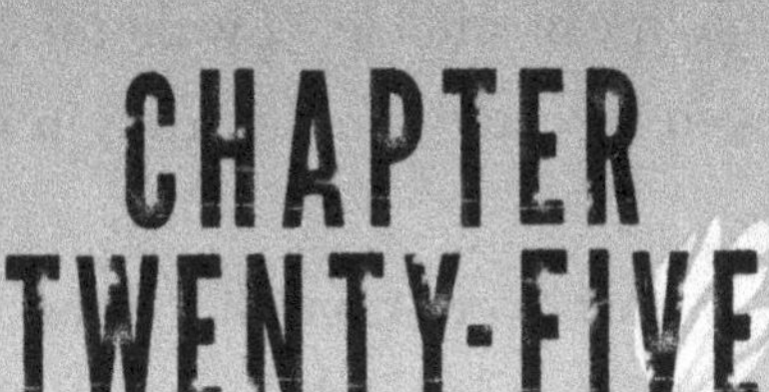

The instant my mouth met Henry's, the world narrowed to nothing but him. His taste. His heat. The way he kissed like he'd been starving. It had only been a few weeks since I'd felt him like this, but it might as well have been a lifetime.

Even so, this kiss felt...different. Like I was finally allowing myself to have him. The last time he kissed me, I hadn't been myself. At least not the person I'd become over the past few weeks.

The person who could choose this, choose *him*, with clear eyes and an open heart.

Now, I was.

He tore his lips from mine with a guttural sound, his breathing ragged. When his eyes locked on mine, they darkened with the kind of intensity that pinned me in place.

"Are you sure about this?" he asked again, resting his forehead against mine.

I lifted my hand to his cheek, brushing my thumb along the rough line of stubble. "I want this. I want you." I met his eyes so he could see the truth in my words. "I trust you."

The groan that tore from his chest was primal enough to turn me to mush. He cupped the back of my head and slammed his mouth back onto mine, kissing me like I'd just confessed something sacred. Maybe I had. Trust didn't come easily to me. He knew that better than anyone.

When he tore away, he held my face in both hands, breathing hard.

"Pick a safe word."

A jolt of nerves lit through me. Not out of fear, but from excitement. Anticipation. The realization that I was truly stepping into something new with him.

Becoming who I was always meant to be.

"Hades," I said, smirking despite the tremor in my breath.

"Hades." His lips curved, a soft huff leaving him. "I like it."

Then his expression shifted, serious and steady. "Just so we're clear, you're in control here. Not me. You call the shots. I'll test your limits, but you hold every ounce of power. You say the word, and I stop. Everything tonight is for *your* pleasure. *Your* empowerment. Okay?"

I nodded automatically.

His gaze hardened. "Use your words, Ariana. Your voice. Whenever I ask you something, answer out loud. Do you understand?"

"Yes. I understand."

"Good." He kissed me again before standing and stepping back several paces.

The air changed instantly. His posture, his eyes, his entire presence sharpened.

"Come here, Ariana."

I started to rise, but his voice cracked like a whip. "No."

I froze. A shiver shot through me, electric and hot, but utterly free of fear.

"Crawl to me."

My breath hitched, core clenching, skin vibrating with need.

I carefully sank back onto my knees with my eyes trained on his, unable to look away from the severity etched into his features. My pulse thundered, my chest tight with adrenaline and want.

Slowly, deliberately, I lowered my hands to the floor and crawled toward him. Inch by inch, the tension between us coiled tighter. His eyes tracked every movement, his desire growing, sharpening, devouring.

By the time I reached him, I was trembling. Breathless. Desperate.

I sat back on my heels, obediently waiting for whatever he planned to ask of me next.

Whatever it was, I'd do it.

He reached out and cupped my cheek, my eyes fluttering shut as I leaned into his touch.

"Good girl."

A visible shiver rolled through me.

"You like that," he murmured. "You like when I praise you."

My nod was small, automatic. Then I remembered his rule. "I do."

"Tell me why."

I tilted my head back, meeting his gaze. "I like knowing I please you."

"Is that what you want? To please me?"

"Yes."

"Good." He dropped his hand from my cheek. "Keep your eyes forward."

"Yes." My voice was breathy, thin, eager.

I didn't move as he stepped out of sight. The soft pad of his footsteps circled the room, followed by the quiet slide of drawers opening and closing. Every sound heightened my awareness as curiosity buzzed through me like static.

But I didn't look.

I kept my eyes forward.

Like he asked.

After what felt like forever, a warmth brushed my back. Every hair on my body stood on end.

He knelt behind me and pressed a slow, lingering kiss to my neck.

"What's your safe word?" he murmured against my skin.

"Hades."

"Good."

Something in his tone made my pulse trip. Before I could process it, he slipped something silky over my eyes, and darkness swallowed me.

I inhaled a breath, sharp and fast. For a split second, panic clawed up my spine, Victor's shadow whispering old threats, old fears.

But Henry wasn't Victor.

Henry would never hurt me.

I wanted this. I chose this. For him *and* for me.

I forced a slow exhale, then another, grounding myself in the warmth of Henry's hands and the steady calm of his presence.

"You okay?" he asked.

"Yes." My voice came out steadier than I felt.

"Good girl."

His mouth found my neck again, and I melted into the sensation as he teased me with a combination of his lips and teeth. I was so focused on this one point of contact, I didn't even notice when he'd taken my wrists and secured them behind my back.

"Okay?" he asked again.

I swallowed hard through the pounding of my heart. "Yes."

"Good girl."

He released me, and cool air swept over my skin where he'd been. I listened, every sound in the room amplified. His footsteps. The faint clink of metal. His belt buckle sliding free.

This was trust in its purest form. Terrifying. Thrilling.

Invigorating.

He pressed his hand to my cheek, his thumb brushing my jaw.

"You are so fucking beautiful," he breathed. "I thought so the first night I saw you. And I mean *really* saw you. Not as someone's ornament. But as a person. As a goddamn treasure."

His voice dropped, turning rough, reverent.

"You weren't my target, but something pulled me toward you that night. And when I heard your voice, saw your mouth move, I couldn't stop looking at you.

Couldn't stop imagining those crimson lips wrapped around my cock."

Warm, bare skin brushed my mouth, his unmistakably hard erection, the bit of pre-cum moistening my flesh.

"Now open those lips for me," he said, his voice thick with hunger. "And please me."

CHAPTER TWENTY-SIX

Henry

Ariana's mouth opened for me without hesitation. The moment I felt the heat of her lips close around me, I had to fight to keep myself from coming undone like an inexperienced teenager.

I looked down at her, and the sight of her nearly knocked the air from my lungs. I couldn't believe she was here. Couldn't believe any of this was real. That she was on her knees. Blindfolded. Trusting me.

When I'd said goodbye earlier, I thought I'd spend the rest of the night replaying the way she looked across Gideon's table. How easily she'd slipped into my world. How badly I'd wanted her. Wanted her more than I wanted air.

I never expected a knock on my bedroom door.

And I certainly never expected her to walk in, strip down, and kneel for me.

This was the biggest fucking turn-on I'd ever experienced.

Not because of the blindfold.

Not because of the restraints.

Not because of the way her lips tightened around me in an instinctive need to take more.

It was her trust that completely unraveled me.

Her surrender.

The fact that she gave them to me freely.

I threaded my fingers through her hair, guiding her gently at first. "Loosen your jaw," I murmured, my voice thick with lust.

Ariana immediately complied, her jaw relaxing.

"There you go. Take me deeper."

She obeyed again without hesitation. Just the fierce, stubborn bravery she didn't realize she possessed.

"Good girl," I groaned, letting my hips move just enough to test her limits. "You take me so fucking well."

Her answering hum vibrated through me, almost making my knees buckle.

I tightened my grip on her hair, holding her in place as I thrust into her mouth with controlled precision. Every sound she made, every swallow, every breathy moan she let slip dragged me closer to the edge.

"Look at you," I rasped. "Mouth full of me. Can't see a damn thing. Hands tied behind you. And you're still giving me everything."

My praise had the desired effect, and she increased her efforts, meeting each thrust with unwavering determination.

"Fuck," I bit out, my jaw clenching so hard it ached. "I love seeing you like this. Trusting me like this," I grunted, every nerve ending in my body on fire.

I was getting close. Too damn close.

As much as I wanted to let go in her mouth, watch as she swallowed every last drop, I wanted everything else with her more.

I pulled out suddenly, gripping her shoulders and hauling her to her feet. Before she could even gasp, I slammed my mouth over hers, kissing her hard, desperate.

When I finally tore my lips from hers, panting, her blindfolded face lifted toward me.

"Did I do something wrong?" she asked softly. "Something you didn't like?"

"Just the opposite." My voice was so rough it scraped out of me. "I liked it too damn much. And I'm nowhere near done with you. There's so much more I want." I skimmed my lips along her temple. "So much more I want to do to you."

A shiver rolled through her, fearless and excited all at once.

I turned her toward the bed, steering her backward as my fingers worked the knot binding her wrists. The moment she was free, I lowered her onto the mattress, my body following, my mouth claiming hers in a slow, possessive kiss.

"Your safe word," I murmured against her lips.

"I haven't forgotten it," she whispered.

"I know." I brushed my thumb across her cheek, softening my voice. "The reason I ask is to remind you that you can use it. Anytime. So tell me. What's your safe word?"

"Hades."

"Good girl."

I kissed her again, deep and lingering, before pulling back and sliding off the bed.

"I've been wanting to do this for a long time." My voice dipped lower, darker.

She swallowed. "What's that?"

"You'll see."

I picked up one of the silk ties I'd set out earlier and lifted her wrist. She tensed at the first brush of fabric, then relaxed as I left a soft kiss on her sensitive flesh. With deliberate movements, I wrapped the tie around her and secured it tightly to the headboard, keeping my eyes trained on her for any sign of distress.

But there weren't any.

Only increasing desire.

So I repeated the process with her other wrist, leaving her open and waiting.

Then I dragged another tie down the center of her torso, watching her breath catch and flutter as I brushed it around her clit.

"You okay?" I asked quietly.

"God, yes," she moaned.

"Good girl."

I moved to her ankles, binding each one to the footboard until she lay stretched out before me, blindfolded, restrained, utterly vulnerable.

And trusting me more than anyone ever had.

I stepped back, and my cock throbbed painfully at the sight of her. "I can see how wet you are from here. Does this turn you on? Being tied up like this?"

"Yes."

"What do you like about it?"

"That I'm completely at your mercy," she breathed. "That you have the power to hurt me, but I trust you won't. That you'll make me feel good."

Her honesty wound through every inch of me.

I climbed over her, caging her body with mine, and brushed my mouth along her jaw.

"I'll never hurt you," I promised. "Not like that. If I

push you, it's only to make the pleasure deeper. You understand?"

She nodded.

I took her nipple between my fingers and twisted.

She gasped, a sound caught between a moan and a cry.

"Remember the rules," I murmured. "Give me your voice. You have a voice. Use it. *Always* use it."

"Yes," she breathed. "I understand."

"Good girl."

I lowered my mouth to her breast, sucking, licking, teasing until she arched and trembled beneath me.

Then I pulled away.

"If anything is too much, tell me."

"I will," she whispered.

Her chest rose and fell quickly, her skin flushed, her breath uneven. She was already sinking into the sensation. The anticipation. The trust. And I wasn't even touching her. God, I loved seeing her like this. Loved seeing how much she craved me. How desperate she was for my touch.

I reached for another item I'd laid out and gently placed the noise-canceling headphones over her ears.

Her breath hitched as her world went silent.

Blindfolded. Bound. Deaf.

Mine.

I'd never felt more responsible for another person.

Never felt more protective. Never been more turned on in my life.

I skimmed my hand along her thigh, smiling when she didn't flinch, completely trusting me.

"God, Ariana...," I whispered, even though she couldn't hear me. "You have no idea what you do to me."

CHAPTER TWENTY-SEVEN

Ariana

The moment Henry lowered the headphones over my ears, the world went silent.

No breath.

No footsteps.

No whispered words of praise.

Just the darkness behind the blindfold and the stillness pressing around me, leaving me with nothing but my racing heart and the anticipation coiling through my body like a live wire.

Every nerve was awake, every inch of skin too aware of the absence of his touch.

I'd asked for this. I *needed* this. The quiet. The surrender. The trust.

But the longer I remained bound and waiting, the more my mind buzzed with a mixture of nerves and thrill.

And beneath it all was the bone-deep certainty I was safe with him.

Seconds stretched into what seemed like an eternity. I didn't even realize I was holding my breath until something feather-light brushed along my ribcage.

I jolted.

Not in fear. In relief.

His touch.

Finally.

But it left too soon, disappearing before I could chase it. Another ghost of contact whispered over my hip. Another down my arm. Never enough. Always gone before I could lean into it.

He was teasing me.

Drawing out every ounce of tension building low in my stomach.

Letting anticipation become its own kind of delicious torture.

Then a sharp scent cut through.

Like a match being struck, with something rich layered beneath it.

Warm. Sweet. Spicy.

Almost like cinnamon.

Did he just light a candle?

My breath hitched, my mind spinning with what he was doing. He didn't give me long to consider before warmth touched my skin.

His mouth.

It closed around my nipple, drawing me into a pleasure so sharp I arched instinctively against the restraints.

But just as quickly, he stopped, leaving me aching.

Then heat wrapped around my nipple again.

This time, it was different.

Not soft.

Not gentle.

Hot.

Wax.

I gasped, the sound trapped inside the silence of the headphones, my back straining off the mattress. The heat dissolved into a tingling coolness, rippling outward in waves that made me shiver. Pain mixed with pleasure. Torment mixed with release.

Henry repeated the pattern on my other nipple, worshipping me first with his mouth, followed by the slow drip of wax, each drop stealing my breath and feeding the fire building inside me.

He continued down my frame, each lick of his tongue and drop of wax pulling me between two opposite sensations. But both catapulted my body higher and higher.

When he reached my stomach, I felt him pause

before warm lips pressed reverently against the place I avoided looking. The scars Victor carved into me. The word that used to define me, whether I wanted it to or not.

He kissed it again.

And again.

My eyes stung, a myriad of emotions filling me as heat traced over the same place, deliberate and slow. Not random drops this time. This was purposeful. Intentional.

Like he was writing something.

I didn't know what.

But my chest tightened with something fierce, something that hurt and soothed all at once.

When he was done, the bed dipped. I couldn't see him, but I could almost feel his gaze traveling along every inch of me, admiring his work.

Then the sweet scent of cinnamon came close again. A drop by my hip. Another a little lower. My body tensed, anticipation knotting so tightly I could barely breathe, especially as he neared my clit.

Was he going to drip wax on me there? How would that feel? Would it be too much?

I braced myself for the pain, knowing Henry would never do anything to hurt me.

But instead of the burning sting of wax, a sudden vibration pulsed against my clit.

I cried out, the sensation almost more painful than the wax. Because it felt so damn good. I surrendered to it, each vibration propelling my body higher until I was on the verge of shattering into a thousand tiny pieces.

Which was the precise moment Henry pulled the vibrator away, leaving me a quivering, panting mess.

Then heat consumed me, a sharp drop of wax landing exactly where the vibration had been.

My scream felt silent in the enclosed world of darkness as I fought against my restraints.

But I still didn't give him my safe word. I needed this. Needed the pain.

Because I knew it would be followed by a pleasure unlike anything I'd ever experienced.

And that was precisely what happened. A wet cloth wiped away the wax before Henry pressed the toy back against me, sending shockwaves through me so intense I couldn't tell where pain ended and need began.

The pattern kept repeating.

Vibration. Heat. Pleasure.

Wax. Pain. Bliss.

His hands steadied me. His breath ghosted over the skin he'd set on fire.

Just when I thought I might break, he brought the toy back up to me. But instead of pressing it against my clit, he slid it inside me, the deep pulse stealing my last coherent thought, especially when he closed his mouth over my clit, consuming and devouring me.

Every sensation collided. The lingering burn. The cool air. The vibration inside me. Henry's mouth pulling pleasure from me in deliberate, torturous strokes.

I spiraled fast. Too fast.

But right before I hit that peak I was desperately chasing, he stopped.

A whimper tore out of me. Or maybe it was a scream. I couldn't be sure. All I knew was his absence was the cruelest form of torture, the pain of being deprived of my release worse than any burning wax.

My breath echoed in my ears, my heart feeling like it was about to burst out of my ribcage as I waited for what was to come.

And then I felt it again.

The wax on my clit. I arched off the bed, panting, moaning, walking the perilous tightrope between plea-sure and pain once more.

He pressed his hand to my stomach, gluing me to the mattress, and repeated the same process.

His mouth.

The vibrator.

The climb.

The sudden withdrawal.

I begged without words.

But he still didn't give me what I needed.

Or maybe he did.

He pushed me to the edge, then pulled me back.

Again.

And again.

And again.

When he'd deprived me of an orgasm for probably the fifth or sixth time, I was practically sobbing. Still, I wanted more. *Needed* more.

The bed dipped, and I held my breath, bracing for another round of exquisite torture.

Instead of wax dripping on my clit, I felt something else rub against me. Something warm.

Then he slammed into me, and the world detonated around me.

Every thrust was amplified.

Every slap of skin on skin.

Every pulse.

Every breath he ripped from me with the force of his body claiming mine.

I couldn't see him.

Couldn't hear him.

Couldn't touch him.

But I felt him everywhere.

Pleasure tore through me in a violent wave I couldn't stop, couldn't soften, couldn't hide. My body arched so sharply the restraints pulled tight, my cry echoing in my ears as an orgasm spiraled through me, relief mixing with need.

But Henry didn't slow down. Didn't drag out my pleasure.

He drove into me again. And again. And again. Pushing me past the edge, past reason, past everything I thought I understood about my own limits.

I climbed again.

Faster.

Higher.

Right as I reached the breaking point, he ripped the headphones and blindfold off me.

It took me a second to adjust to the light. When I did, Henry was there.

Fire-bright eyes.

Jaw clenched.

Chest heaving.

Peering at me like I was his salvation and damnation all in one.

Just like he was mine.

I didn't look away.

I couldn't.

He was my anchor. My center. My true north.

Our bodies moved together like two puzzle pieces snapping into place. His groan mixed with my cry, my vision blurring as a climax tore through me a second time. Harder. Brighter. Leaving me shaking uncontrollably. He let go at the same time, his body jerking and trembling through his own release.

When he had nothing left, he crushed his lips to mine, breathing into me. And I greedily accepted every last exhale.

After he finally got his breathing under control, he quickly undid my restraints one by one, leaving a tender kiss on each place he'd tied me.

The moment I was free, he gathered me into his arms and held me against his chest. His lips found my forehead, my cheek, my hair. Every kiss was soft, every touch gentle.

It broke me.

Tears spilled hot and sudden down my face, so many emotions overwhelming me at once.

"I'm sorry," I choked out. "I don't... I don't know what's wrong with me."

"Hey." His voice was low, steady, grounding. He touched my chin, forcing my eyes to meet his. Not letting me hide from him.

"It's okay. You've had to bury your feelings for too damn long. Let them out. If you need to cry, cry. If you need to scream, scream. You're safe with me."

I closed my eyes, drawing in a steadying breath. When I returned my gaze to him, I pushed back his tendril of hair that always seemed to spring loose.

"I know I am."

He kissed me soft and slow, proving he meant every word he said. Then he released me and stood. "Be right back."

With one last kiss on my temple, he padded into the bathroom, returning a few seconds later to scoop me into his arms and carry me with him. Steam curled from the oversized bathtub as water poured from the spout.

He set me gently on my feet, extending his hand to help me into the tub, but I shook my head.

"I want to see first."

He scrunched his brows in confusion as I turned toward the full-length mirror.

Mirrors used to be my enemy.

I'd avoided them for years, only studying my reflection when necessary, hating how trapped I was in my own skin.

My body had always felt like a cage.

Now when I looked at myself, I no longer felt trapped.

Where Victor's mark once stood out stark and cruel, Henry had written something new in bright red wax.

Something beautiful.

"Warrior," I whispered, tracing the cooling letters.

Henry stepped behind me and wrapped an arm around my waist, brushing his lips against the curve of my neck.

"It's what you are," he murmured. "The wax will

wash away. But it doesn't change who you are. Or how I see you."

Emotion squeezed my chest, and I spun in his arms, grabbing his face and kissing him.

Fierce.

Grateful.

Alive.

CHAPTER TWENTY-EIGHT

Henry

The first thing I noticed was the light, thin, golden slats cutting across my bedroom as the sun crept through the blinds.

The second was Ariana.

She lay on her side, facing away from me, the sheet tangled low around her hips, her hair spilling over my pillow. I didn't move. Just watched her breathe. Slow. Peaceful. The kind of peace that was cathartic. That could only be felt from finally facing your fears.

I knew the sex would be good. With her, it always was.

But what I hadn't expected, what I hadn't been prepared for, was the trust.

Her trust.

Last night she'd put herself in my hands. Unequivocally. Completely. The weight of it hit me harder than anything I'd experienced in years. Maybe ever. And I wanted more of it.

Something squeezed at my chest as I admired her in the morning light. It wasn't the first time I'd watched her sleep. But it was the first time she looked like she wasn't carrying a weight that was about to crush her.

Instead, she looked lighter. Softer. Almost like the last piece of her past had finally loosened its hold on her.

Her breathing shifted, and without opening her eyes, she rasped, "I can feel you watching me."

A laugh rumbled out of me, quiet and low.

I slid my hand along her stomach, pulling her back into my chest, savoring the warmth of her skin against mine. My thumb brushed over the faint scars marring her stomach. Unlike every other time I'd touched her here, she didn't flinch. Didn't tense.

She let me touch her.

She *trusted* me with every scar and imperfection.

"You can feel me watching you?" I murmured.

She rolled to face me, her blue eyes bright as they locked on mine. Her fingers threaded through my messy hair, tugging just enough to make my pulse increase.

"After last night," she said, her voice a rough whisper, "I'd like to think I'm becoming an expert on what your eyes feel like on me. Not like I had much choice." A small smile tugged at her mouth. "It was one of the few senses I had left."

My brows lifted. "What's that?"

"The sense of feel," she breathed.

I brushed my thumb along her hip, unable to stop touching her. Wanting her. *Feeling* her.

"And what did you feel?"

"Everything, Henry." She leaned in, ghosting her lips against mine. "I felt everything."

Every last ounce of restraint snapped, and I crashed my mouth against hers, my body reacting before I could stop it. And I didn't want to stop. I was driven by one thing and one thing alone. The insatiable need this woman sparked inside me.

She hooked her leg over my hip, pulling me closer, and need unfurled low in my stomach, especially when I felt her heat against my throbbing erection.

"Did you enjoy it?" I asked against her lips.

She huffed a soft, incredulous laugh. "You know I did."

"Do you regret it?"

"No." Her gaze didn't waver. "Do you?"

"Not for a fucking heartbeat."

I kissed her again, our tongues tangling in a desperate dance. I pulled her even closer as I pulsed against her, craving her in a way that didn't feel entirely sane. She arched into me, her breathing uneven, her nails digging into my back. Into the scars marring my flesh. The pain it caused only made me want her more.

"I wouldn't mind a repeat," she murmured. "Feel free to tie me up anytime you want."

A rough sound escaped me. "I plan on it."

I rolled her onto her back and hovered over her. Her hair fanned across the pillow, making her look like an angel.

"But right now..." I rasped as I buried my head in the crook of her neck, nipping and licking at her sensitive skin. "I need your hands on me. Need to feel you everywhere."

I slid into her, slow and steady, and she gasped, wrapping herself around me. Arms. Legs. Heart. Soul.

And in this moment, I couldn't tell where I ended and she began. We moved together like we'd been doing this for years, some instinctive rhythm neither of us had to think about kicking in.

Last night had been fire.

Sharp. Intense. All-consuming.

This was something else entirely.

This was connection.

Raw. Terrifying. Addictive.

With every slow roll of her hips, every soft sound that fell from her throat, something tightened around my heart. Something I'd never experienced before. Something I never believed I could. Not after the blood on my hands. The people I'd failed. The losses that had carved me from the inside out.

I didn't deserve this.

I didn't deserve her.

But the thought of letting this go, letting *her* go, was worse than any fear I'd ever faced.

Her lips brushed mine, her fingers gripping my shoulders as we climbed together, the intensity building until it was almost unbearable. I tried to fight it, but Ariana wouldn't let me. She pulled me closer, her legs circling my waist like a vice. It wasn't just the way her body moved with mine that undid me. It was the feelings she brought out of me.

Years ago, I swore I'd always remain in control.

Control was the one thing no one could take from me. After everything I'd been through, it was the only shield I trusted.

But every day with Ariana had chipped away at that armor. The way she looked at me. The way she challenged me. The way she didn't cower or shrink away from me.

The way she saw who I really was underneath it all.

And when she kneeled before me last night, trembling but trusting, it wasn't only her surrender on the floor of my bedroom.

It was mine, too.

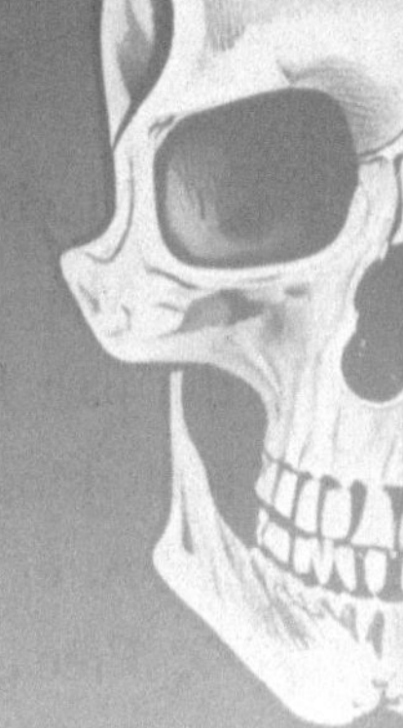

CHAPTER TWENTY-NINE

Ariana

The scent of coffee and bacon drifted through the kitchen as I sat perched on a barstool by the island, drowning in one of Henry's shirts while morning sunlight streamed through the floor-to-ceiling windows. The city buzzed beneath us — cars moving, people living, the world turning. But up here, everything felt still.

And right.

For all the time I'd spent wanting to escape Henry, terrified of what choosing him would mean, now there was nowhere I'd rather be.

It made me rethink everything I thought I knew about freedom.

Maybe freedom wasn't distance.

Maybe it wasn't running.

Maybe freedom was the first breath you took when the past loosened its grip long enough for you to feel something good again.

After last night, I finally felt free.

Free from my past.

Free from the blame.

From the version of me Victor had broken and twisted.

I took a long sip of coffee, welcoming the nutty flavor, as Henry moved around the kitchen. I'd watched him cook countless times by this point.

But watching him this morning felt different.

Because now there was nothing between us.

No more lies.

No more secrets.

Everything was finally out in the open.

He knew my scars and appreciated each and every one.

And I knew all his imperfections and wouldn't trade them for anything.

"What are you thinking about over there?" Henry's voice cut through my thoughts as he flipped bacon in the pan.

"What do you mean?"

He glanced over his shoulder at me. "I can feel you thinking."

"Oh, really?"

He nodded once, setting the tongs down before walking toward me with that slow, predatory pace that made my pulse stutter.

"I'd like to think I've become a bit of an expert at reading your body by now, Ariana," he murmured as he caged me in, his proximity overwhelming me.

"Is that right?"

He dipped his head into the crook of my neck, so close yet still painfully out of reach.

And he knew it drove me crazy.

"That's right," he rasped.

"Then instead of *asking* me what I'm thinking, you should be able to *tell* me what I'm thinking."

He grinned that wicked, devastating smirk as he slid his palms up my thighs, fingers teasing at the thin cotton between my legs. I sucked in a breath, the scrape of his stubble against my neck sending a shiver through me.

"You're thinking how you want me to fuck you, Ariana," he began, teasing me through my panties. "How you want me to pull you off this chair, haul you over to the couch, pin your stomach against it, then slam into you from behind. How you want me to pull your hair, spank you, make you teeter on that perilous tightrope between pleasure and pain."

With every word he spoke, my breathing grew ragged until I was practically panting for him.

"Isn't that right?" he asked, his voice rough.

"Yes," I whispered, pulsing against him, squirming for him to touch me where I needed him.

But he didn't.

Instead, he stepped back and widened his stance, arms folding over his chest again in a display that made my insides twist.

"Then tell me."

I blinked, caught off guard by his sudden retreat. "What?"

"You heard me." He leaned close once more, his mouth brushing mine without kissing me. "Tell me to fuck you, Ariana."

I didn't question it. Didn't argue. I was so desperate for him, I'd do anything to put me out of my misery.

"Please, Henry." I swallowed hard. "I need you to fuck me."

He didn't move right away. Just stayed a breath away, time seeming to stand still.

Then he spun around, heading toward the stove. He turned it off and removed the pan from the heat before returning to me. Without hesitation, he slammed his lips against mine, thrusting his tongue in my mouth in a way that stole my breath.

Forcing my legs around his waist, he gripped my thighs and lifted me off the barstool, carrying me across the open living space, his lips never leaving mine. And I never wanted them to. Never wanted to stop kissing this man.

But I wouldn't get my wish. Too soon, he tore his lips away and carefully set my feet on the floor. Reaching for my t-shirt, he tore it over my head and spun me around, bending me over the back of the couch. He yanked my panties down my legs, then pushed my thighs wide, his motions rough and desperate.

His body folded over mine, his lips soft as they made their way up my spine. His breath warmed my neck, causing all the tiny hairs on my body to stand on end.

"If it's too much, tap the couch three times."

I glanced over my shoulder at him. "What about my safe word?"

"You won't be able to talk."

"I won't?"

A devilish grin tugged on his lips as he brought my panties up to my mouth.

"Open."

My heart stuttered, a tiny voice in my head screaming at me not to do this. Victor used to gag me, too. He'd stuff my mouth, then cover my nose so I couldn't breathe. The way he'd look at me with delight as he held my life in his hands was something I'd never forget. Why would I willingly put myself in the same situation?

But this *wasn't* the same situation.

Henry wasn't Victor. He'd proven that repeatedly.

Especially last night.

So I parted my lips, allowing Henry to shove my panties into my mouth.

Unlike when Victor did the same thing, it turned me on, heat flooding through my veins.

"You like this, don't you?" he murmured, his voice low and husky as he slid his fingers through my center, coating them in my desire. "Does it turn you on to have your mouth full of your panties?"

My only response was a moan. I closed my eyes as I basked in the feel of Henry's fingers teasing me. Torturing me. Pleasing me.

"Now you'll taste and smell the same thing I am."

In a heartbeat, Henry replaced his fingers with something warm. I whimpered as he flicked his tongue against my clit, pushing a finger inside, followed by another. I was so blissed out, I barely registered when his tongue slid back, nearing my ass.

I instantly tensed, my breathing increasing.

"Relax," Henry soothed, his motions careful and reverent.

Unlike whenever Victor would force himself on me back there.

"Let me make you feel good."

I drew in as deep of a breath as I could and tried to relax. And when I felt his tongue against me, I couldn't reel in the moan.

"You like that, don't you?"

I didn't want to admit it. I shouldn't like it. Not after all the times Victor forced himself on me. After all the times Victor savagely thrust inside me there, causing me inexplicable pain.

But with Henry, I didn't feel anything even remotely close to pain.

All I felt was pleasure.

"He hurt you here, didn't he?" he remarked, sliding his tongue over the sensitive hole as his fingers gently teased my clit.

I nodded.

"Do you want me to stop?"

I hesitated long enough to feel the old fear try to claw back up my throat. But I pushed it down, shaking my head.

Henry briefly removed his tongue, and the lack of his touch left me wanting, writhing for more.

"Give me one second. Don't move."

I nodded, remaining in place as I stared out the floor-to-ceiling windows at the city below, my breathing seeming to echo in my ears, drowning out the sound of Henry's retreating footsteps.

My mind raced with what we were about to do, but I was more excited than anything. I needed this. *Wanted* this.

When Henry returned, he placed gentle kisses along

my spine. My hips. My ass. Slowly working his way back to my hole. I braced myself to feel his tongue once more. Instead, something cold landed on me.

I glanced over my shoulder to see him squirt some baby oil on me before teasing me with one of his fingers.

"Is this okay?"

With my eyes locked on his, I nodded.

"Good."

He rubbed more baby oil onto me, then carefully slipped a finger inside.

I released a groan, burying my head in the couch as I struggled to make sense of the warring feelings inside of me.

"You feel so fucking incredible, Ariana," he rasped as he worked his finger in and out of me. Instead of resisting, I moved with him, each thrust and twist flooding me with desire.

I felt him bend over me, his chest hair tickling my skin. Then his teeth clamped onto my earlobe.

"Do you want me to show you how good it can be?"

My pulse spiked once more, my mind reeling.

"You can say no," he continued when I didn't immediately agree. "Don't think you have to do this for me. I want you to do this for you. I want to make you feel good. That's all."

I squeezed my eyes shut, torn between fear and desire. But I knew he'd make it good for me. And more than anything, I wanted to take back everything Victor stole from me. Didn't want to live under his control anymore. Didn't want to be afraid of intimacy anymore.

So I gave Henry a small nod.

"Look at me, Ariana," he demanded.

I followed his command, my eyes meeting his.

"Are you sure?"

I held his gaze, hoping to communicate how certain I was.

Then I nodded once more.

He yanked the panties from my mouth with his free hand and thrust his tongue inside, the combination of his ravenous kiss and his finger working my ass almost too much. I barely had time to catch my breath before he shoved my panties back in, peppering kisses down my back.

I expected him to replace his finger with his erection, but he didn't. Not right away. Instead, he took his time, stretching and preparing me.

I didn't think I'd ever enjoy someone touching me like this, but everything about it felt incredible. His slow, deliberate motions. His murmured words of praise. His warm kisses along my skin, encouraging me.

I wasn't sure how much more I could take. I was already overcome with pleasure.

But then his touch disappeared, his finger slipping

out. I was about to glance back at him when I felt another squirt of baby oil on me.

Then something pressed against me.

Something much bigger than a finger.

My pulse spiked, and I gripped the couch tighter.

Henry leaned over me, leaving soft kisses along my shoulder blades.

"When I tell you, I want you to take a deep breath. Okay?"

I nodded.

He nudged himself against me, every muscle in my body becoming taut.

Maybe this wasn't a good idea. Henry was so much bigger than Victor.

But I wanted to do this. Wanted to reclaim every last piece Victor stole from me.

This wasn't about giving Henry what he wanted.

It was about giving myself what I wanted.

What I *needed*.

And I needed Henry to do this.

"Okay, baby. Deep breath. Inhale for three."

I did as he asked, inhaling through my nose as he counted.

"Now exhale."

I released my breath as best as I could through my gag. As I did, he pushed inside.

My exhale turned into a muffled cry, my grip on the

couch tightening even more as so many sensations fought for attention. There was pain, but it didn't hurt like I thought it would.

Instead, I felt a sort of pleasure I didn't think possible.

Henry didn't move right away, toying with my clit before slipping a finger inside my pussy. I squirmed, fighting against the orgasm already building.

"Are you ready for more?" Henry asked, his voice filled with barely restrained need.

I met his eyes and gave him a nod.

"Good girl."

He started to move inside me, slowly at first, giving me time to adjust.

And my god, it was unlike anything I'd ever experienced.

"You're fucking incredible, Ariana," Henry grunted, his motions slow and measured as he treated me to more pleasure than I thought possible.

Before Henry, my life was nothing but torture, torment, and pain.

But Henry changed everything. He helped me find a side of me I'd forgotten about.

And a side of me I didn't know existed.

"You should see yourself right now," he continued. "Your ass filled with my cock. Your cunt filled with my fingers. You're fucking soaked."

Even if my mouth wasn't being gagged with my panties, I didn't think I could even attempt to formulate a response.

Piece by piece, breath by breath, Henry coaxed me into reclaiming a part of me I thought was gone forever. A part Victor had ruined.

And it felt...incredible.

Empowering.

Like stitching together a wound I'd been pretending didn't bleed.

I let him guide me.

Let my body respond.

Let pleasure replace fear.

Soon, that familiar sensation built low in my body. I wanted the release, but at the same time I never wanted this to end.

"Come on, baby," Henry said, peppering rough kisses along my back, biting my shoulder blades. "Let go. Let me feel you clench around me. I need it."

That was all it took for the tension to snap inside me, my release tearing through me so intensely I screamed into my gag.

This wasn't just an orgasm.

It was a reclamation.

I'd barely had a chance to come down from the bliss rolling through my body when Henry pulled out and tugged me to my unsteady feet, his hand stroking his cock.

I didn't have to ask what he wanted. I knew.

Spitting out my panties, I lowered myself to my knees and parted my lips, the sight of him stroking his glistening cock setting me on fire all over again. He gave himself a few final tugs, then let go, ejaculating on my tongue, my chin, over my chest.

Once he was done, he yanked me to my feet, slamming his lips to mine, not caring that I tasted like him. And I didn't care that he tasted like me. If anything, it turned me on even more.

Tearing away, he leaned his forehead against mine, his ragged breaths echoing around us.

"Thank you," he murmured.

"For what? Letting you fuck me?"

"No." He pulled back and pushed a tendril of hair behind my ear. "For trusting me. For choosing me to be the one to help you reclaim this part of you. I'm not sure I deserve it, but I'll do everything I can to prove I do."

Emotion stung behind my eyes, my throat heavy from the sincerity in his words.

I lifted onto my toes and brushed my mouth against his. "You already have."

He kissed me again, deeper this time, but the sound of his phone vibrating on the counter broke the moment.

He groaned, pulling away and glancing at it. Blake's name flashed on the screen.

"Do you need to get that?" I asked, extracting myself from his embrace.

He looked torn. "I probably should."

"Talk to him. I need a shower anyway."

"I'll make it quick so I can join you." His mouth curved into a hungry smile. "Then maybe we try breakfast again."

"Sounds good to me."

I headed upstairs, warmth spreading through me at the weight of his eyes on me as I disappeared down the hallway and into his room.

In the bathroom, I turned on the shower, allowing it to warm up before stepping under the stream. I released a long sigh, the water soothing the muscles Henry had worked so thoroughly. But it was a good ache.

A reminder of what I'd taken back.

I'd barely gotten my hair wet when the shower door opened and Henry slipped inside.

"That was quick," I remarked.

"Yeah."

Something in his voice made my stomach tighten. "What is it? Did something happen?"

He hesitated. "Blake found Schaffer's files. The sterilizations. He wouldn't tell me much over the phone. Said I needed to see it for myself."

Ice slid through my veins. "Do you think he found something on Sarah?"

Henry pushed out a breath that sounded like defeat and dread tangled together. "I don't know."

"Then we need to get back," I said.

His shoulders dropped further. "I know how much you needed this. Getting away. Having space. Not being trapped in that so-called 'prison' anymore."

I stepped toward him, looping my arms around his neck. "It's hard to consider it a prison when the warden makes me come so hard I see stars."

He studied me for a beat. Then he laughed. A real, unrestrained one that vibrated through me.

When he looked at me again, something warm flickered in his eyes. "Think you'd mind the warden sneaking into your cell tonight?"

"I do have a cellmate," I teased. "Maybe I should sneak into the warden's room instead. Or..." I paused, searching his face. "Maybe the warden wants me to move into his place?"

His expression softened. "Only if it's what you want. If it's what you choose."

"It is," I whispered against his mouth. "I choose you, Henry."

CHAPTER THIRTY

Ariana

The drive back to the farm felt nothing like the one to Atlanta.

Henry kept my hand in his almost the entire time, his thumb brushing lazy circles across the back of it like he wasn't even thinking about it. Like it was instinct now. Natural.

And I'd be lying if I said I didn't enjoy every second of it.

I'd gotten used to the sound of the road beneath us, the soothing strains of jazz music coming from the speakers, the warmth of his palm wrapped around mine. If I could have stayed in this bubble — just the two of us, no shadows from the past, no imminent danger — I would have.

It was surreal to think it was only twenty-four hours ago that we were in this same car on our way to Atlanta.

It felt like a lifetime ago.

I wasn't the same woman who'd left Henry's property yesterday morning. I'd been carrying so much weight. Trauma that had burrowed deep in my marrow. Pain I'd convinced myself I deserved.

But over the past twenty-four hours, Henry had peeled it off, piece by piece, without me noticing.

He helped me let go. Of my past. Of Victor. Of everything.

He fulfilled the promise he'd made last week.

That he'd help me find the woman I was always meant to be.

And because of Henry, I was starting to do something I never thought possible.

I was learning to love myself again.

When the farmhouse finally appeared at the end of the long gravel drive, it didn't look like the place I'd once considered a prison.

It looked like safety.

Like protection.

Like *home*.

Or maybe it was Henry who made me feel all those things.

He parked the SUV and stepped out, running to

open my door before I could even reach for the handle. He extended his hand and I took it, allowing him to help me out, my shoes crunching against the gravel. He retrieved our bags, then steered me toward the front door.

When I walked inside, everything was exactly as I remembered. The grandfather clock in the living area. The birch beams throughout the cathedral ceiling. The smell of lemon and eucalyptus.

But it felt different. It felt...peaceful. Like this was where I belonged.

"I'll walk you to the guest house," Henry stated, leading me toward the great room.

"You don't have to," I replied. "I'm sure you're itching to see what Blake found."

"He can wait while I walk you to your door." A hint of a smile tugged at his mouth.

"So you're a gentleman now?" I teased.

"You don't think I am?"

I paused as we approached the French doors leading outside, lifting myself onto my toes. "I could be wrong, but the things you did to me last night weren't very gentlemanly." I smirked. "Or this morning."

He brushed his mouth against mine, the ghost of his kiss setting me on fire. "I didn't hear any complaints. In fact, all I heard was you moan my name."

"Did you not enjoy hearing me moan your name?"

He yanked me against him. "I fucking loved it, Ariana. Can't wait to hear it again. But next time, I don't want you to just moan my name."

"No?" I arched a brow.

"No." He gave me the same devilish smile that always seemed to make my heart skip a beat. "I plan on making you scream it."

He lingered for a moment before pulling back and opening the French doors, his absence causing a chill to overwhelm me.

"Are you coming?" he glanced over his shoulder at me.

"Unfortunately not," I retorted, walking toward him.

"Don't worry, baby." He placed a soft kiss on my head. "I'll make sure you do later on."

"I'm going to hold you to that."

We made our way through the back garden, the scent of pine drifting from the woods beyond the property. Everything felt sharper somehow. Brighter. More awake. As if the world had shifted.

When we reached the guest house, I stopped and faced him, erasing the space between us.

"Thanks again for everything. I had a really good time."

"I know." He waggled his brows, and I playfully punched him.

"Can you get your mind out of the gutter for two seconds? I'm trying to be serious here."

"It's hard around you." He gave me another mischievous smile, and it felt like my heart was ready to burst out of my chest.

I barely recognized the Henry who emerged from the shadows in the snow as the man in front of me now. I liked to think I had something to do with it. Just like he played a big part in the change in me.

"But I'm glad you enjoyed yourself," he said, his voice shifting. "I did, too. And not because of the sex, although if I'm being honest, it was fucking incredible." He pulled me closer. "But I liked being able to just...be with you."

"I liked it, too."

His lips curved into a heartwarming smile. Then something vulnerable flickered behind his eyes. "If you meant what you said earlier, you're welcome to move back into the main house. Into your old room." He hesitated, as if gauging my reaction, before adding, "Or mine. Whatever you choose, I'd still like you in my bed tonight."

"I'd like that too," I whispered.

"Good."

He leaned in, treating me to an open-mouthed kiss that managed to break me and put me back together again. When he pulled away, he leaned his forehead against mine.

"You make it hard for me to let you go. I just want to forget the world exists and lose myself in you."

"I know," I exhaled. "But you need this." I met his gaze. "We both do. We need closure."

"And I'll do everything to give it to you, Ariana."

He kissed me again, one last lingering press of his mouth against mine.

"I'll see you later," he murmured.

"Can't wait."

I watched him walk away, admiring his broad physique, purposeful stride, the way the sun hit him. Then I turned and walked into the house.

And was instantly met with my mother's teasing grin.

"Did you have a nice night?" she asked from her place on the couch. Cato was curled beside her, as if they'd known each other their entire lives.

He was that way with me when I first met him.

Guess he'd moved on to someone new.

Traitor.

"It was...fine."

Mom and Cato exchanged a look so perfectly synchronized I couldn't even pretend I hadn't noticed.

"I have a feeling that man is capable of much more than 'fine'."

My cheeks heated, and I tried to hide my smile, but failed miserably. I dropped beside Cato on the opposite side of the couch.

"It was amazing," I gushed, my grin breaking free. "*He* was amazing. *Is* amazing."

"I'm guessing you finally worked through your differences," she teased.

"That's one way of putting it."

Talking to her like this should have felt strange. What woman wants to talk about sex with her mother? But I'd lost so many years with her, and I wasn't wasting another second. I'd always yearned to have a mother with whom I could have a close relationship.

Now I did.

"Tell me all about it." She shifted on the couch, devoting her full attention to me.

So I told her all about my getaway with Henry.

Well...not *everything*. I left out the blindfold, the gag, the way surrendering to him had felt like reclaiming something Victor had stolen. Those details weren't necessary.

What mattered was that Henry had given me control when I'd had none for so long. And I'd given him my trust.

By the time I finished, my mother was watching me with a softness I hadn't seen in years.

"You're glowing," she said.

"I'm happy," I remarked, unable to hide my disbelief. "I mean, I know he's older, and I probably shouldn't want anything to do with him because of how we met—"

"Stop letting your head get in the way, Ari." She reached over, tucking a strand of hair behind my ear like she used to when I was little. "Too many people spend their whole lives fixated on all the reasons something is a bad idea. And in the process, they talk themselves out of what could be the best thing to happen to them. Remember the color you saw when you thought about Henry?"

"Green," I exhaled.

"The color of hope. Of rebirth. You may not want to admit it, and granted my memory is still a bit foggy. But in just the past few weeks, I've seen a change in you. He tended to you like you tended to your garden when you were a child. He learned what you needed and gave that to you. If you ask me, *that's* what's important. Nothing else. Not age. Not circumstance. Just that he understands your needs and can meet them."

A warm feeling swelled in my chest. An emotion I'd learned to suppress years ago.

But whenever I thought of Henry, it was there.

At first, it was subtle, but over the past few weeks, it had grown stronger and stronger to the point where I could no longer ignore it.

Maybe it wouldn't last.

Maybe life was about to shift again in ways I couldn't predict or control.

But right now?

I could breathe.

I could hope.

That was all I cared about.

CHAPTER THIRTY-ONE

Henry

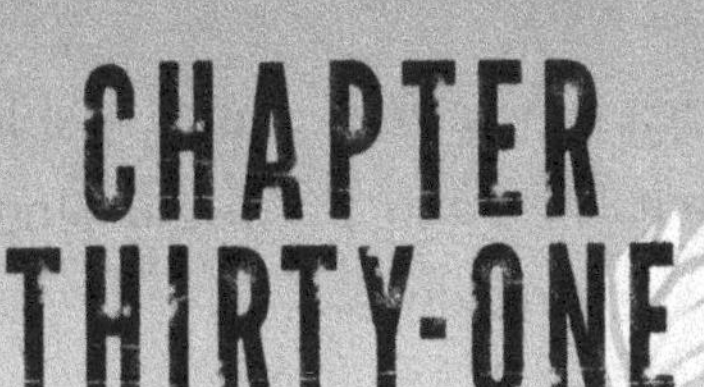

Blake was already in my office when I walked in. Black suit. Crisp shirt. Dark hair styled with precision. Facial hair neatly trimmed. The only thing out of place was the chaos swallowing my office.

Four Banker's boxes rested on the floor near the coffee table, overflowing with manila files, the smell of paper and dust thick in the air. Blake sat on the couch, flipping through papers like a man possessed, the edge of his jaw tight.

"What's all this?" I asked, furrowing my brows in confusion.

"The files you wanted," he said, not looking up. "The women Victor had Schaffer sterilize."

"What are you talking about? This isn't just a few like he claimed."

He finally met my eyes. "This is why I wanted you to see this. He lied."

"Where did you find these?" I asked, taking in all the files.

"His charity runs a few clinics in Florida. I found these at one outside Tampa. I'm guessing it's where he performed all the procedures."

"Fuck..." I exhaled.

"Exactly." Blake returned his attention to the papers in front of him as I joined him on the couch.

"I'm running their names through a program I built. It'll crawl through every state database — DMV, court records, even old social media caches. See if I can find a common denominator other than Victor paying Schaffer to sterilize them."

"Anything yet?"

"I've only checked five names so far, but I haven't found much connecting them except for the fact that the last transaction on their bank accounts was a few days prior to the date Schaffer performed their procedures, according to his records."

"What the fuck was he involved in?" I asked, although I feared I already knew the answer.

"I can only think of one reason Victor would want to make sure this many women couldn't get pregnant."

Blake gave me a pointed stare. "And I doubt it's because he was keeping them all as mistresses."

I squeezed my eyes shut, pinching the bridge of my nose. "You're right."

This was so much bigger than I'd expected. I'd wanted these files in the hopes of finding a list of mistresses on the off-chance it might lead us to Victor's hiding place.

Instead, we'd uncovered proof of something much worse.

A goddamn human trafficking operation, if my gut was right.

"Guess I'd better make some coffee." I pushed up from the couch. "Looks like we'll be here a while."

The kitchen was quiet except for the persistent drip of the coffeemaker. I braced my hands on the counter and stared out the window, trying to steady the chaos in my mind.

Victor Kane had always been a sadist. I'd seen the evidence of what he'd done to Ariana. But this... This was industrialized cruelty. Organized. Systematic.

I wished Schaffer were still alive so I could kill him again for the role he played. And for lying to me about it.

The only silver lining was the fact that Victor was still alive.

I'd make him suffer for all of this. For Sarah. For

Ariana. And for every single one of the women in those files.

I'd make sure justice was served.

Even if it was the last thing I did.

Once the coffee finished brewing, I poured two mugs and brought them back to the office. Blake glanced my way as I entered, then returned his focus to the folder, his mouth tightening before he tossed it aside.

"Everything okay?" I asked, sitting beside him and placing a mug in front of him.

He gave a short, humorless laugh as he took a sip of coffee. "Yeah."

"You sure?"

"I just..." He sighed, scrubbing a hand down his face. "Never mind. Let's see what we can find out about these women. See if they can lead us to Victor... Or them."

"Are you sure you're okay?" I dropped my voice. "Is this about the girl you keep looking for? Chandler something?"

His shoulders stiffened. Then he pushed out a long breath. "I guess a part of me was hoping she'd be in here," he admitted quietly. "But at the same time, praying she wasn't."

I knew that kind of hope. The kind that tore you apart either way.

"Who is she?"

"Just someone I used to know."

"Did you—"

"Sarah's not in here, either," he said before I could ask.

I didn't know if it was a good thing or not. My gut told me there had to be a connection between this recent development and everything else that was going on — Sarah's death, Ariana's abduction, the Bratva.

I could feel us getting closer. But with every new piece of information, new questions arose.

"Well..." I sighed, taking a fortifying sip of coffee. "Let's get to work."

***

Hours later, my office looked like a war room. Files littered every surface, a map of the U.S. dotted with colored pins marking each woman's last known city and date hung on the wall. Another wall held rows of photographs — young women smiling in frozen snapshots of ordinary lives.

"Now what should we do?" Blake asked, rubbing his neck.

I didn't answer right away, unable to shake the feeling we were missing something. I focused on the various cities. Santa Fe. Santa Monica. Austin. Chicago. Boston. San Francisco. Miami.

If the women had been concentrated in one area,

maybe it would have made sense. But they were spread out. Dozens of cities over the course of several years.

I kept staring at the map, something about these cities in particular standing out in my mind.

"What is it?" Blake asked, obviously sensing the wheels spinning.

"It's probably nothing."

"Remember what you taught me. Leave no stone unturned. What are you thinking?"

"These disappearances," I began, walking up to the map and pointing to the pin by Flagstaff. "One of Sarah's last videos was from there. And around the same time, if my memory is correct."

I grabbed my phone and navigated to Sarah's social media feed, scrolling to the video from Flagstaff. Then I checked the date against when Wendy Allen had last used her debit or credit card.

Only one week prior to Sarah's post.

I scrolled again, landing on a video from Sonoma. Posted ten days after Susan Wynter disappeared. Then a video from Boise. Posted six days after Gretchen Storm vanished.

"What if Victor wasn't having an affair with Sarah?" I asked excitedly, my brain spinning with possibilities. "What if she was investigating him?" I gestured toward the map, toward the web of pins and faces. "Santa Fe.

Sonoma. Boise. Flagstaff. She visited all these cities shortly after these women disappeared."

Blake's eyes narrowed, scanning the map again. "It could just be a coincidence."

I shot him a look. "You know how I feel about coincidences. Sarah was on to something. And Victor realized it. Now we just need to prove it."

Blake blew out a long sigh. "Looks like we'll need some more coffee."

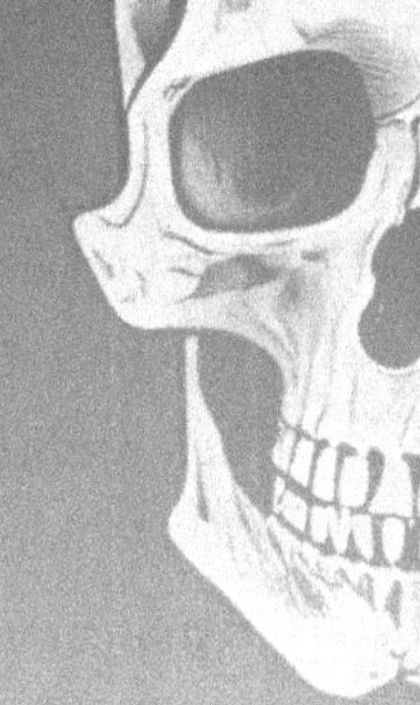

CHAPTER THIRTY-TWO

Ariana

It was after four in the morning when Henry's bedroom door finally creaked open.

I'd left the lamp on for him hours ago, hoping the soft light would make the room feel less empty. He'd told me he wanted me in his bed tonight. That he wanted to fall asleep with me in his arms. So even though I knew Blake must have found something important, I still expected Henry to come earlier.

But the man who stepped through the doorway looked like a ghost of himself — exhausted, drained, carrying the weight of whatever awful truth he'd uncovered.

"Henry..." I pushed up on an elbow as he shut the door behind him.

He didn't speak. Just tugged his shirt over his head, pushed down his jeans and slipped beneath the covers, reaching for me immediately. His body was hot, tense, heavy with fatigue.

When he wrapped his arms around me, I felt the exhaustion down to his bones.

He buried his face in my neck, breathing me in. I sighed, melting into him, letting his hands roam over me, slow and possessive.

"I'm sorry I kept you waiting," he murmured against my shoulder, leaving soft kisses along my skin.

I rolled over and met his eyes, brushing a tendril of hair away from his face. "You're here now."

He gave me a halfhearted smile, something flickering behind his gaze.

"Is everything okay?" I asked softly.

But he didn't respond. Not with words anyway. Instead, he responded with a kiss.

Not a gentle one, either. A hungry one. A desperate one.

He pulled me against him, his arms wrapped tightly around me. He dug his fingers into my hair, tilting my head to the side to deepen the kiss even more, every stroke of his tongue igniting a spark, every circle of his hips sending fire through my veins.

As he tore his lips away, he eased me onto my back and settled between my legs, his eyes locking on mine.

Then he slid into me, filling me so slowly it felt like torture.

Every time with Henry was different. But tonight was...more. More needy. More desperate. Just...more.

I tried to wrap my arms around him to pull him even closer, not wanting a single breath between us, but he caught my wrists in his hands and pinned them above my head, his fingers firm but tender, holding me still as he moved inside me with deliberate restraint. His eyes stayed locked on mine the entire time, like he was trying to read something in me, or write something into me. Something he didn't dare say out loud yet.

Whatever demons he'd met tonight, he was chasing them away with my body.

And I let him.

If this was what he needed, I'd give him everything. My body. My soul. My trust. I'd surrender to him completely.

There were no desperate grunts. No carnal declarations of want. The only sound was that of our ragged breathing and our bodies becoming one.

Too soon, I felt that familiar warmth building low in my core, spreading through me like a fire I couldn't extinguish. And I didn't want to.

Henry sensed it, too.

He released one of my wrists, trailing his hand down my frame and bringing it between us, rubbing my clit.

"Let me feel you, baby," he pleaded.

I couldn't deny him. So I let go, both of us finding our release together.

Breathless and spent, he collapsed onto the bed and pulled me close again. As if he couldn't stand being apart.

For a few long moments, we just lay there. His heartbeat gradually steadied beneath my palm, but the tension didn't leave his body.

"Want to talk about it?" I traced my fingers over his chest. "Did Blake find something important?"

"He did," he replied with a sigh.

I waited, but he didn't continue.

I lifted my eyes to his. "If you're worried I'll be upset you confirmed Victor was cheating on me, don't be. I know he was. Honestly, I looked forward to the times he went out of town. It meant I could breathe."

"This isn't about Victor's mistresses."

I furrowed my brow. "But you said Blake found Schaffer's files. The women he sterilized for Victor."

"He did."

"Then...?"

"It wasn't just a few, like Schaffer claimed." His voice was barely audible. "There were a hundred and forty-seven."

My stomach dropped, an unsettled feeling trickling down my spine. "I-I'm not sure I understand."

Henry pushed out a long breath. "Victor wasn't cheating on you. Not the way we thought. I could be wrong, but I find it hard to believe he had that many mistresses."

"Me, too," I admitted. "So what do—"

"I think he was trafficking those women. And that's why he paid Schaffer to sterilize them."

The room tilted as a myriad of thoughts and questions consumed me. One louder than the others.

"Your daughter," I began reluctantly, unsure I wanted the answer. "Did he... Was she..."

"She wasn't in Schaffer's files," he answered.

Relief hit so hard that I sank into him, relishing in the warmth of his body against mine. He pressed a kiss to the top of my head, smoothing his fingers through my hair.

"But I think she figured out what Victor was doing. Or she got too close."

I met his gaze. "What do you mean?"

"I tracked the disappearances and compared them to Sarah's travel history." He swallowed hard, grief sharpening his features. "For months before her death, she visited every city a week or two after each woman went missing. And that's not all."

"What else?" I prompted.

"They all interviewed for jobs with Kane Hotel Group."

I shot up, blinking. "They worked for Victor?"

"They were never hired," he replied. "But Victor had access to all their information. Applications. Interviews. Background checks."

"And you accessed them," I whispered.

He nodded.

"Every woman had two things in common," he continued. "they all applied for a job with Kane Hotel Group. And they came from unstable backgrounds. Nobody who'd push for answers if they vanished."

"Oh, god..." I covered my mouth, a wave of guilt washing over me.

"I've seen how this type of thing plays out. Maybe not firsthand, but in my line of work, you see how sick and depraved some people truly are. My guess is that Victor used his access to their personal information to target them."

A chill washed through me so violently I wrapped an arm around my stomach, as if I could keep myself from splintering.

I'd known Victor was cruel. I'd suffered from that cruelty. I wore it in my scars.

But this?

This was monstrous.

"I had no idea," I whispered, my voice breaking. "All those poor women... Maybe if I had—"

"No." Henry sat up, clutching my cheeks in his

hands, forcing my gaze to his. "Do *not* blame yourself for this. It's not your fault. This is all on Victor."

"But those women. Where are they now?"

"I'm not sure. But I'll find them. And I'll find him."

"How?"

"I'm working on it. Victor has resources, but so do I. I *will* find him, Ariana. And I will make him pay."

I stared past him, bile burning my throat.

Over a hundred women. Gone. Disappeared. Vanished.

Sold to god knows who for god knows what.

For ten years, I'd been draped in diamonds, fed caviar, wrapped in privilege. All paid for with their suffering. Their pain had been the currency of my comfort.

It made me sick.

And strengthened my determination to take him down.

To make him pay.

By any means necessary.

"You can use me," I announced.

He darted his eyes to mine. "What?"

"You mentioned Victor most likely tried to have my mom killed in order to draw me out."

His jaw clenched. "Yes."

"Then use me. If he's desperate to find me, turn that

desperation against him. If he wanted me dead, I'd already be dead. Those Bratva soldiers had plenty of chances. He wants me alive for a reason. If I reappear with some story that I went out of town to meditate or something equally cliché for a rich, trophy wife, it'll be front-page news. He won't be able to resist stepping into the spotlight as the relieved husband. He'd *have* to in order to keep up appearances. This could end everything."

"And throw you into the lion's den?" he bit out. "Absolutely not."

"Henry…"

"No, Ariana. I can't let you do this. *Won't* let you."

I scrambled out of bed, fire scorching my veins. "You won't *let* me? I don't need your fucking permission, Henry. This is *my* life. And my choice. I overheard you talking to Gideon the other night. He suggested the same thing."

"And I wanted to punch him for it," he said, jumping out of bed and stalking toward me, gripping my biceps. "I can't… I can't lose someone I love. Not again."

I opened my mouth to argue my case further, but then snapped it closed when his statement finally hit me.

"You…love me?" I squeaked out through the lump forming in my throat.

A part of me expected him to take it back. Claim it slipped out. That he didn't mean it. That he was caught up in the heat of the moment.

Instead, he moved his hands to my face with nothing but complete certainty in his expression.

"I do. I love you, Ariana Summers."

He curved toward me, seeking out my lips. But before he could brush his mouth to mine, I placed a finger over his.

"Then prove it."

He tilted his head. "What do you mean?"

"If you love me, show me you trust that I know what I'm doing. I put my trust in you when it was one of the hardest things for me to do. Now it's your turn to trust me."

"I do trust you. It's Victor I don't."

"Please, Henry."

I grabbed his hand and brought it up to my mouth, leaving a soft kiss on his rough knuckles.

"I don't want to hide for the rest of my life. I want my freedom. I want to cut the chains he wrapped around me." My eyes locked on his, unwavering in my resolve. "If we're to ever have a future together, I need to settle my past. So do you. Otherwise, I don't see how we can ever truly move on together. Not like we deserve."

"How will we move on if you're dead?" he shot back, his voice heavy with emotion.

"How do you expect me to just stay here, knowing what those women are suffering?" I retorted. "I know what kind of hell they could be enduring. I lived it for ten years." With each word I spoke, my voice shook a little more as all the years of torture and abuse came rushing back.

Which was exactly why I needed to do this.

"All that time, I would have given *anything* to be free. For someone to realize the truth and help me escape that hell."

"Ariana…"

I held up a hand, cutting him off. "I have the power to save these women, Henry. To finish Sarah's work, if your theory is right. Don't let her sacrifice be in vain. She gave her life for this." I swallowed hard. "Let's make it mean something."

I saw the moment I finally got to him.

He released a reluctant sigh and wrapped me in his embrace.

"You are so fucking stubborn," he said into my hair. "But you're also a goddamn warrior." He pulled back enough to meet my eyes. "If this is what you choose…"

"It is," I breathed.

"Then I'll support you." His thumb brushed my cheek. "On one condition."

"What's that?"

"We don't rush this. We'll come up with a foolproof plan. And part of that plan will include training with me. Learning self-defense."

"I can get on board with that." A slow, wicked smile

curled my lips as I draped my arm over his shoulder, hoisting myself onto my toes. "Why don't we start with you teaching me how to break out of zipties?"

"Zipties?" he murmured, steering me the few feet toward the bed.

"Could be fun. Although, if I'm being honest, I'm not sure I'd want to break free around you."

He helped lower me onto the mattress and crawled between my legs, grabbing my wrists and holding them in his firm grip. "Then I'll be sure to make them extra tight."

CHAPTER THIRTY-THREE

Henry

"**R**eady for me to kick your ass again, old man?" Ariana joked as I entered the home gym after taking Cato for a walk.

She was already stretching, wearing fitted leggings and a tank top that did absolutely nothing to help me keep my head straight. Her hair was pulled into a high ponytail, exposing her neck...as well as the bite marks I'd left hours earlier.

It had been a few days since I'd agreed to use her as bait in order to lure Victor out of hiding.

I still hated it. Every damn part. The idea of her being anywhere near Victor made my skin crawl.

But she wasn't wrong.

Victor had paid the Bratva an obscene amount of

money to have her abducted. If she suddenly reappeared with our carefully crafted story — that she'd taken a few days to "disconnect" while her husband was out of town — he wouldn't be able to stay away.

He'd need to play the part of the caring, concerned husband for the world to see.

Then, we'd end this.

In the meantime, Blake and I had doubled our efforts to locate him. We'd put tails on several Miami Bratva members, including Nikolai Volkov, the Obshchak Victor had spoken with the night before Ariana's botched abduction. So far, nothing led us to him. It was as if the earth had swallowed him whole.

But I wasn't giving up. Not now. Not ever.

And while Blake's team hunted, I spent every morning training Ariana in my home gym.

If she insisted on being bait, she'd damn well know how to defend herself. I'd also taken her shooting so she'd be comfortable handling and firing a gun if it came to it. I hoped it didn't. But she needed to be prepared.

"Old man?" I closed the distance between us, my mouth hovering over hers. "Correct me if I'm wrong, but if I were really an old man, would I have been able to treat you to three mind-blowing orgasms this morning? Have you begging for more while you rode my cock?"

"They *do* make pills for that," she teased.

I pulled her against me, gently thrusting so she could

feel what she did to me with just one touch, one look, one smile.

"I don't need any pills when you're around." I covered her mouth with mine, hopelessly addicted to her. In such a short time, she'd invaded my every waking thought to the point where I couldn't imagine my life without her.

Where I happily told her I loved her.

She hadn't said it back yet, but I didn't care.

I'd lived with enough regret. I didn't want to add this to the growing list.

After the shit she'd been through, she deserved to know she was loved.

And hopefully, one day, she'd trust her heart enough to say it back.

"Let's get started," I said, pulling out of the kiss.

"Yes, sir." Ariana mock saluted, and I couldn't deny a thrill rushed through me when she called me "sir".

Maybe we'd add that to our bedroom repertoire.

We went through warm-ups, then reviewed basic strikes, blocks, escapes. She caught on fast. Almost too fast. Victor trained her without meaning to. Surviving him required instincts no normal person should ever have to develop.

Seeing her improve by leaps and bounds every day solidified what I'd told her the first time I saw her scars. What I tried to make her feel every day.

She was a warrior.

"Let's practice a new hold," I said after a while.

"Which one?"

"The bear hug."

"That doesn't sound all that scary."

"No, but when you're in the heat of the moment, one wrong move could be the difference between life and death. You need to know the best way to weaken your opponent in order to escape."

"Okay." She took a sip of water. "What's the bear hug?"

"I'll approach you from behind," I began, keeping my voice steady, my gaze studying her for any hint of apprehension. "Then wrap an arm around your upper body and pin your arms to your sides."

Her expression faltered slightly. I knew exactly what she was thinking about. That night in Maine when I'd performed this exact hold on her, which led to a panic attack.

"We don't have to do this today," I said when I noticed her face grow pale.

She closed her eyes, taking a deep breath. When she returned her gaze to mine, it was full of determination.

"If Victor attacks me, he won't ask what hold I'd prefer. I need to be ready for all of them."

Fair point.

"When I restrain you, drop your weight, shift your hips, aim for a soft target, and strike."

"Got it."

"Ready?"

She nodded. "Ready."

I moved behind her carefully, giving her time to adjust as I slid my arm across her chest and pinned her arms to her sides. Her breath hitched immediately, her muscles going rigid.

Uncertainty crawled up my spine. If she panicked like this in front of Victor, she could end up dead. The mere idea had my stomach in knots.

Then, just as quickly, her unease seemed to subside, her body shifting.

Before I had time to register it, she dropped her weight, twisted her hips, and drove her elbow back hard.

Pain exploded beneath my ribs.

The next second, she executed the sweep I'd shown her a few days ago, and my back hit the mat.

"Like that?" she asked, standing over me, her chest heaving.

I blinked up at her and grinned. "Exactly like that."

She extended a hand to help me up. I grabbed it, flashed her a devilish grin, and yanked her down on top of me. She let out a startled laugh, her palms bracing on either side of my shoulders.

"If this is what I get when you take me out," I

murmured, sliding a hand along her hip, "I'm happy to let you kick my ass all day, every day."

Her laughter softened, and she dipped her head to kiss me. Slow, lingering, the kind of kiss that made me want to forget about Victor Kane entirely.

This was the effect Ariana had on me. She made me want to shut out the world and focus on her and her alone.

But we couldn't.

Not until she was finally free from her past.

Suddenly, the gym door swung open, startling both of us.

I snapped my head in its direction as Blake came to an abrupt stop.

"Shit. Sorry." He looked between Ariana and me. "Didn't realize I'd be walking in on...anything."

"You didn't. Just me kicking Henry's ass." Ariana smirked as she rolled off me.

I loved Blake like a brother. But right now, I wanted to kill him for interrupting us.

"He needs a good ass-kicking every now and then. I'm Blake, by the way." He extended his hand toward her.

"Nice to finally put a face to the name," she said as they shook. "I'm Ariana."

"I know." He winked at her before turning to me. The lightness left his face instantly. "We need to talk."

I got to my feet and grabbed a towel, wiping the sweat from my brow. "Did you find something?"

"I did."

I shot Ariana a look. "We'll pick this up later?"

She nodded. "Go."

I pressed a quick kiss to her temple before following Blake out of the gym and into my office.

He dropped into the chair beside the monitors and tapped a key. Footage popped up of a man standing next to a pickup truck, pumping gas.

"What am I looking at?" I asked.

"Victor Kane," Blake said.

My pulse slowed, sharpened. "Where?"

"Near Lake Okeechobee. Used his credit card this morning. I got an alert, so I hacked into the system at the station to check the footage. It's not great and I can't make out his face, but he has the same height and build."

"I've never known Victor Kane to wear anything but designer suits. Certainly not jeans and a flannel."

"He's probably hoping no one recognizes him."

I considered this for a moment, then asked, "Do we know where he is now?"

He hit another button, and footage of a cabin on a lake popped up with the same truck from the gas station parked in the driveway.

"He also turned on his cell phone this morning to

make a phone call to an electrician. I was able to track it to this cabin."

Relief punched through me so fast I had to brace a hand on the desk. We wouldn't need Ariana as bait. We could end this without putting her at risk.

"What do you want to do?" Blake pressed.

I stared at Victor's shadowed face as he pumped gas. My jaw clenched. My daughter's face flashed before my eyes. Then Ariana's. Then the dozens of women whose photos hung on the walls around me.

"We go there," I said. "See if it's him."

"And if it is?"

"We end this. Tonight."

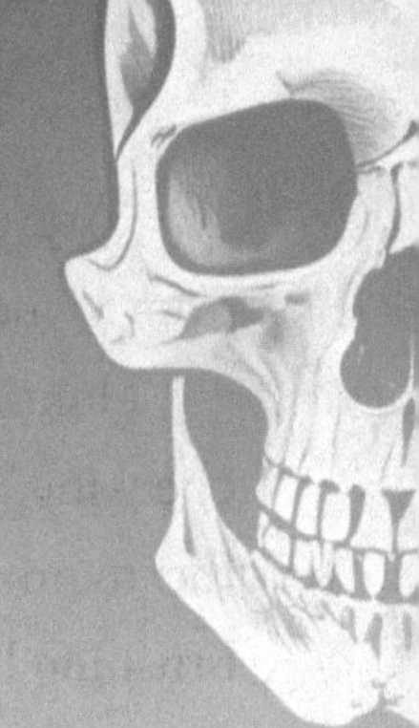

CHAPTER THIRTY-FOUR

Ariana

I sat on the edge of Henry's bed, my knees drawn up as I watched him pack. Not clothes. Guns. Knives. Extra magazines. Every piece checked and placed with a level of care that made my anxiety increase.

When he'd first told me Blake might have found Victor, I felt relief. Hope for a future I'd barely allowed myself to imagine.

But as I watched Henry pack for any and every situation they may encounter, all I felt was the sharp edge of something twisting low in my gut.

It was too simple. Too convenient. Why would Victor disappear without a trace for several weeks, then show up at a gas station in central Florida, allowing Blake to track him to a lakeside cabin?

"Are you sure about this?" My voice sounded small, even to me.

Henry clicked the magazine into the gun he'd been checking, then set it gently into the case before crossing the room toward me. He cupped my cheek, his thumb brushing lightly over my skin.

"It'll be fine," he said softly.

"I just... It seems too...easy. You've been searching for him for weeks, and suddenly he just...shows up? There's been no trace of him. Phone turned off. Credit cards not being used. No hit on any of his cars. No sign of him at any of his properties. And now he miraculously turns on his phone and uses a credit card to buy gas? I don't like it, Henry."

"The fact that so much time has passed is probably exactly why he stopped being so diligent. He probably figured it was safe. I told you he'd eventually slip up. And he did." Henry dipped his head, his gaze steady. "You don't need to worry. We're just going to check it out. See if he's there."

"And if he is?"

"Then you'll finally be free. Free to go wherever you want. Live wherever you want."

"So I won't have to be your prisoner anymore?" I playfully waggled my brows.

His thumb traced my cheek again, slow and tender. "I don't think you've ever truly been my prisoner." He paused. "But yes. You'll be able to leave here." His throat worked in a hard swallow. "Leave me."

The mere thought was like a punch to the gut. Not leaving this place, but leaving Henry. The idea of not waking up beside him, not feeling his arms around me? I hated everything about it.

"What if...," I began, my heart pounding as I stared into his bright green eyes. "What if I don't want to? What if I want to stay here? With you."

He exhaled a long breath, a small smile curving on his lips. "You won't hear any complaints from me. But only if it's what *you* want, Ariana. Not because you think it's what *I* want." His lips twitched. "I mean, it *is* what I want, but I won't force you to stay. I want you to choose me freely."

"Henry..."

"Yes?" It came out almost like a breath.

I touched a hand to his cheek, relishing the roughness of his unshaven jawline. "I choose you. Always." My throat tightened with all the emotions fighting for attention. But one overpowered the rest of them. "I love you, Henry Fontaine."

He stared. Blinked. Swallowed. Stared more. Then he crashed his mouth against mine, coaxing my lips apart, our tongues tangling in a dance they'd done hundreds of times by this point. Yet this kiss felt bigger than all the others.

Because it came from a place of love.

"You have no idea how long I've wanted to hear you say those three words to me," he murmured against my mouth.

"I'm sorry I didn't say it after you told me."

He shook his head. "I don't want you to tell me something because you think it's what I need."

"I knew I loved you then. I guess my brain was still trying to tell my heart how to feel."

"And how does your heart feel?" he asked, brushing a strand of hair behind my ear.

"Like it can't beat without you."

His eyes darkened. "It'll never have to."

He kissed me again, pushing me down onto the bed and crawling on top of me. His hands were gentle, reverent, the opposite of the man who'd ripped me from Victor's world. He took his time undressing me, his fingers lingering on every inch of skin he uncovered, as though he were revealing a priceless treasure.

And that was exactly how he made me feel. Like I was treasured. Like I was adored.

Like I was loved.

And I was.

He didn't bind my wrists. Didn't keep me pinned with his weight. Didn't bare his teeth against my skin or drive into me with the same devastating force I'd grown to crave.

This was different.

He moved slowly, his hips rolling against mine in lazy circles, his fingers laced with mine, our breaths mingling in the quiet between us.

Henry didn't just fuck me.

He made love to me.

He made me feel his love with every caress, every kiss, every soft sound he gave me when he pressed deeper. I'd never experienced anything like it. Not even close.

This was what I used to imagine love would feel like when I was a little girl dreaming of fairy tales. The kind where the girl wasn't just saved. She was cherished.

Sure, maybe my version of a fairy tale was more like *Beauty and the Beast* than *Cinderella*, but that didn't matter.

It was my story. My life.

And I was ready to finally live my life, regardless of what the future may bring.

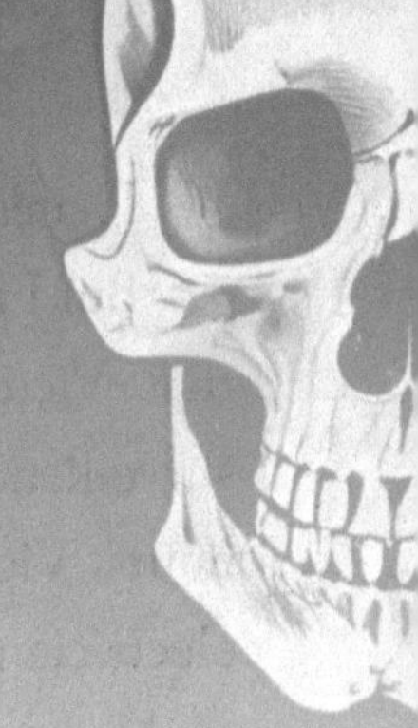

CHAPTER THIRTY-FIVE

Henry

The highway had long since given way to the back roads, narrow two-lane strips of cracked asphalt threading through endless forests and stagnant, moon-lit marsh. Central Florida at night had a way of swallowing sound, of making the world feel hollow and forgotten. The kind of place where bad things could happen quietly, without anyone ever knowing.

I kept one hand on the wheel and the other loose on my thigh, resisting the urge to check my phone for the tenth time. Ariana was safe and secure at my farm property. The perimeter sensors were on. The alarms. The locks. Everything.

Better yet, she had Cato. If all else failed, he wouldn't. He was loyal to a fault.

I hated leaving her.

But I found a small slice of comfort in the knowledge that Victor was nowhere near Georgia. And Blake's surveillance on this cabin had held steady for over twelve hours. Victor hadn't left once. The only activity was an electrician stopping by this afternoon to fix a breaker problem, as Blake confirmed with the electrical company.

It *did* seem too easy, like Ariana cautioned. But like *I* assured her, Victor had probably gotten lazy.

His laziness was about to cost him everything.

The road narrowed as we approached the turnoff. Spanish moss hung from the trees like skeletal fingers, brushing the roof of the SUV as we eased forward. I flipped the headlights off and let the residual glow from the moon guide us the last quarter mile.

"It's around the curve," Blake murmured beside me, studying the feed on his tablet. "We should park here."

I nodded, rolling to a stop well before the gravel driveway. The night hit me the second I opened my door — dense, warm, buzzing faintly with mosquitoes. I checked my pistol and followed Blake toward the tree line, the two of us moving like shadows through the darkness.

When the cabin finally came into view through the gaps in the pines, I blew out a slow breath. Completely dark. Two stories. No exterior lights. A wraparound porch. A small dock stretching into the lake, the water black and glassy.

Nothing about it screamed hotel magnate. Nothing screamed anything at all. It looked like a place a fisherman might rent for a long weekend.

Or somewhere to go so no one would find you.

But we found him.

Like I knew we would.

Blake crouched down behind a fallen tree, bringing his binoculars up to his eyes. I mirrored him, scanning the structure from roof to foundation, looking for anything that seemed out of place. But there was nothing. Just a regular fishing cabin.

Still, Blake let out a sigh.

"What is it?" I whispered.

"It just...feels wrong," he replied. "I don't know. Maybe it *was* too easy."

"We've had eyes on the house all day. Victor's in there. Alone. It's him. He used his credit card at the gas station we passed a few miles back. His cell phone is pinging from this location. The only thing easier would have been if he walked out with a bow tied around his neck."

Blake didn't argue again, but the tension in his jaw told me everything. He didn't like this. I wasn't thrilled with it, either, but this needed to happen. If for no other reason than to prevent us from having to use Ariana as bait.

"I'll go in by myself if you'd rather," I offered. "You can stay on watch out here."

"And let you have all the fun?" he replied with a smile. "No way in hell."

"Then let's go."

We deftly moved through the night, the only sound the faint rustling of raw earth beneath our feet. When we neared the back door, I met Blake's eyes.

"Ready?" I whispered.

He gave a single nod and got to work on picking the lock, one of his specialties. He had the door open in less than ten seconds, and we quietly slipped inside.

The air hit me like a wall — stale, unmoving, heavy with the damp wooden smell old cabins tended to have.

"I'll take the upstairs. You take down here."

"Copy," Blake said, and we went our separate ways, sweeping each room.

The first bedroom was empty. As was the second. The last room showed some sign of life, the bathroom light still on and the bed unmade.

But even after looking in the closet and under the bed, there was no sign of him. I even checked the linen closet and laundry room.

Still nothing.

I headed back downstairs, meeting Blake in the living room.

"Anything?" I asked.

He pushed out a breath. "Nothing. Maybe he's in the garage."

"Let's check it out."

We moved toward a door off the kitchen that led to the attached garage, and Blake eased it open. A thin line of moonlight stretched across the cement floor.

At least, what could be seen of the cement floor.

The garage was filled with every manner of fishing gear — poles, tackle boxes, spools of fishing line. There was even a workbench with a disassembled motor on top.

But that wasn't what caught my attention.

Instead, it was the form of a man sitting in a chair, the moonlight like a spotlight.

"Victor?" I said, my grip tight on my gun as I slowly moved across the space toward him.

No response.

"Victor?" I repeated, my dread increasing with every inch I erased.

And when I stepped in front of him, I let out a shaky breath.

Because this man wasn't Victor Kane.

He was dressed like the man we'd seen in the surveillance video. Same jacket. Same jeans. Same boots.

But as I shined my flashlight over his face, there was

no mistaking it. He may have had a similar bone structure. Similar hair. Similar build. Enough to pass for him at a distance. Or even up close.

But I'd spent the better part of the last year studying Victor Kane. Learning everything about him.

"Who the fuck is that?" Blake snipped out.

"Someone who looks a hell of a lot like Victor Kane. Who someone wanted everyone to think was Victor Kane. Who wanted *us* to think was Victor Kane." A ball of dread tightened in my stomach, and I felt like I was going to be sick. "It was a fucking trap. You were right. Fuck!"

"No time for 'I told you so'," he rushed out, quickly moving toward the exterior garage door. "We need to go."

But just as he opened the door, he froze, darting his eyes toward me. "Henry! Stop!"

I halted in my tracks. "What are you—"

Then I saw it.

A thin plate beneath Blake's foot.

I pointed my flashlight at it, following the wires along the floor and toward the workbench.

At first, it was nothing but a tangle of black and red lines disappearing under the legs. But then I noticed them coming out from behind it.

Right to the gutted boat motor.

Only it wasn't gutted.

Not in the way I'd assumed. It had been taken apart and repurposed for something else.

My stomach bottomed out.

"Jesus Christ. It's a fucking bomb."

Blake went still, like he didn't dare breathe.

I returned to him, following the wiring every step of the way. "This plate is a switch. You lift your foot, the circuit closes." I straightened, my heart slamming against my ribs as I scanned the garage once more. "There has to be a bypass—"

"You need to go, Henry." His voice dropped. Calm. Steady.

"The hell I do." My light stayed locked on the plate under his boot, like if I stopped looking at it, it would detonate. "I'm not leaving you here."

"Yes, you are. If you stay, we both die, and Ariana ends up right back where you dragged her from. You want Victor to win? Because that's how he wins." He held my gaze for a beat, then surveyed his surroundings, moisture forming in his eyes. "Never thought I'd die in a garage that smells like fish guts and mildew." He pushed out a nervous laugh. "Or that your ugly mug would be the last thing I'd ever see. But here we are."

"Blake..." I shook my head, emotion tightening my throat. There was so much I wanted to say. Other than Gideon, he was the only true friend I had.

And I'd just gotten him killed.

"I'm sorry, Blake."

"Go, Henry. Please. Get the fuck out of here."

It was the please that did it.

Blake never said please.

My jaw clenched. My eyes burned, but I did as he asked.

I took a step back. Then another. And another, until the doorframe was at my back.

"I'll send help," I promised.

"I'll be here," he whispered.

I held his gaze as I backed into the house.

"Go," he said once more.

And while I hated abandoning him, I knew he was right. If this *were* a trap, Ariana could be in danger. So I spun around and sprinted out of the house, not stopping until I reached the SUV.

I cranked the engine, the tires spitting gravel as the cabin disappeared behind the curve of trees. Every few seconds, I glanced in the rearview mirror, growing hopeful with each heartbeat that passed without hearing an explosion.

But that hope was dashed when the world behind me erupted, a violent burst of red and orange swallowing the sky.

My vision tunneled.

My hands tightened on the wheel.

But I didn't slow down.

I couldn't.

Not after Blake's sacrifice.

I had to get to Ariana.

And then I'd kill Victor Kane, once and for all.

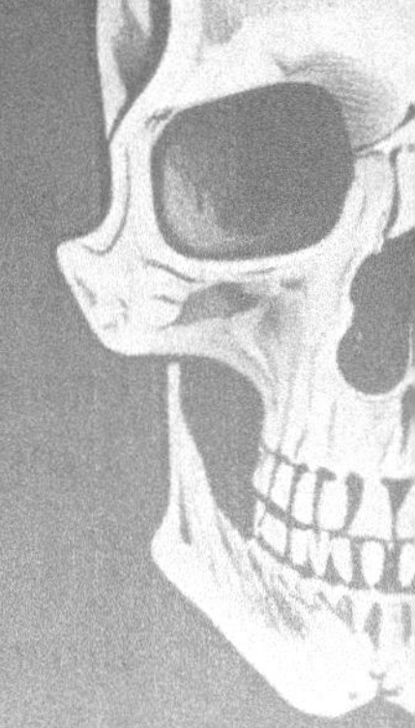

CHAPTER THIRTY-SIX

Ariana

I woke with a jolt, my heart punching against my ribs like it was trying to escape. The room was dark. Too dark. The sheets were cold beside me, the emptiness so sharp it felt like a knife sliding along my skin. Something felt...off.

Wrong.

I told myself it was just because Henry wasn't here. The uneasiness creeping along my spine. The pressure in my chest. The way my breath wouldn't settle. That was all this was.

Nothing more.

I tossed the covers off and grabbed my robe, slipping it on as I padded across the room, needing some water to quench the dryness in my mouth.

Rubbing my eyes, I opened the door and stepped into the hallway.

I immediately froze.

A silhouette filled the darkened space.

Tall.

Broad.

But not Henry.

My pulse stuttered, my stomach dropping as I peered into two dark eyes I prayed I'd never see again.

Victor.

His lips curved into a slow, sinister smile that made all the tiny hairs on my body stand on end.

"Hello, wife. Happy to see me?"

"What are you doing here?" I whispered, backing up as he stalked toward me until my spine slammed into the far wall.

"I'm here to take back what's mine." He gripped my hair so hard tears blurred my vision. "And make no mistake, Ariana. You *are* mine."

He flung me across the room and onto the bed like I weighed nothing. The mattress thudded beneath me, adrenaline causing my movements to be jerky and unsteady.

I tried to remember what Henry had taught me. Tried to remain calm. But around Victor, it was a losing battle. Still, I attempted to scramble off the bed, but he was on top of me before I could, pinning me down.

"Seems like you need a reminder of who you belong to."

He pulled out a knife I'd become quite familiar with and pushed my t-shirt up, exposing my stomach. Exposing the word he'd carved into me over and over until I believed it.

I tried to buck him off like Henry had trained me to do, but my muscles felt heavy. Like they were filled with wet sand. My head was foggy, my surroundings blurry.

Was I drugged?

It didn't matter. I needed to fight. Needed to get away from Victor. Get to one of the many guns Henry had stashed around the house. But my arms wouldn't move correctly. My fingers slipped uselessly against his wrist. Like some unknown force was keeping me pinned here.

"Ariana," Victor purred, dragging the knife along my skin, "you should have known you'd never get away."

His smile widened, becoming even more wicked, as I fought to lift an arm. Anything.

I couldn't. All I could do was stare in horror as he plunged the knife deep into my stomach.

A blood-curling scream echoed through the room, and I finally managed to move, bolting upright in bed.

But the room was empty.

No Victor. No knife. No hands pinning me down.

Just shadows and moonlight and the harsh rasp of my breathing.

I looked down at my stomach. No blood. No fresh scars.

"It was just a dream," I whispered to myself. "It was just a dream."

But my body didn't get the message. Sweat soaked through my t-shirt. My hands trembled. My legs felt weak.

I went to the bathroom and splashed water on my face, repeating it was just a dream over and over, sucking in deep breath after deep breath.

It still didn't make me feel any better.

I should have taken my mother up on her offer to stay here tonight. Or spent the night with her and Cato in the guest house.

After that dream, I didn't want to be alone, so I changed out of my sweat-soaked pajamas, slipped on a pair of sneakers, and crept toward the door.

As I reached for the knob, I hesitated, the memory of Victor's face flashing in my mind, causing fear to snake up my spine.

But it was just a dream. He had no way of knowing where I was. Henry repeatedly assured me I was safe. That Victor couldn't get to me here.

And I trusted Henry.

I turned the knob slowly, blowing out a relieved breath when I was met with nothing but emptiness.

I slipped down the hall, one hand gliding along the railing as I descended the stairs, my legs still unsteady from the nightmare clinging to me like a second skin. The house was dim and quiet, the only light a soft glow from the kitchen. I headed that way, intending to grab a bottle of water and the flashlight Henry kept hidden in the junk drawer.

But I only made it a few steps before a shape emerged from the shadows, solid and unmistakably human.

My breath froze.

I blinked, once, twice, harder, convinced my mind was still tangled in the dream. "It's only a dream," I whispered. "Just a dream."

Victor's laugh slithered through the dark, cold enough to ice my blood.

"If this is only a dream," he murmured, "would you feel this?"

He closed the distance with a swift, practiced motion and fisted a hand in my hair, yanking my head back.

Unlike when he did this in my nightmare, pain exploded, making me realize this was real.

Victor exposed my throat as he secured me against him, his front to my back, the cold edge of a knife kissing my skin.

The same knife that had carved me into someone else.

The same knife that had turned my skin into maps of pain.

The same knife I'd seen in my nightmare minutes ago.

Before Henry, that knife had defined me.

Before he made me feel beautiful.

Before he made me feel loved.

I refused to let this knife turn me back into the woman I used to be.

My eyes darted across the kitchen. Henry had shown me every place he'd hidden a gun before he left. At the time, I'd thought he was being paranoid.

Now I was grateful.

All I had to do was get to the drawer at the far end of the counter. Then I could end this.

End *him*.

Victor's lips brushed my ear, his voice low and smug. "I bet you're wondering how I found you."

"How?" I asked, not because I wanted to know, but because I needed to stall.

I could just picture the grin forming on his lips. He always enjoyed the idea of being the smartest person in the room, even if he wasn't.

"When I sent my men to retrieve you and someone else answered one of their phones, I knew I'd heard that voice somewhere. Took me a bit to place it, but I always remember people. Especially people who look at my wife in a way I don't like."

"I'm *not* your wife."

I rammed my elbow into his stomach, desperate and sharp. The blow landed hard enough to make him grunt. He released me, and I stumbled away, sprinting toward the drawer with the gun.

But Victor was faster. Bigger. He snatched my arm and slammed me against the wall.

"Yes," he snarled, his breath scorching my skin, "you are."

"If you think I'm going to stay married to you now that I know what kind of monster you truly are, after you tried to have me abducted, you're crazier than I thought."

He tilted his head, studying me like a puzzle he thought he'd already solved. "You've fallen in love with him, haven't you?"

I didn't answer. I wouldn't let him stain Henry with his filth. Henry was kindness and loyalty and fire beneath steel. Victor didn't deserve so much as to speak his name.

"Well, I hate to tell you this, sweetheart..." Victor's smile sharpened, and a ball of dread formed in my stomach.

I'd seen this smile before.

It was the way he looked at me whenever he was about to deliver a devastating blow.

"Henry's dead."

His statement hit me with the force of a boulder. My lungs seized. A wave of cold swept through me so fast I felt nauseous.

No. He couldn't be dead. I'd know. I'd *feel* it.

"You're lying," I hissed.

"Once I realized who that voice belonged to when I'd called the man I hired to find you," Victor continued, almost giddy, "I tracked his movements here. Had someone override his security system. Henry's not the only computer genius out there. But I needed to lure him away." His smile stretched, slow and vile. "What better way than to let him think he'd found me?"

My stomach heaved, regret coiling deep inside.

I should have fought harder. Insisted Henry slow down. Stayed by his side. Something, *anything*, other than letting him leave when I knew what Victor was capable of.

Now I'd have to live with that regret.

"So you see... There's no reason for you to stay anymore. Time for you to be the obedient wife I trained you to be and come with me." He shoved me toward the door.

For one disorienting moment, I let him, my grief turning me back into the version of me he'd built. The docile, hollow woman who survived by disappearing inside herself.

But then a single thought broke through like a crack of lightning.

Henry.

Henry, who told me I was brave.

Henry, who made me believe I could fight.

Henry, who laid down his life so I could finally be free.

Was I really going to let Victor drag me back into hell?

Back into being his punching bag?

I couldn't. Not when Henry gave his life for me.

I planted my feet, my muscles trembling but locked.

Victor jerked back toward me, surprise flickering across his face. Then I slammed an open-palm strike into his nose, the cracking sound echoing around us. He howled, bringing his hand up to his face to stop the flow of blood, disoriented long enough for me to drive my knee straight into his groin.

He folded with a strangled grunt, and I ran toward the side table a few feet away where I knew there was another gun.

"Kitty grew some claws," Victor sneered from behind, but I didn't look back. Not when every second counted.

I yanked the drawer open with shaking hands, found the gun, and spun around.

But Victor's blood-covered hand shot out, knocking the weapon from my unsteady grasp just as I managed to pull the trigger. The gun clattered across the floor, skidding toward the kitchen as the bullet fired upward and shattered the light fixture, glass raining down around us.

"I've always liked a woman with a little fight in her," he drawled, stalking toward me, blood dripping down his face. "Makes it taste even sweeter when I win. And I always win, Ariana."

I backed up, step by step, toward the kitchen counter. Toward the knife block. Toward the second gun. Toward any chance of survival.

"Is that why you targeted all those women?" I asked, my voice low and steady, even though my heart was thundering. "Because they had fight in them?"

"Women?" He arched a single brow.

"The ones you had sterilized."

His grin widened. "You think you have it all figured it out. Don't you?"

I blinked, a hint of doubt creeping in, but I pushed it down. This was what Victor did. Gaslit me. Made me question my own reality.

Not anymore.

"I do. And I also know that's why you killed Henry's daughter," I said, letting his name crack through me.

"Sarah. You killed her because she learned the truth, too. Because she outsmarted you."

His expression flickered for a fraction of a second. Victor hated the idea of anyone outsmarting him, so I knew my statement would hit a nerve.

At least, I *thought* it would.

Instead, he threw his head back and laughed.

Loud. Wild. Untethered.

When his eyes snapped to mine, something feral lurked there.

"I didn't kill Sarah," he explained calmly. "Although she goes by Nova now."

The world tilted, my heart dropping to the pit of my stomach as my brain struggled to keep up with what he just admitted.

"What do you mean? Is she alive?"

"She is. She was chosen."

"For what?"

"The same thing you were. So let's go."

He reached for me, and I didn't hesitate.

I spun, grabbed the cast-iron skillet off the stove, and swung at his head.

He stumbled back, and I ran toward the gun on the floor.

But Victor tackled me, slamming me onto my back. Pain exploded up my spine as he wrestled the gun from my fingers and pressed it toward my face.

"I don't want to kill you, Ariana, so stop fighting," he hissed. "You won't win. You should know that by now."

My arms trembled, muscles screaming, but I pushed back with everything I had.

"Never." My voice tore from my throat, raw and fierce. "I'll never stop fighting you."

His smile slithered across his face as he forced the gun closer.

"Have it your way."

The barrel hovered inches from my forehead.

His finger tightened on the trigger.

And something strengthened inside me.

Not fear. Not submission.

Something sharp.

Something wild.

Something that felt a hell of a lot like freedom.

I wrenched my body sideways at the same second he fired. The deafening crack detonated beside my ear, splintering the hardwood floor inches from my skull. The recoil rocked him back just enough for me to shove upward, scrambling out from under him as he swore and tried to adjust his grip.

My hands fumbled uselessly against the floorboards until my fingers brushed something cold.

Metal.

His knife.

I lunged for it, my breathing ragged.

But before I could, Victor grabbed my ankle and yanked, sending pain tearing up my leg. I crashed forward, my chin slamming into the floor so hard stars burst across my vision. Still, I refused to give up, my nails scraping wood as I reached for the handle.

"Ariana," he growled, dragging me back. "Enough."

But he didn't understand.

Enough happened years ago.

Enough was the last time he carved the word *whore* into my skin.

Enough was when he made me believe fighting was pointless.

I twisted, kicking with every ounce of panic-sharpened strength I had, my shoe striking something solid, but it barely slowed him. He launched himself at me, his weight crushing down on my hips, my ribs, pinning me flat on my back.

His breath was hot and furious against my face, his teeth bared, eyes burning with that same look of possession he'd always had.

"I told you," he panted, his hand moving to my throat. "I always win."

His fingers tightened.

The pressure was instantaneous. Brutal. A vise around my windpipe.

Air shredded in my lungs, what little was left escaping in an ugly gasp. My back arched, body thrashing on instinct, but he adjusted his grip, cutting off every desperate, clawing attempt at breath.

Black dots obscured my vision like falling ash. I gripped his wrist, nails digging in, trying to pry him off, but he only squeezed harder. My chest burned, every muscle screaming for oxygen I couldn't reach.

Maybe he did always win.

Until now.

Because even as my vision dimmed, even as the edges of the world blurred and curled inward, I felt something crack open inside me. Something fierce. Something Henry couldn't teach me, but something he helped me uncover.

I was a warrior.

And warriors didn't surrender.

My arms fell to the floor, heavy and uncontrollable, fingers fumbling. Searching.

And then I felt it again, the welcome metal of Victor's knife.

"You may have always won before," I choked out, my voice strained as I struggled for one last breath. One last second. One last chance. "But not anymore."

The world narrowed to a pinpoint as darkness threatened to consume me.

And then I wrapped my fingers around the knife.

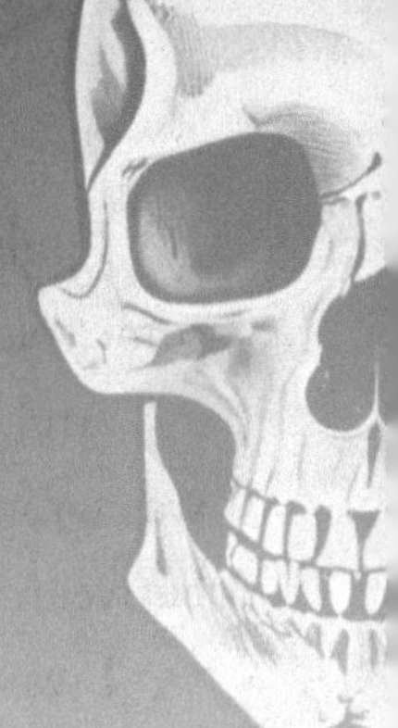

CHAPTER THIRTY-SEVEN

Henry

The tires on my SUV screamed as I tore down the last stretch of road leading to the farm.

I bought this place for the quiet. For the serenity it offered. Peace was supposed to live here.

Tonight, every second it took to reach the house felt like it carved a deeper wound in my chest.

I checked my phone again, refreshing the security system, even though I'd done it a dozen times in as many minutes.

No breached doors.

No broken windows.

No motion sensors tripped.

Nothing.

I pulled up the feed of Ariana sleeping, trying to find some solace in it.

And yet I couldn't shake the feeling that something was wrong. Something I couldn't see. Something slipping between the cracks of the system I built.

I was never one to pray. It was hard to believe in God when life dealt me one harsh blow after another.

But tonight I prayed Ariana was okay.

I hated to consider the alternative.

When the farmhouse finally came into view, I was relieved to find nothing appeared out of the ordinary. But I wouldn't relax until I was sure. I pulled up to the gate and pressed my thumb to the scanner.

But instead of the gates swinging open as they normally did, they remained locked.

My heart dropped to the pit of my stomach, but I wiped my hands on my jeans and tried again.

And again, they didn't budge.

Suddenly, a gunshot reverberated through the night sky, piercing the still tranquility.

I didn't hesitate.

I jumped out of the SUV, sprinting the quarter mile along the nine-foot brick wall and toward the tree I'd been meaning to get rid of.

Now I was glad I hadn't.

I quickly scaled the tree, slid across one of the branches, and leapt onto the ground. I only allowed myself a second to get my footing before I darted toward the house. My ankle throbbed from the sprain that still hadn't fully healed, but that didn't matter to me. Not when Ariana was in danger.

By the time I reached the front door, my gun was already drawn. The moment I stepped inside, I heard it. A broken, ragged sound that punched every ounce of air from my lungs.

I moved through the foyer, and when I rounded the corner to the kitchen, the world stopped.

Victor Kane was in my house.

On the floor.

Bleeding out.

A crimson pool seeped beneath him, spreading across the hardwood like a slow-moving shadow. His limbs twitched weakly, his breath coming in wet, desperate gasps.

Ariana straddled him, her cheeks streaked with tears, her hair wild, her entire body taut as she dragged a knife across his abdomen, the blade sinking into his skin with a sickening, deliberate precision.

I froze in the shadows, my breath locked in my throat as I watched her carve a word onto his flesh.

Weak.

"Please," he rasped, his face scrunched up in agony. "This isn't you. You've gone mad."

Ariana's eyes flashed with something I'd never seen

in her expression before. She pressed the blade deeper, and Victor howled, the sound echoing through the rafters.

"Funny," she hissed, shaking with rage but smiling. "You never seemed to mind madness when it was yours."

"Ariana," he choked. "P-please d-don't do this."

He tried to push her away, but his body refused to cooperate. Blood poured faster when he struggled.

"Please?" Ariana echoed, her voice soft in a way that made my skin crawl, but at the same time filled me with immense pride. "That's interesting coming from you."

"I'm begging you. I—"

She let out a short, humorless laugh. "You want mercy?"

She leaned closer, lowering her voice to a whisper, but it still carried across the room.

"You didn't give me mercy. Not once. Not when I begged. Not when I cried. Not. Once."

"Ariana, listen—"

"No." She tightened her grip on the knife. "You listen. For the first and last time in your life."

His breathing quickened, panicked, shallow.

"This," she said, dragging the tip of the blade down his sternum, her cut slow and deep, "is for every woman you've hurt."

The knife moved lower. Another stroke. Another blood-curdling scream.

"For Sarah."

His eyes rolled back, pain overtaking everything else.

"For Henry," she continued as she drew another deep line, her voice cracking around my name.

"And this," she whispered, curving toward him so her face was inches from his. A flicker of worry flashed through me, but I pushed down my innate need to protect her.

She needed this.

She needed to be the one to end him.

"This is for me. You often told me the only way I'd get out of this marriage is in a body bag."

She straightened and raised the knife.

"You first."

Victor shook his head frantically. "Ariana. No. Don't. Please!"

She didn't hesitate.

She plunged the knife into his heart.

His body convulsed, a wet gasp ripping from his throat. His gaze locked on hers, pleading, disbelieving, terrified, before the light in his eyes went out.

The silence that followed was thick and absolute.

Ariana remained frozen for several seconds, her chest heaving, hands soaked in blood. Then her shoulders slumped. The knife slipped from her fingers and clattered onto the wood.

Only then did she finally look up.

Her gaze found me.

She jerked back like she'd been electrocuted, eyes wide and unfocused, breath escaping her in short, broken bursts. She wiped her face with a trembling hand, smearing Victor's blood across her cheek.

"Henry?" Her voice cracked, tears spilling down her cheeks. "No. I'm hallucinating. You're not... You're supposed to be dead."

I stepped out of the shadows, and slowly made my way toward her.

She stood, reaching for me, tentative at first, then desperate.

"Are you real?"

Her hands cupped my face, sliding over my cheeks, my jaw, my mouth, as if memorizing every feature. I didn't care that her palms were coated in Victor's blood. I held her wrists gently, grounding her.

"I'm real," I responded, my voice rougher than I intended.

Her body crumpled, and she melted into me, gripping the front of my shirt as she sobbed into the fabric.

I wrapped my arms around her, pulling her tight against me, her heartbeat racing against mine. I didn't tell her to calm down. Didn't tell her it was over. I just held her.

Like the fucking warrior she was.

"You're alive," she breathed, and I had a feeling it was more for herself than anything else.

"I'm alive," I managed, anchoring her against me because I didn't trust my legs to keep me upright otherwise.

She clutched me like she didn't intend to ever let go. "I was so scared you were... He said you—"

"I'm fine," I whispered into her hair. "I'm right here."

When she pulled back, her gaze darted past my shoulder and her face fell. "Where's Blake?"

I swallowed hard, but it didn't help. Nothing would.

"He didn't make it. When we realized it was a trap. He...he sent me back here. Made sure I'd get to you."

Her eyes welled. "Oh, god. Henry, I'm so sorry. I never meant—"

"It's not your fault," I cut in, gripping her jaw gently so she'd look at me. "All he cared about was making sure you were safe. That Victor couldn't hurt you again."

I scanned her frame, her t-shirt and arms stained with blood. "He didn't hurt you, did he?"

"No." She swallowed, then shook her head. "But..."

"What is it?"

She hesitated, then lifted her eyes to mine.

I sensed whatever she was about to tell me would change everything.

"Sarah," she whispered.

Everything inside me went still. "What about Sarah?"

Ariana drew in a trembling breath. "Victor didn't kill her, Henry."

"Who did?"

"No one."

My world stuttered. Paused. Waited to fall apart.

"What are you saying?"

"Sarah's alive."

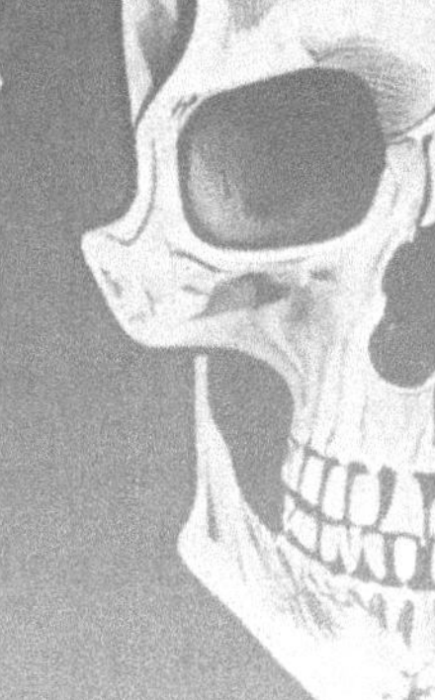

CHAPTER THIRTY-EIGHT

Sarah

The screams started again.

Thin, ragged pleas scraping down the hallway like metal dragged against stone. I squeezed my eyes shut, pretending the sound didn't slither under my skin the way it always did. But the fear it invoked never went away.

That was the point. They instilled compliance through fear. Most people fell into line so as to not endure whatever occurred behind closed doors.

Not me.

I refused to give up my humanity.

In this place, it was the only thing I had left.

So I held on to it with everything I had, even if it meant I'd pay in the long run.

I drew in a deep breath and focused on the walls caging me in, tuning out everything else.

Despite the horrors this room bore witness to, beauty surrounded me.

Pale silk drapes that stirred faintly when the air vents kicked on. Soft carpeted floors. A chandelier dripping crystals that scattered light across walls covered in pale gray.

It was the kind of room you'd find in a luxurious hotel.

Not a place you'd be chained in like an animal.

No. Not an animal. I was better than an animal, at least according to *him*.

I was a vessel.

Chosen.

Footsteps sounded beyond the door, slow and measured.

My breath caught, not out of fear, but with something worse. Anticipation coiled in my chest, sharp and confusing.

I should have wanted him dead. And I did.

But months of nothing except him — his voice, his presence, his rules — had chipped away at my hatred until I didn't know what I felt anymore.

He was my captor. My tormentor.

But he was the only human connection I had.

And I *craved* human connection.

The door opened with a soft click, and I scrambled to my feet as he stepped inside.

Tall. Immaculate. Calm in a way that made my skin crawl.

His gaze slowly moved over me. Assessing. Possessive. Like I was something he built and was deciding how best to use me.

"Good morning," he said gently.

His voice was warm. Practiced. The kind of voice that convinced people to bow down before him. And they did.

"Are you going to willingly fulfill your divine duty today?"

My chin lifted on instinct. "Never."

He smiled. Slow. Unbothered. The kind of smile that said he already knew my answer and didn't care. That said he liked it when I fought him. That he liked the challenge.

"We'll see about that, Nova."

Heat prickled my skin, along with anger. Shame. Something darker I wished I could rip out of myself.

"I told you..."

I moved toward him, even though fear pulsed behind my ribs, the chain at my ankle rattling like a warning bell.

"My name is Sarah."

Thank you for reading *The Pawn*! I hope you enjoyed the continuation of Henry and Ariana's story.

Where is Sarah? And why were she and Ariana "chosen"? Find out today in *The Chosen*. Just scan the code below to grab your copy.

I thought I knew what evil looked like. I was wrong.

Thank you so much for taking the time to read this book. If you enjoyed it, please let your friends know by leaving a review so more people can fall in love with Henry and Ariana.

THE
CHOSEN

She was supposed to be a pawn. Now I'll burn down the world to keep her safe.

I thought I knew what evil looked like.

I was wrong.

For years, I believed Victor Kane was the monster at the center of everything...

The man pulling strings, destroying lives, and hunting the people I love.

I was prepared to burn down the world to stop him.

But Victor was only a distraction.

The truth is darker. Older. More sinister.

And it's been watching me far longer than I ever realized.

Now Ariana is caught in the crosshairs of something far bigger than revenge.

Something that doesn't just want power.

It wants obedience. Devotion. Sacrifice.

I've hunted monsters my entire life.

But this time, the monster isn't in the shadows.

He's been standing beside me all along.

ACKNOWELDGMENTS

There's a certain magic to writing the first book in a trilogy.

Everything is new. The characters are just revealing themselves. The danger is still taking shape.

The second book?

That's where the real work begins.

By now, you know these characters. You understand what drives them. You know their wounds, their fears, and the lies they tell themselves. But this isn't the moment where everything explodes just yet. This is the part of the story where they start making intentional choices. Where they begin shedding the versions of themselves they were when the story began... Before they ever met each other.

It's challenging. Messy. Uncomfortable at times.

And for me, it's also the most rewarding part to write.

This book wouldn't exist without the support of some incredible people.

First and foremost, thank you to my husband, Stan, and my daughter, Harper Leigh. Your patience, encouragement, and love mean more to me than I can put into words.

To my amazing PA, Melissa Crump. Thank you for keeping me organized, on track, and sane through every deadline and curveball.

To my wonderful beta readers, Melissa and Stacy. Thank you for always showing up, reading early drafts, and helping me make these stories better, even during the hectic holiday season.

To my review team, thank you for not only reading but for taking the time to share your thoughts and support publicly. It truly makes a difference.

To my reader group. My super-fans. Thank you for being my safe place, my sounding board, and my reminder of why I do this.

And most importantly, thank *you*, my readers. Whether you've been with me since the beginning or you just found your way here, I'm endlessly grateful you chose to spend your time with these characters and this story.

Henry and Ariana's journey isn't over yet.

And I can't wait to show you where it leads next.

Love & Peace,

~ T.K.

ABOUT THE AUTHOR

T.K. Leigh is a *USA Today* Bestselling author of romance ranging from fun and flirty to sexy and suspenseful.

Originally from New England, she now resides just outside of Raleigh with her husband, beautiful daughter, rescued special needs dog, and three cats. When she's not writing, she can be found training for her next marathon or chasing her daughter around the house.

facebook.com/tkleighauthor

instagram.com/tkleigh

tiktok.com/@tkleigh

bookbub.com/authors/t-k-leigh

pinterest.com/tkleighauthor